SAINTS & HEATHENS

An International Anthology of Stories

Edited by Dixiane Hallaj and
Richard Bunning

S & H Publishing, Inc.
Purcellville, VA

Dixiane Hallaj/S & H Publishing, Inc.
P O Box 456
Purcellville, V A 20134
www.sandhpublishing.com

Publisher's Note: This is a work of fiction. Names, characters, places, and incidents are a product of the individual author's imagination. Locales and public names are sometimes used for atmospheric purposes. Any resemblance to actual people, living or dead, or to businesses, companies, events, institutions, or locales is completely coincidental.

Ordering Information:
Quantity sales. Special discounts are available on quantity purchases by corporations, associations, and others. For details, contact the "Special Sales Department" at the address above.

Saints & Heathens/Dixiane Hallaj and Richard Bunning, ed. — 1st ed.
ISBN 978-1-63320-048-5
Ebook ISBN 978-1-63320-048-7

SAINTS & HEATHENS
An International Anthology of Stories

Table of Contents

(NOTE: Spelling and punctuation vary by country of origin)

A short story is a précis: an essential essence,
a sharp quality distilled from quantitative narrative.

— *Richard Bunning*

THE DEATH OF
DONALD EDWARDS

Lenora Rain-Lee Good

Matthew Jerome St. Cloud, Homicide Detective, Seattle Police Department stood in the cold Seattle drizzle and grumbled at the corpse at his feet. He had a head cold, and wanted nothing more than to return home to his bed, its electric blanket, and a bottle of single malt scotch. March, in Seattle, is anyone's month. Sunny, warm, pleasant, or, when Matt had a cold, March was always windy, wet, and miserable. Detective St. Cloud muttered his mantra, "Five more years, then Tucson, here I come!"

Annoyed, Matt stood in the alley. Death always annoyed him, and that this man should have chosen this time, and, most importantly of all, this cold, wet, place to die, further annoyed him. How come, he thought as he looked down at the mangled corpse, you had to choose now, to reveal your ugly, mangled self? Huh? Because of you, I gotta stand in this freezing drizzle getting sore joints. Oh well, at least my cold means I don't have to smell you.

God? Are You listening? I hate Seattle!

A uniformed officer approached Matt and waited respectfully to be noticed. "Well, Officer," Matt paused before continuing to address the young man, looking for his nametag and not seeing it on his yellow slicker. "Do we know anything yet? Who he was? How he got to be here? How he got to be such a mess?"

"I'm Olson, sir. Stuart Olson. And no, sir. Nothing. Sure looks like dogs got him, though, doesn't it? I saw dogs go after a rabbit once—less of the rabbit was left than here. But I swear, not much."

Matt barely managed to swath his raw nose in a clean handkerchief before asking, "Who found him?"

"A kid. He works at the Met—night janitor...."

"The Met?" Detective St. Cloud asked. "As in Opera? As in New York? Here? In Seattle?" Honest disbelief colored his voice.

"No sir, not as in the opera. As in health and well-being. The Metropolitan Health Club—it's a hole-in-the-wall gym. The main entrance is around on Third, and down the stairs. This door," Officer Olson pointed to a locked, unmarked, heavy metal door opening onto a stoop five steps up from the alley, "is the back exit. Only the owner, Reeves, and the kid have a key to this door. It's a nice little gym, really."

"Yeah, I'm sure. So, where's the kid now? The one who found...this?" Matt waved his hand at the body as the Medical Examiner's crew placed it on a gurney and covered it with a yellow plastic tarp.

"Mary took him home."

"*Who* took him home?"

"Excuse me, Detective. Officer Mary O'Rourke. She comes down here in the mornings, to work out before reporting for duty, and parks her car next to the kid's. That's his, there." Officer Olson pointed to a pale silver-blue Honda parked across the alley in a small lot. "I tagged the car so it wouldn't get towed. The kid was too shook to drive. Mary, ah, Officer O'Rourke, said she'd get it later today."

"Did Mary, ah, Officer O'Rourke, give any indication of what happened before she spirited off our prize witness?" He made no attempt to hide his sarcasm and discontent.

"Yes, sir. She did." Officer Olson checked his notebook before he responded further, oblivious to the sarcasm.

"Craig Connelly, the kid, got here his usual time, at 0400. He walked from his car, there, to the door, here, and let himself in. There was no one in the alley. He cleaned the gym, and Reeves showed up about 0530. Reeves unlocked the front door, let himself in, and he, and one or two other early birds, began their workouts."

"You mean," interrupted Matt, "that people willingly get up this early? And then come downtown to *exercise*? Total insanity. God herself isn't up this early! I'm sorry, continue."

"Uh, yes sir. People actually do get up this early. To work out. Do it myself. But anyhow, Reeves said he noticed nothing untoward, nor did any of the other early birds. Then Craig left at 0630, he had to get ready for school."

"University?"

"Uh, no sir. He goes to West Seattle High."

"Well, you said he was a kid."

"Yes, sir. He grabbed his bag and baseball bat, and—"

"Baseball bat? I thought this was a weight-lifting type gym," interrupted Matt.

"Yes, sir. It is, and yes sir, a baseball bat. This isn't exactly the nicest part of town for anyone to be wandering in, especially at 0400 in the morning. He carries an aluminum baseball bat."

"Smart kid! And..."

"And he opened the back door and came out. The door

had latched before the scene registered. Even then he says the dogs..."

"Dogs? Plural? As in more than one?"

"Yes sir. He said there were six or seven. All big. Like shepherds. At first he said he wasn't scared, he likes dogs, and they like him. Then he realized they were fighting over something, growling, snapping, even charging at each other over pieces. He said he'd never seen anything like it. They'd grab a piece and toss it.

"Anyhow, he raised his bat and beat on the dumpster here by the door, and yelled at them. They stopped. Looked at him, and scattered. He came down the steps to see what they were fighting over, and found the body. Or rather, what was left of it.

"He doesn't really remember what happened next. He said the face, what was left, reminded him of someone he knew when he was a kid. Mary found him, over there," Officer Olson pointed down the alley about twenty feet, to a building corner. "He was leaning against the building, white, shaking, and dry heaving.

"She called it in, and took care of him once we showed up."

"Yeah. I don't blame him. Death is never kind to view, especially like we see it. But this? My God, this is the worst I've seen in quite a while. Maybe ever." Matt blew his nose, then dismissed the uniformed officer.

"Thank you, Officer Olson. You've been a help."

"Oh, Detective? Mary said to give you this. It's the kid's address. Said to tell you she'd come in after she got Craig home and settled. It's her day off..." Officer Olson explained at the raised eyebrow.

Detective Steve Kyrklyn, Matt's partner, came through the gym door. "Matt, there's nothing more in here. Why

4

don't you go on back to the office? I can finish up here, and you can start the paper work in the dry and warm."

Detective St. Cloud sneezed his assent and slid his six-foot-two-inch, two-hundred pound bulk behind the steering wheel of his car. I'm getting too old for this, he thought. Murder was exciting when I was a kid, a hundred years ago. But this... Thoughtfully, he drove the few blocks to the police garage, parked, and took the elevator to the fifth floor and his desk.

"Matt." Matthew looked up as Steve crossed the room to his desk. "The ME's office found some papers in his pocket. From what I hear, I'm surprised they even found a pocket. Anyhow, his name was Donald Edwards. He served nine years behind the Walls—his Department of Corrections identification card barely had dry ink—as a pedophile. Y'know, I think I remember the case—he was an officer of a local company, vice president of Seattle Air, as I recall. Yeah. Raped a bunch of little boys. A real predator."

"Revenge, maybe? What do the lab rats say? Have they found anything yet?"

"Yeah—he had eaten a couple of hours before he died. No alcohol or drugs. They think he fell and the dogs jumped him—but the body was so torn they can't tell for sure. Cursory look-over says no bullet or knife wounds, only teeth marks."

"Steve, dogs? We were there, we saw it. But a pack of wild dogs? In downtown Seattle? It doesn't make sense. And wait until the papers get hold of this one. My god, they'll have them all rabid, and a new panic will strike the city." Matt paused, then smiled as he continued, "Well, then again, maybe it'll get a lot of dogs their long overdue rabies shots, eh?"

"Matt, we're next up on the homicide roster, but I really don't think we've got a murder here, do you?"

"Pardner, I don't rightly know. But my shoulder blades truly do itch over this one. Maybe it's just the strangeness of having a pack of dogs where there shouldn't be. I don't know. Something's not quite right."

Matt poured himself another cup of toxic sludge, that passed as coffee, into his cup, and called Records for all they had on the late Donald Edwards. He also called his buddy, Rick Braun, over at the Seattle Sentinel, for anything he could add. Turned out that Rick had worked the case as a crime reporter.

Matt rummaged in his desk drawer for a packet of sugar and one of cream, to see if he could cut the edge from the sludge. He found a stale buttermilk donut, three packets of salt, one of pepper, and six beverage stirrers. He looked up, toward the coffee pot, to see if there was any cream and sugar there, when his field of vision was suddenly limited by the approach of a girl.

Woman, he self-corrected; yes, definitely: woman. Five feet, six inches, 130 pounds, natural blonde, and whatever her problem is, I hope she confesses the error of her ways to me, the lecherous old man of Homicide. Be still my beating heart.

"May I help you?"

"Are you Detective St. Cloud?" At Matt's nod in the affirmative, she continued, "I'm Officer O'Rourke. Mary O'Rourke."

Jeeze. That figures. She's a cop! And now I know why the uniformed kept calling her 'Mary.' I'd like to call her 'Mary,' too. Sigh! "Have a seat Officer O'Rourke. Thanks for stopping by. Would you care for a cup of sludge? Coffee?"

"No, thanks. It's a taste I've never acquired. And the

way all you guys who do drink it, complain about it, I think I haven't missed much. Have I?" Her smile was quick, friendly, and amazingly disarming. Matthew St. Cloud knew he would die a happy man for having received that smile.

Mary O'Rourke, he thought, I don't think you've missed a thing. Not with those big and innocent-looking blue eyes. "Nope. Not a thing. 'Scuse me, I gotta dilute mine with some cream and sugar." Matt was silent as he fiddled with his coffee until it was more or less palatable, and he was sure he could get his mind back on the job and off the angel in the chair next to his desk. "Now, tell me, you know the kid, how did he take it?"

"Pretty rough. The weirdest thing was he kept saying it looked like an ex-neighbor of his, from about ten years ago. Some airline executive who went to prison as a pedophile."

"Did you talk to Craig's mom when you took him home?"

"No. She's out of town. I took Craig across the street to Aunt Molly."

"His aunt lives across the street?"

"No," smiled Mary, "Aunt Molly's a doll maker. She's the 'auntie' to the whole neighborhood. She's lived there since before Craig was born, and is sort of surrogate mom when needed. She makes dolls, babysits the local kids, and bakes cookies. Great cookies. Be sure and have one when you talk to her.

"And, Detective St. Cloud, I know I probably should not have taken Craig home, but he's a good kid, and I've known him since I've been going to the Met. I told him he was to watch no television, listen to no radio, and, literally, to talk to no one but Aunt Molly until the investigating detectives could talk to him. I emphasized that to him *and* Aunt Molly. They both gave their word, and I believe them."

Mary O'Rourke told Matt the same story that Officer Olson had related. By the time she left, Matt's coffee was cold and tasteless, his stomach growled, and he swore he heard a cup of espresso calling him by name from the nearest Starbucks.

"Stebe," Matt growled through his congestion, laying it on just a tad, hoping for the sympathy he didn't get, "I'm gonna go ged lunch, and maybe drop by dis here Aunt Molly and talk to da kid. Wanna come?"

"No, you go ahead. Get some decongestants while you're out. I've got a call in to the State Penitentiary at Walla Walla about this guy. I agree with you, it's strange, but I truly don't think we've got a real homicide. I think it's just a body. Bon appetite!"

Matt shrugged into his coat, crushed his fedora on his head, signed out at the board, and went to lunch at Starbucks. He had a latte and two amoretti cookies, neither of which he could taste, then drove to the address in West Seattle where young Craig Connelly lived.

The neighborhood was single-family homes. Five years ago they were probably moderately priced, but now, he realized, way out of his price range. He noticed that they all seemed to be in good repair, not a single trashed house to be seen.

Matt pulled up across the street from Craig's house, in front of Molly's home. He really hoped Craig was in his own home, as he wanted to talk to Molly Jones, and saw no reason to bother the kid any more. At least not for now. The frozen drizzle of the early March morning had blown away, to be replaced by a hard and hungry rain. The wind whipped the soaking torrent into a frenzy not to be daunted by raincoats, hats, or bumbershoots. Seattle, thought Matt, is too damn wet and windy. I gotta find me a place in the desert. Tucson, maybe. Or Phoenix. With a sigh of resignation, Matt pulled his hat down and his collar up, blew his nose for good measure, and stepped into the tempest. The only good thing about all this, is that the air smells fresh — and it's always green. I sure would like to try for dry and yellow sand.

He climbed the ten or so steps to a deep covered porch as wide as the house, which protected him from both the wind and the rain. Like an old dog he shook as much of the water off as possible before reaching for the doorbell. He stopped as he read the sign on the door: "Aunt Molly, Dollmaker. Please Step In."

Matt opened the door, and heard the gentle music of glass wind-chimes sing his entrance. He stepped into a long, narrow, and warm living room. It was hard to tell what color the furniture upholstery was, assuming things were upholstered — the couch and love seat were full of dolls. The end tables and coffee tables were covered with dolls. No two were alike, as far as he could tell, not even cut from the same pattern. Each doll was a different size, and each face seemed unique.

The far end of the living room merged into the dining room. From there came the sound of a well-cared-for sewing machine as it hummed at its task. Matt smiled at the sound, it reminded him of his grandmother, and his mother as they sewed for the family. Matt looked in the direction of the sound and noticed the top of a head as it intently bent over the machine. The head spoke without looking up, "I'll be with you in just a moment. Please look around."

9

Matt looked. Some of the dolls were whimsical. There were green dolls, and purple dolls, all dressed in costumes that reminded him of old science fiction comics he had read when he was a boy — and that his daughter read now.

Some of the dolls were styled as adults, both by their features and clothing. But the greater number of dolls were children or babies. All the dolls were made of cloth, and on closer inspection, Matt suspected they did, in fact, come from the same pattern, but some were thin, some fat, and the faces, although embroidered, were surprisingly realistic. He was sure they were all made by the same person.

"Now then, what can I do for you?"

Matt turned and looked into the brown and lined rounded face of a Native American. Her black eyes searched his blue ones. Her salt and pepper hair was mostly salt and short, in a ragged crew cut.

"Ma'am, I'm Detective Matthew St. Cloud. Homicide. Are you Molly Jones?"

"Yes, I am. This must be about Donald Edwards?" Matt wasn't sure if she was telling him, or asking him. He decided she asked. And wondered what she already knew about the case to bring up his name so quickly. He noticed her face went from easy-to-read friendly to an unreadable neutral. Ah, he thought, the inscrutable Indian.

"Yes ma'am, it is." Jeeze, one more "ma'am," thought Matt, and I'll start asking for "just the facts!"

Molly stood her ground, like a she-bear ready to defend her cub, "I hope you don't want to talk to Craig. He's asleep."

"No, ma'am...."

"And please," she smiled, again friendly, "Call me Aunt Molly. Everyone does." Her smile broke her face into a galaxy of laugh lines. Matt could see why everyone called her Aunt Molly — she radiated genuine warmth.

Matt smiled, and noticed that Aunt Molly's eyes twinkled a bit more at that. "Yes ma'am. And, if you're going to be my aunt, I guess you'd best call me Matt. You said Craig was sleeping? Is he here? I thought Officer O'Rourke said he was home."

"He's upstairs. Delia, his mom, had to go out of town for a few days, and I didn't want him alone just now. He has been alone before, and just checks in with me, but I want him here. I fixed him a bowl of oatmeal, gave him a stiff shot of firewater," she grinned wickedly, "and put him in the upstairs bedroom. He should sleep quite a while."

"Firewater? As in whiskey?"

"No," laughed Aunt Molly, "As in rose-hip tea. It's pink, and I tell all my children it's firewater. It's also healthful and relaxing. And good for colds," she pointedly added.

"Uh, thanks. I'll pass on the firewater. But I'm glad he's sleeping. I really would like to talk to you, and see no point in upsetting him right now more than necessary."

"Well then, let's have coffee. I always do better with coffee. Cream? Sugar?" Before he could answer, she walked to the kitchen and soon returned with a tray holding two mugs of steaming coffee, a small creamer of milk and a bowl of sugar. And, noticed Matt, homemade cookies, just like Mary said.

"Help yourself. And you'll probably find that chair more comfortable than it looks." She indicated an antique rocker, plain as the Shakers who had inspired, if not made it.

"Mrs. Jones, er, Aunt Molly, I understand you were the one who originally reported Mr. Edwards and his shenanigans to the police? Some years ago, I believe?"

"Yes. I did."

"Was one of your children involved? I mean, why you and not a parent? Why did the boys tell you, I guess, instead of their family?"

"Well, Matt, I'm everybody's Aunt. The boys didn't just tell me. Enjoy your coffee while I explain."

Actually, thought Matt, the chair is comfortable, the coffee's good — and I'm in no hurry.

"When I moved here almost thirty years ago, I made dolls as a hobby. Then little Bettianna took sick. She was the neighborhood darling. She was not yet three, had long blonde curls, big blue eyes, and was the sweetest tempered child. Still is — though she's certainly no longer a child.

"Aunt Molly..."

"Don't interrupt, young man. It all ties in. Trust me." Molly smiled at the last remark. Matt responded in kind, and settled back to hear her story, grateful he didn't have to pry, as he so often did, for even one word, one syllable, answers.

"Anyhow, Bettianna was in the hospital, and we all thought she was dying. The doctors couldn't figure out what was wrong, but something surely was. John, her brother, asked me to make her a doll. He brought me a favorite, and outgrown, dress and I made her a doll that looked like Bettianna — long blonde hair, pink cheeks, healthy, happy — the works. Her parents took the doll to her and two days later she was home. Well."

She held up a hand, and smiled again. "Trust me." Matt ate cookies that reminded him of his grandmother and her warm kitchen that always smelled of fresh snickerdoodles.

"Later, someone else got sick and I made another doll — they got well. Soon, all the children in the neighborhood had dolls — and no more illnesses."

12

"Are you telling me, Aunt Molly, that your dolls are magic. That you're a witch?"

"Magic? I don't know about that. I'm certainly no witch. I am, however, a shaman. But if you look around you, you'll see dolls that represent real people. Some are dead, most living. Anyhow..." Molly shrugged and went back to her tale.

"When Donald Edwards moved in, he had a house full of 'boy toys'—a Nintendo and all the games, a real pinball machine, a VCR with all the action movies. A gym in his basement—everything that would appeal to boys. Plus, he liked having the boys around. Most of these homes are single parent homes—moms and kids, so the moms were happy to have a good, positive, male image for their boys. Someone who enjoyed having them around, who would take them camping, fishing, teach them to swim—all the things Dads are supposed to do. The moms all adored Donald Edwards. And many set their caps for him, after all, he was single, well-educated, good looking, vice-president of a growing local airline. What boy would, for that matter, *could*, tell his mom the truth?"

Before Matt could swallow his cookie, Aunt Molly's pause ended.

"I noticed that Donald Edwards limped. He told me he had broken his hip when he was thirteen and it had never healed properly—but it didn't cause him much pain. He lied, at least about the pain. And I knew it, but he preferred to ignore it, so I didn't say any more.

"Then the boys started coming to me. Asking me to make a Donald doll, and make him right. For my children, I'd do anything. They even got me an old shirt of his, stole it from the rag drawer, they said.

13

"I made the doll, but it was never quite right. One day, one of the younger boys came to me in tears. 'Aunt Molly,' he sobbed, 'you just have to make Don right. You just have to.' When I began to explain about Don's hip and my efforts, he became almost incoherent with tears. 'No! No! Not his hip. His, his...' here he stumbled over words and thoughts, 'I don't know. He said to never tell. That we couldn't play at his house any more if we told.'

"Well, that did it! I sat him right here," she patted her lap, "Held him close, and asked him questions. I was so angry when I got the story, I wanted to kill Donald Edwards myself! Of course, I couldn't let my boy know how angry I was, so we talked, and he calmed down, and when his mom came home from work, I walked him home. I told her, and called the police, and then called the rest of the parents."

"Did you kill Donald Edwards?" Matt asked, almost afraid this kind, gentle neighborhood healer would say "yes."

"Hunh!" snorted Aunt Molly, "Wait 'til I'm done, then ask me." She paused as though collecting her thoughts. "Anyhow, there was the trial. My, there were angry moms, and hurt and confused boys. They knew Don had done wrong, but they still felt guilty sending him to prison. The judge sentenced him to life in prison. We thought it was over, until after slightly less than ten years we got our victim notification from the Indeterminate Sentence Review Board. They had found this sexual predator worthy of parole. He was to have no contact with his victims and could not come within five miles of our neighborhood.

"In all that time, I kept working on the Donald doll. Still trying to get it right."

The story was interrupted by the insistent ring of the

telephone. Molly answered it, listened a moment, and handed it to Matt. "For you. Steve Kyrklyn." She then picked up the empty coffee mugs and walked back to the kitchen.

That, thought Matt, is a hell of a gesture. To leave me some privacy, when she's gotta be dying of curiosity. Most people would have sat there and hung on every word. Aunt Molly, you have just gone up ten notches on my respect indicator.

Aunt Molly remained in the kitchen until Matt hung up the phone. She returned with two more cups of steaming coffee, more cookies, and a plastic grocery sack.

"That was my partner." Matt told her. "The M E, excuse me, Medical Examiner, now knows how Mr. Edwards died. It was...."

"No," interrupted Aunt Molly, "Let me tell you. He was mauled by dogs and eaten by ants. Number one, there are no dog packs in downtown Seattle, and number two, it's March, and still too cold for ants."

"Were you listening on the extension?" asked Matt, privately angry at this invasion of his privacy as well as his wrong assessment of Aunt Molly.

"No. I don't have an extension. That's a cordless phone. It goes anywhere I want to take it. Drink this while it's hot.

"Yesterday, I had the Donald doll out and had taken it into the kitchen for some reason. I left it on the table. Rebecca, the seven-year-old across the alley came over for a social visit after school. She had a cracker with a bit of honey with a glass of milk. She must have dribbled some honey on the doll. Anyhow, before I went to bed, I was washing up the dishes, and I noticed the doll looked odd. It was black. It was crawling with ants! I decided that was as good a reason as any to finally dispose of the doll, and took it out to the garbage.

"It wasn't until later this morning, after Craig was asleep, that I wondered about the commotion I heard around five o'clock or so out by the garbage can, and went out to check. There, in the alley, was the Donald doll. It had been pulled from the garbage and had been mauled..." She pulled a Ziploc bag out of the grocery sack. Inside was a rag doll, badly ripped and shredded. It was covered in ants.

"So now, Matthew St. Cloud, you tell me—did I kill Donald Edwards?"

Matt almost choked on a sip of coffee before replying. "No, Aunt Molly. No, the ME's office said they could find no evidence of foul play—except by seven different very large dogs!"

Matt set his empty coffee mug on the table, stood, placed his hat on his head and walked over to Aunt Molly. He shook her hand as he bade her goodbye and was pleased at her firm grip. "Aunt Molly, it's been a pleasure meeting you. And thank you for the coffee. And the cookies. They're even better than Officer O'Rourke described them." He smiled and added as he opened the door. "I may be back—to order a doll for my daughter."

"Order one for yourself, Matthew Jerome St. Cloud. Get over the aches and pains of cold and wet weather. And give up the idea of moving to Tucson or wherever. Too hot. Too dry. Too far away from your friends and family. Oh, and tell Steve hello for me, will you please? I remember him from before."

Matt closed the door and hurried to the dry safety of his car. He parked in the police parking garage and almost reached his desk before he realized he had not told Aunt Molly of his dislike of cold, wet weather, or the accompanying aches. Nor had he told her of his dream to move to the warmth of the desert. And he certainly had not told her his middle name!

———

Lenora lives in the high desert of Washington State where she writes poems, novels, and radio plays. When not writing, she reads, quilts, makes jam, and takes road trips. Her historical novel, Madame Dorion: Her Journey to the Oregon Country, *is published by S & H Publishing, Inc.*
http://sandhbooks.com/story/madame-dorion/
Find Lenora at https://www.facebook.com/MadameDorion

PEACH PIE

Terry Korth Fischer

It was slim pickings in Browning Township. Nonetheless, Donna Pritchard intended to throw her hat into the ring. And although she wasn't convinced that extending the meal invitation was the best idea she'd ever had, she patted her hair to make sure it covered her hearing aids, and headed back to the dining room and her two gentleman callers.

Earl Clarence and Bob Reed Senior sat facing each other across the round oak table. Together they represented the entire field of eligible bachelors in Browning. One divorced and the other widowed, the men ran in the same social circle. They played an occasional game of dominoes at the American Legion, and even though they no longer fought fires, both were active members of the Township Volunteers.

"It's said that your peach pie has a way of making a body forget anything else but the sheer pleasure of eating it, Donna," Bob Senior said. Dressed in his starched uniform, he offered his police chief smile. "I've enough room left for one gigantic slice."

"Amen," Earl said. A Baptist minister, Earl had lost his wife more than a decade earlier and using the last piece of dinner roll to sop up the gravy on his plate, he added, "Just like Mom used to make."

Donna's hearing aid whistled as Earl asked, "Bob, I suppose you intend to preside at the county fair this year?"

"It's a matter of pride," Bob Senior said.

What was Bob talking about? It's a *matching bride*? Donna reached for her ear, stopping herself in time to divert her hand and tug at the collar of her paisley blouse instead. She looked at Bob Senior through her cat-eye framed glasses. He had a smug look on his face, what had been called, in her day, a canary-eating smile.

Earl nodded. "County fair and the bond issue, all we hear nowadays."

"Don't get me started on the bond issue."

Confound that whistle. What did Earl say? What *blonde statue*? As if the whistle wasn't bad enough, a beeping started. The insistent chirp meant the batteries were running low. Donna excused herself and retreated to the kitchen in search of relief. 'Matching bride' and 'blonde statue' could only mean one thing; the Hollis twins had managed to somehow get hold of the only eligible men in Browning. And, the Hollis' hair wasn't natural, not in their sixties, wigs or bleached straw. The thought made her shudder.

Opening the drawer in search of batteries, Donna found the silver polish and cloth she'd used earlier in the afternoon. Always the perfect hostess, she'd polished the silver. The task was part of the ritual passed down from her mother, the routines she lived with, and the conventions she used to fashion her expectations. Like other women of her generation, her dreams extended as far as marriage and family. And, when you married, there were things you did, like getting fine china, picking a silverware pattern and using the things collected in your hope chest. Donna happily went from being someone's daughter to being someone's wife. She transitioned from wife to mother, and two years ago, found herself someone's widow. At sixty-eight, Donna knew that regardless of the situation, a respectable lady held on to her beliefs and conducted herself accordingly. And in that accord, she'd polished the silver and set out the fine china for gentlemen callers. It was time to move on, and Bruce would understand. Locating the Energizer package, she slipped the hearing aids from her ears and began the task of exchanging the batteries.

In the dining room Bob Senior and Earl were wiping their mouths in anticipation of the famous Pritchard peach pie when the doorbell rang. "Donna?" Bob glanced at the kitchen.

"I'll get it." Standing, Earl crossed to the door, and recognizing Bob's son, Robert Junior, still dressed in his police uniform, opened it, asking, "What's up?"

"Sorry to disturb ya." Robert Junior swiped the cap from his head as he stepped into the room. "We've got a situation at the station." He craned his neck in an attempt to locate his father. "Thought I'd search out Pops and get some advice. He's here, right?"

"Sure, sure. Come on in. We're just getting ready to have dessert. You know Mrs. Pritchard's famous pie? Best in town."

"What kind of situation?" Bob Senior joined them in the living room with a cloth napkin still tucked into the open neck of his shirt.

"Nothing earth shattering, Pops. You know that cat burglar that's been bothering people? Well, it looks like it might be Jimmy Snodgrass. We caught him stealing around the Henley place with an empty fifty-pound potato sack and a homemade lockpick in his possession. We've got him down to the station house and are holding him on suspicion. Haven't booked him yet, but he's handcuffed to the desk. We're gonna sweat him until he starts talkin'." Robert Junior gave a whisker-licking grin that mirrored his father's.

"Man-o-man," Bob Senior said jerking the napkin from under his chin and shoving it into Junior's hands. "I gotta get a piece of this!" He snatched his hat from the rack and headed for the door. His last words were, "Tell Miss Pritchard I'm sorry," and, "You're welcome to my piece of pie." Then he was gone.

They had no sooner settled at the table, Robert Junior with the napkin serving as a bib over his uniform and in the seat vacated by Bob Senior, when Donna emerged from the kitchen with their pie. "I hope you gentlemen are ready for dessert," she said, placing one dish before Earl and genteelly moving into position behind the gentleman she thought was Bob Senior. She looked up in time to see Earl beaming at her from across the table. He nodded his head at the seated policeman. It seemed like he wanted to say something, but good manners and a mouthful of pastry prevented him.

Donna smiled awkwardly. What was up? Something felt odd. As she leaned in to deliver his serving of peach pie, Donna noticed the police chief's haircut; a little thicker and slightly darker than usual. Then the square, broad shoulders, thinking he certainly kept in shape. And finally, the wedding ring on his left hand. She set the dish down abruptly without looking directly at Bob, and immediately retreated to the kitchen feeling rather flustered.

What had she been thinking? Bob Senior had already wed one of the Hollis twins, and now she was entertaining him at Friday night supper? No wonder he'd been divorced. That heathen! She decided that while her nerves

21

calmed, she'd eat her pie alone in the kitchen. It was the place she and Bruce would have enjoyed a slice together, and she felt comfortable there with the 35th and 40th anniversary plates on the wall, their grandchildren's pictures on the fridge, and Bruce's old sweater on a hook by the mudroom door. The whole situation of *other* men in her house made her feel foolish. Using a finger to absently pick up a smear of peach pie goo, she began licking the sweet filling, hoping her muddled mind would regain its bearings.

In the dining room, Robert Junior said, "Say! You're right this *is* the best pie I've ever had."

"Just like Mom used to make," Earl said, using the back of his fork to collect the pieces of pie crust still remaining on his plate.

The doorbell rang, followed by a mellow voice asking, "Hello? Anyone at home?"

"Sure, come on in. The more the merrier," Earl answered, waving in a young man wearing a Roman collar.

The newcomer, the Assistant Minister at First Baptist, Pastor Franklin entered timidly saying, "I just left the hospital where the newest member of our flock was ushered into this world. I'm on my way home and saw your car parked at the curb, thought you'd want to know."

"Praise the Lord," Earl said, indicating the empty seat between him and Robert Junior. "We're having some of Miss Pritchard's peach pie. Best in the county."

"Hillary Hollis' first," Pastor Franklin offered, taking a seat. "Mother and baby are doing well. Nine pounds, two ounces. The proud papa is passing out cigars." He patted his breast pocket where two pink wrapped cigars peeked over the fabric, and his cheeks flushed to match the wrapping.

"Bet Miss Pritchard will be interested. She's best friends

with the Hollis twins," Earl said. "Why back in high school the Hollis girls, my late wife, Gracie, and Donna were quite the thing, all bell-bottomed pants and Puka beads. Yes, quite the rebel-angels back then. Thank Heavens, no trip to Woodstock and no bra burnings. Course, Donna settled down, when Bruce Pritchard came back from Southeast Asia and made her his bride. Isn't Hillary the Jergen girl that married one of the Hollis grandsons?"

"Did I say this *is* great pie?" Robert Junior asked lifting his plate in tribute. "Do you suppose Miss Pritchard has another slice?"

"I'll just poke my head in and see." Young Pastor Franklin took Junior's plate and headed for the kitchen.

* * *

Donna removed her glasses and began to wipe the tiny smears on the bifocals. Looking up, she saw the minister with his empty plate, and suddenly felt very old. Earl and Bob Senior had aged well. Neither appeared to wear dental, audio or visual aids. Her sagging body would be a rude awakening to either of them. She left her eyeglasses lying on the counter as she dished up Earl's second piece of pie, and sighed.

"Hillary Hollis presented us with a baby girl this evening," Pastor Franklin said with a smile and patted the cigars in his pocket. "Mother and daughter doing fine. Such a blessing."

The minister's face beamed above his Roman collar, appearing boastful and proud. Egad! Not one of the Hollis twins, one of their offspring. The barbarian! How could Bob Senior dine out while his wife lay in the hospital? This was beyond belief. And, to think she was party to it all. The young minister headed back into the dining room, while Donna took Bruce's sweater from the hook.

She shrugged the saggy old garment onto her shoulders and smoothed the front lapels. Gosh, she missed Bruce. Crossing to the counter, Donna cut herself a substantial slice of pie and sat down in the kitchen nook.

* * *

Robert Junior's radio squawked. "Reed," he said. "Uh-huh." Nodding his head as his eyes grew wide. "No! I'll be there in a sec."

"I gotta go, fellas," he said, grabbing his hat and clipping his radio back on his belt. "That was Pops down at the station. Snodgrass managed to hurt himself in a tussle while the boys were moving him into a cell. They can't stop the bleeding and he's going in and out of consciousness."

"I'm a first responder," Pastor Franklin said as he too stood in preparation to leave.

Earl Clarence took one final finger lick across his pie plate and adjusted his belt, saying, "I'll say goodnight to Donna and meet you there."

Earl poked his head into the kitchen doorway. "Donna, fine meal. I'd say, you've outdone yourself. There's an emergency, you'll have to forgive us. We've got to run. Delicious pot roast. Great pie!"

Straight lie? Donna watched him disappear, wondering what he meant. No whistle—no beep, but she didn't hear so well these days. She adjusted her hearing aids and realized she'd forgotten to turn them on after the battery replacement. She felt the floor boards dip. Fresh air circulated as the front door opened and closed. Donna didn't hear any movement in the dining room. No chairs scooted, no fabric rustled, no last minute words of thanks. Perhaps they had stepped onto the porch to enjoy their cigars. Donna raised another mouthful of pastry to her lips in appreciation, savoring her moment alone, and Bruce's memory.

"Peach pie," she thought, "it certainly has a way of making a body forget anything else but the sheer pleasure of eating it."

———

Terry Korth Fischer lives in Houston, Texas. Retired from a career in IT, she uses her time to read, write, and relax. Her work recently appeared in The Write Place at the Write Time, *and* Clear Lake Area Writers Selections—Summer 2016. *Terry is a member of Sisters in Crime International, Clear Lake Area Writers, and Pennwriters Inc.*

THE ODD CASE OF WIDOW MEROVIGIAN

C. M. Stucker

I, Alejandro Guevere, am not usually a kind or altruistic fellow and I certainly cannot for the life of me say why I got involved with the strange fellow who came to town. It was late in the day, the sun on the horizon, when he rode in. Tall, lean and young, with long white hair flowing out from under an old-fashioned black hat. Earlier that same day, while I was enjoying my lunch, I'd heard disturbing news from a local guard, gossiping over a pint, in the local public house. He reported that during the last week several guards had gone missing during night patrols. Unsurprisingly, he and his remaining colleagues were nervous. As the newcomer dismounted, I noted the foreign look of both his cloak and the basket-hilt of his arming-sword. Information from abroad always interests me, so I called out, "Ho stranger, what news?"

He glared at me through spectacles of deep green glass. "I might ask what news you could give me."

"Happy I am to help a stranger," I started in, for I am a friendly fellow. "There is little to tell. We are but a humble town. Our grapes grew well last season and the wine is quite fine. Are you interested in carrying some of the trade elsewhere?" I did not hesitate, for others might deal with him. His accent placed him from Genoa or thereabout,

26

which is renowned for the cunning of their merchants. His youthful appearance lent me hope that I might get the better of him. Proud fathers oft send their sons on purchasing missions ere they are truly fit to carry on the family business.

"What of recent disappearances?" Despite his subtly unsettling appearance, his voice was friendly. Nonetheless, I began to wonder what whim had possessed me to take up with this fellow. Still, in for a penny, in for a pound, as the islanders say.

"Why, the only wine which has disappeared has been that which we can well account for, having drunk it ourselves." I smiled genially, for I did not care to discuss the guard's troubles with a stranger. Too, perhaps he was testing me. They say that the king's men go about in disguise to spy on the people, and I had no care to become embroiled in some doings of theirs. "Indeed, it is such a splendid vintage that we have trouble keeping it in the bottle long enough to sell any at all."

"I meant the guards." And well, I must give him some measure for directness, yet I have always felt that a blunt manner was the mark of those who could not afford better. I was tempted to say as much, but the quality of his clothes, the drape and fit of the fine fabric, spoke eloquently of a man blessed with ample coin. Coin which I hoped to acquire, despite his odd turn of phrase.

"I am certain that such would not interest you." Here, I was cut short, for with a look of ire he pointed a finger at me, interrupting as if he were my better, a situation which I doubted prevailed. The king's writ recently declared all free men of equal status within a set of specific parameters which allowed advancement only through the attainment of a patent of nobility. No noble I have ever met would let you forget that he was far above you in station, even those so impoverished they were scarce better than workers in the field. Yet here he was pointing and interrupting, tempting me to tell him what I thought of such rude manners, though I held my tongue. Perhaps it was some ingrained sense of etiquette, for I was raised to be polite, or perhaps it was some sense of dread, for the fellow had an odd manner which was entirely unsettling.

"I have no time to waste. I am hunting the thing that took your guards. If you cannot help, tell me who can." At this point I noticed the symbol worked into the back of his glove and I shuddered, for it was the mark of a holy hunter, an Inquisitor sanctioned by the church to seek out those things which go in the darkness. I had seen this mark but once before, on a magistrate who came to town with a company of guards and burned seven suspected witches. What this fellow might expect to accomplish alone I knew not, yet I was doubly afraid, for if he took the notion I had a hand in abducting the guards, then the accusation alone would condemn me.

"Seven guards in seven days, each at night." The whisper escaped my lips. It is one thing to listen to a guard and wonder who might have a secret hatred for them, yet another to see a grim young hunter implying I might have done it. For why else had he approached me?

"Yes?" His question hung in the air. I watched the sun sinking below the horizon as we talked. It gave me a slight start to realize this could be the last sunset I might ever see. If the stranger wished me burned, he would likely arrange it for the next sunrise.

"I had nothing to do with it. Ask anyone about the wine merchant, Alejandro Guevere. They will tell you I had company two days of the last week. It could not have been I." Again he interrupted me, though I was so distraught with terror that I scarce noticed the inequity. Then too, as an Inquisitor for the church, he held ample rank to silence me — permanently should he wish — so I felt little rancor.

"I never thought so." His smile could have as easily been a grimace, "I am Donato Lamberti, a hunter for the church. I need a guide. Will you help?"

What could I do? I was trapped by my own earlier offer of aid. To refuse now would have been churlish. "Of course, you had only to ask." To my annoyance, the words sounded forced, even to my own ears.

* * *

The next several minutes passed in a blur. Lamberti led me to the local church where he showed Father Oberto his commission of holy orders and asked his leave to use the church as a place to rest. He also commended me to the padre as a brave and helpful soul. This made me uncomfortable as I know the priest, who found my faith lacking, had been asked to speak at the local baronial court about a small situation where I had been accused of cheating a fellow. Yet here was an ordained paladin of his church commending me to him. I am not normally uncomfortable expanding upon the truth, yet having this grim youth say it in such a manner somehow made me feel like a cheat. Not that I would ever relate that to anyone, as the matter could cost me a fair sum if the lord were to find against me.

Next, with scarce a breath wasted, we sped straight to the Three Hens public house which the watch captain typically patronized. I had barely related the information to Lamberti before we had crossed the street to stand before the captain, and were informing him of the intent to pursue the thing which Lamberti believed was preying upon the captain's watchmen. At no point did he state explicitly what he believed the thing was, yet I had the uncomfortable feeling that he suspected some specific foul creature. If it was not some band of thieves attempting to intimidate the constabulary, a trick they used in the past; to the extent that the Baron had sent a band of veterans to police the streets with orders to hang anyone caught out after dusk. On that occasion, it had taken but two nights and seven hangings ere no one ventured forth after dark and within the month the matter had been deemed settled. Then, the dead had been placed to insure that the watch would be intimidated, which they were. Yet this time the bodies had not been found, and it had led to all manner of speculation among the guards as to the true cause. The captain, unlike the priest, has always been a friend of mine and one I have some confidence in. I wished him well as he stood facing the witch finder. He responded to Lamberti with his typical bravado.

"Good sir and well met. I am Juan de los Nueces, and I see you are a friend of my friend, Alejandro, and so it does me much pleasure to greet you in the hopes we will be like brothers in our fond affection for one another." I had never before noticed how dissipated Juan appeared. Though he is still young and, like most youths yet firm of flesh, his countenance bore little resemblance to the stark and fierce visage of the one who faced him.

"I am Donato Lamberti, an Inquisitor. I need to know where the missing guards were last seen." With the first words of interruption, Juan had started to turn angry, for his ire is easily raised, yet the thought of crossing an Inquisitor chilled him visibly. As well it might, for a watch commander might be held to blame for losing so many of his men.

"Of, of course, Signore Inquisitor," Juan gasped, rising to his feet. "How can I help you?"

"Tell me where your men were, and be quick about it." Lamberti's voice snapped like a whip, the first sign of temper I was certain I could attribute to him and not my own dark musings.

"Naturally, ah they were, let me think." Juan was too rattled to remember, for this shock on top of having men vanish each night of the last week fuddled his brain. Too, the wine he had imbibed ere we came to meet him was working on slowing him to more of a dullard than the simplest farm hand. Despairing, he called for his aide. "Giovanni, where did the missing men patrol?"

Giovanni, just coming to set a pair of tankards on the table, was unaware of anything amiss. He answered easily, "Why in the wine pressing district sir. Remember, we decided to make the watch double after the second night. Even with that, Thomas vanished on the third night while his partner, Petros, saw nothing. Have you a new idea?"

Lamberti motioned me outside without waiting for any more information. As soon as we were cloaked in the darkness, he answered many of my unspoken questions. "I need you to carry a lantern and show me the way to the wine pressing district."

I was perhaps too bold, yet Juan is still a friend of mine, so I found myself asking, "What of Juan? Do you plan to punish him?"

He turned to me and it seemed as if his eyes glowed behind the odd green glasses he wore. "Punish a man because he was the victim of some 'thing' in the darkness? Don't be absurd."

At that, I became afraid, for he seemed certain that what we were facing belonged to no human agency. The dark seemed to loom over the glow of the lantern that I had taken from the rack reserved for the watch's use when they went forth on their nightly rounds. Then I followed the receding form into the darkness, fear driving my feet to a staccato beat on the cobblestones as I labored to catch up with my companion. "Signore, could we not ride? It must be near to half a league as the roads wander, and my feet tire easily. Yet I have a fine steed, near the match of yours, and am certain that if your mount, noble beast that it is, be weary from this day's travel that my good friend Juan would gladly loan you one of his, for he is an agreeable sort of fellow." At his stare I lost my voice, which happens so seldom that it is a thing to be remarked upon, though it seems that this Lamberti is the sort to manage that with near anyone.

"Two points." His voice was a scant whisper, of the sort which makes one strain to hear for fear that you will miss something important. He lowered his glasses and it seemed that his eyes glowed red as coals in the reflected light of the lantern. "First, the thing we hunt might spook the horses if it comes near and I do not care to be thrown upon these stone cobbles. Second, I listen for sounds of it passing. Iron shoes would drown any faint trace which got past your talking."

With that he turned again to the road and motioned me to lead the way. With a start, I recalled he needed me to show him the path to the wine pressing district. I was sorely tempted to detour about, for surely in the dark none could be expected to know precisely where they were. In the morn, he could get another guide. I am not such a coward, yet there was a chill in the air which set the hairs on the back of my neck twitching. A sense of impending doom filled my heart and it was all I could manage to not quail in terror. It was with a slight tremor that I placed one foot in front of another and found myself reluctantly leading the fierce Inquisitor toward the wine pressing district.

I know I must seem the world's lowest knave, particularly when compared to the stalwart and implacable avenger with whom I traversed the deserted streets. An otherworldly aspect engulfed us with a surreal grip that set my heart racing as if a gang of reavers chased me. Each step led to new terrors until I was quite certain that I would have been luckier to be sent to the fires of the Inquisition rather than forced to tread these dark streets beside the strange specter of a hunter who strode silently beside me.

Suddenly, a terrified scream rent the night. With a wail sounding like the trump of doom in my ears, a young guard came dashing toward us, arms and legs flailing as he raced from whatever apparition had so alarmed him. Being a naturally cautious fellow, I would gladly have allowed the guard to pass, both to avoid being bowled over and to get a better start on eluding whatever nightmare creature must have sent him in such panicked flight. Yet Lamberti, that dour caballero, raised a gloved hand and, in a voice which brooked no refusal, called out, "Stop." A single word, yet it worked upon the fellow to the point that he not only halted his headlong rush, but stood at attention as if Juan de los Nueces himself were berating him for a lack in his uniform or carriage—ironic given Juan's own poor posture. I am not known for being ineffective in my speech, rather the opposite, yet Lamberti, for all he uses them so sparingly, seems as much a master of words as I, for every command he utters bears some unseen imprimatur causing others to heed his each and every demand as though obeying him were the most natural thing one could imagine. In truth, it seemed a single beat of my heart was greater than the time required for the young guard to halt and snap to, so unhesitatingly did he respond to Lamberti's demand.

Even as the youth gasped for breath, Lamberti strode further up the road, as though the entire incident were unworthy of comment, yet after what seemed only a very few moments, he turned to me, and with a quiet whisper, addressed my fears, which still rattled my bones till they might have been castanets in the hands of a skilled dancer. "I fear the trail grows cold. The creature fed already. We will return to the church and rest until dawn, then make further inquiries."

* * *

Seemingly, no sooner had I settled into sleep, than a rough hand was shaking me awake. With last night's wine in my head, I told the servant to let me sleep. It had given me the oddest dreams. Then, Father Oberto shouted my name and this startled me back to wakefulness. It took half a cup of Madeira before I could organize my thoughts sufficiently to recall the day prior. With this awakening, the deep-seated sense of dread returned, and I was utterly loathe to travel further with that mad champion, Lamberti. Let him gather another to aid him in his quest. I am a respected citizen in these parts, with enough status and wealth to excuse me from such intolerable work. I was quite certain that, as soon as I stated my needs, he would graciously allow me to return to my own life. With that conviction, I sought him out by the well in the courtyard of the small house adjacent to the church wherein Father Oberto makes his lodging.

I had just begun to open my mouth to speak, when Lamberti, having dashed a ladle of water over his head, turned and saw me. At that point, I took a terrible fright, for the Inquisitor's eyes were red as flame. This was not the red of a man who has had too much drink the night before, where the whites of his eyes are bloodshot, rather he was possessed of eerie red pupils which seemed alight with an inner fire. The look in those eyes silenced me even though I was still resolute in my determination to not waste another day chasing after phantoms. Hunting apparitions seems best left to those experienced in such matters. Had I not done enough, introducing him about the town to the priest and the watch captain? Then, as if I were a hero, did I not stalwartly accompany him on his mad search just yesterday evening?

As he raised the strange green glasses to his eyes, I was so struck by the realization that the color was not for some arcane purpose; to reveal evil or some such, but rather merely a method to disguise his uncanny eyes, that I near lost track of his words. "I need to speak with several people today. I would like your assistance."

Never have I regretted such a simple phrase before. Had I merely been a bit less garrulous, and not answered his question yesterday with that foolish phrase 'Happy I am to help a stranger' I would not be in such a state. Yet that response, a common politeness around our fine city, had bound me to this man—if man he was and not some terrible thing constrained to the service of the church. I saw no escape possible. This left no choice but to acquiesce and, with my nod, another round of horror began.

As blithely as if he were about shopping for new gloves, Lamberti set forth for the streets of the city, his long legs and tireless stride carrying him forth at such a rate that I was hard put to keep apace of him. I was naturally in a state for I had not obtained a single chance to change my clothing from the day prior, nor had I broken my fast beyond the cup and roll which Father Oberto had pressed on me at my rising. Further, I had managed but scant rest, plagued both by terrors, and by the narrow, hard bed—

which was reserved in the most part for mendicants from diverse orders who are wont to seek shelter in the church. It certainly did not compare in any favorable way to the warm, comfortable four-poster which is my normal habitué when I sleep at home. Nor did I have gentle company to make the bed softer by its presence. I suspect, from the vigor with which he carried himself, that the grim hunter was inured to hardships, and unimpressed by the delights of the fair sex. Perhaps any civilized comfort is an unnecessary luxury to him. Such characteristics are not at all what I would expect of a man of such status. Any Inquisitor has the right to demand the best which might be offered by any of the common folk. Certainly, the only other Inquisitor who had ever come across my path had partaken liberally of all our town had to offer, and railed at us for the quality into the bargain.

At this point, a mad fancy took me and I began to speculate as to whether some fiend had possessed the real hunter, which might well and enough explain his uncanny eyes, and that even now I was on my way to some ill-fated meeting. Mayhap monsters would sup on my blood and ponder its dainty qualities ere they roasted my flesh like a joint of mutton. I knew nothing of this fellow beyond his appearance. That itself was quite fantastic, for he had owned no more chance to repair his appearance than I, yet his red jacket was unwrinkled, his hat seemed well brushed, and even his boots looked to have been given a rubbing of wax, they gleamed so in the morning sun. I was so struck that I found myself commenting on it. "Good sir may I inquire," at this he shot me such a look that I nigh to faltered, yet with a moue of his lips and his nod I continued, "I am in quite a state this morn, yet you seem to have had a company of squires to attend your appearance, and I had begun to wonder how such a thing might occur, if not with supernatural aid."

To my utter amazement he stopped in his tracks, and I trembled at the prospect that I may have uncovered something best left alone, yet only for a moment, as his merriment burst forth in a mighty peal of laughter which would have done my friend Juan proud. "I let you sleep," he managed while wagging his finger. Then as quickly as it had come his mirth departed, and Lamberti was again the grim hunter, seeking perilous prey. "So we have no time to waste. If you cannot manage a better pace, borrow a horse from the watch captain and be quick." As fate, or one might convincingly argue Lamberti's planning, would have it, we chanced to be just outside the guard barracks when he spoke those words. I do not oft frequent the place, and what reasonable man would as the senior officers are seldom if ever therein, and the common soldiers are so dreadfully common. I had only just begun to make the expected pleasantries leading to my request for the loan, when Lamberti pushed into the small room which housed the officer of the watch. The officer was not Juan, he never rises so early, but an older lieutenant, whose lesser family connections meant he would certainly retire at that same rank. Lamberti spoke in the abrupt manner which seems very much to be the only way he knows. "Lieutenant, two horses saddled in the front yard. Alejandro, do you know of any recent widows?"

"Only one, the Widow Merovigian, a fine lady. Young as well, for her late husband, who was easily old enough to be her father, perished suddenly of a seizure, as heavyset men his age are wont to do." I did not add that I knew the widow quite well, at least from before she had been widowed. She entertained me often enough when her husband was about on his business, so I know there is no witch's mark upon her. Naturally I could not say such to the gallant caballero for he might think ill of me for succumbing to her ample charms. Who can say they have never been tempted by raven tresses? As well, it was not I who betrayed any wedding vow, but the lady herself. No sooner had these thoughts crossed my mind than Lamberti, with the grace of one born to the horse, swept upon his loaned steed and waited for me to gather myself for the task of riding with him on his appointed errand. It is not my nature to be overly proud, but I am a man of certain accomplishments and my skill as an equestrian is remarked on by many who are cavalry officers, yet I found myself suddenly as bereft of skill as the newest novice and clambered awkwardly into the saddle. No sooner was I seated than we set forth at a grim pace. Most worrisome, as I knew the route we followed and he did not, I was forced to lead and I was reluctant to be known as the man who had brought the inquisition to the doorstep of the lovely widow. Not only would those men who doubted the holiness of the Inquisitors shun me, but other attractive women might also deny me their company for fear that I would later turn on them. Thus, I hung my head in dreary acceptance of the wretched fate which had brought me to the state in which I now found myself. Had I but known what horrid beast lay at the end of our journey I might have turned back then, but I was not so wise that morning as I am now.

After a ride both far too brief and of interminable duration, we found ourselves at the home of the merry widow. Lamberti flowed from the saddle and had the door open, silent as a cat stalking a mouse, while I struggled to keep up. The widow's house was a fine city manse, with three full floors, a cellar, and attic rooms for servants, all decorated in a slightly out of date fashion which still showed good taste and lavish wealth. Until I stepped past the doorsill, I did not notice the dim gloom of the interior, and I was forced a moment to wait so my eyes might adjust, and in that briefest of instants my companion disappeared into the gloom of the house's interior, leaving me in a conundrum as to how, or even whether, I might follow without upsetting his plans. As I contemplated, a chill wind blew across my neck, without disturbing a single lock of hair, and sent a shiver down my spine.

"Hello, lover," the widow's dulcet voice breathed into my left ear. "Why did you bring such a man here? He will murder me without hesitation and call it justice, yet you know that I am innocent of the crimes he lays at my step."

It was at this point that I managed to work past the dread in my heart and turn to face the lady. My shock was great, for her skin, once fair with a blooming hint of blush, was pale as moonlight, while her lips were more crimson than I recalled and her raven locks moved, stirred by a breeze I could not feel. Lust and terror fought for control of my actions. She was more desirable than any I had ever seen, but it was an unholy beauty, the sort reserved for only the wickedest of folk. Gazing into her eyes, I realized she was right about Lamberti's intentions. Demons and monsters are born of ignorant peons' superstitious dread. I am an educated man, able to quote philosophy and logic from classical antiquity. Lamberti, a man of the church, sought an otherworldly explanation for the deaths that were surely the result of wicked men, for monsters do not exist. I eased my hand into my coat and wrapped my grip about a slim mazzagato, a fine small pistol from skilled Milanese artisans. As quietly as I might, I opened the small priming pan and checked to be sure the powder was yet

39

there. Then I sought out Lamberti, intent on insuring he would not murder an innocent while I might do aught to stop him.

The corridors, remembered from happier sunlit times when she was a wife and I her handsome paramour, twisted in the shadows until I became confused about my location. Only my determination to save her remained clear, all else blurred. Cobwebs and dust seemed to fill corridors which should have been clean and bright. A shadow moved beyond a turn in the stairs. I had no clear recollection of climbing them, yet I was as sure as I have ever been that I was on the second floor and my mysterious companion haunted the third. Red orbs glinted in the shadows and a voice pulled at me, "Alejandro Guevere, give up your pride and return to the truth."

The words startled me, and I thought about them a moment. Who would call to me in such a familiar manner? I hesitated, suddenly unsure what mad fancy had brought me to the Widow Merovigian's home. Then another voice, one I had oft heard in my dreams, came from beside my ear. "Your enemy is before you. Strike before he can murder us both."

My purpose restored, I raised the pistol, determined to strike with my first shot, aiming for the shape I could now discern in the darkened space. What true hunter would fail to bring light into such a place? Lamberti was a greater fraud than the earlier Inquisitor who had arrived with a full church company. Sighting down the barrel, I squeezed the trigger, and I am a fair shot. The ball sped straight and true, not veering aside as happens when the wadding is akilter. A flash and a cloud of smoke when, with a grunt, Lamberti staggered, then sped past me, brushing me aside with an uncanny ease. Ere I could turn, a violent scream rent the still air and a flash of light, bright as the sun breaking over the mountains at dawn, lit the air a brief moment turning the lingering gun smoke into a fantastic swirl of color. The light ended, plunging me into a blackness more complete than any I have ever witnessed.

"You should have waited outside, Alejandro. She almost killed you." Lamberti's voice sounded by my shoulder and I knew another moment's fear, this one rooted in earthly solidity. I had certainly shot an Inquisitor and such a crime would see me burned alive. Then a lamp lit and Lamberti, clutching at his left side, a dark stain spreading from beneath his fingers, nudged the prone form of the widow with the toe of his boot. "Wrap that in a blanket and carry it downstairs would you? I would spare others the risk of touching her."

"And what, pray tell, of me?" I began, somewhat indignant, for had I not already accompanied Lamberti here when I might have left off the night before? The Widow still looked herself, yet not. She was as beautiful as ever, but somehow not exactly of this world, though not enough to put a finger on. I feared to touch her, for there was no telling what power yet lay in her. Lamberti's glasses sank down his nose, exposing the uncanny red eyes, gleaming with unholy fire in the light of the lamp, and my voice stilled.

"You are already stained by contact with her, no more will rub off than has already." With that he said no more, and fearing for my life if I crossed him, I did as I was told.

After that, the trip back to the church was unremarkable. The Priest already had a spot for the thing to be buried. One from which it could never escape to trouble our town again. Lamberti took but a short rest while the father tended his pistol wound ere he rode off. I did not catch what transpired between them, but Father Oberto has never mentioned the bullet with which I had shot an Inquisitor.

———

C. M. Stucker is literally a rocket scientist. After NASA's successful completion of the space shuttle program, Charles started a personal challenge. He strives to make ends meet with his writing. The result is a new diet program — eat what you can afford — which fuels his writing élan. He writes science fiction, fantasy and mystery.

THE HEFT OF SORROW

Jane Buchan

It was Lucien Morrow's habit to rise at four so he might take his time with shaving and breakfast before he left for work in town. Arlene Morrow complained about this habit, wanting him to be there when she got up at six to share coffee time and a proper goodbye kiss. She reasoned that his drive, an hour in bad weather, half that in good, put him at work long before eight, the official time for his day to begin at Thomson's. Arlene was assistant produce manager for the local Price Chopper and on principle didn't punch in until seven fifty-nine for her eight o'clock shift. She couldn't comprehend why Lucien felt the need to leave for Thomson's so early.

Lucien was the sort of man who liked to accommodate others. If he could have changed this habit for his wife of thirty years, he would have. He adored Arlene. But arriving early for work was as important as arising early to be open to the possibilities of each new day. Something sacred expanded into this space he made for his predawn life. At least that's how he felt about it. He told Arlene a proper kiss, and by this he meant one she was conscious for, was not worth the anxiety of starting out late for a drive on which anything might prevent him from arriving at Thomson's on time. She laughed at his worries over the drive to town, and over his meticulous care with car maintenance and snow tires, and even over his observations of the sky before bed, a good natured, familiar laugh he heard without rancor. Lucien and Arlene had been together since childhood. Each admitted privately, and on occasion to members of their unwieldy, combined family, that they had been blessed to find such easy going companionship along with the teenaged passion that smacked them head over heels into an early marriage that pointedly did not bear children for another five years.

Lucien's drive took him over an "outer space" that resonated with his love of expansive time. A two-lane black top road that heaved in winter and melted in summer, this route, traveled mostly by locals, had been known to host spectacular single car and truck accidents from time to time. Lucien once came upon a crash as first responders lifted a small dead child from a mangled SUV that had rolled over several times after skidding on black ice. The sight of that small dead child left him pondering the concept of time for months.

Despite the occasional lessons in caution, his early departure gave Lucien a proprietary feel for the road. On this particular morning, while keeping an eye out for the worst, he reveled in the familiar deer yards and moose crossings he passed, and in the secret fox dens he sensed camouflaging themselves in the bracken beneath the birch and maple and tamarack that the road, his road, carved through so precisely. Winter and summer, he drove with the windows cracked to admit the faint smells of moss and rotting logs. He felt these scents connected him to a primitive version of himself—a cave man of earlier eons—so that whenever the moon or early dawn called into existence the few homesteads set back from the road, he was startled to find himself among modern men and women.

These signs of human habitation set him wondering if these people, still tucked within their warm beds, knew of his early, solitary journey. Did they turn in their sleep at the sound of his passing? Did they interpret the sound of his truck as a comforting sign that all was still well in the world beyond their toehold in the vast wilderness?

He passed seven homes on his way to work, each of them unique in the way they burrowed into hill or valley or wood so as to appear grown, like giant toadstools, out of the land. Over the nine years of his drive to Thomson's, these homes remained closed to him, but on this day in January, a week before his forty-eighth birthday, a surprise awaited him. The fourth homestead, one he knew as The Morgentallers, Dirk and Friedl, because of the hand-painted, bright red, stylized letters on their mailbox, and because their nephew, Charlie Fander, was one of Thomson's several apprentices, had lights shining from every window when he cruised by at five.

Lucien drove past the lighted windows until his mind began to niggle at what he'd seen. Pondering those lights, so unusual at that hour, he pulled off the road. All at once he imagined he'd arrived at work at the usual time, exchanged the usual convivial remarks with his mates, and asked Charlie Fander if all were well with his Aunt and Uncle Morgentaller. A shiver went through him as Charlie Fander answered, quite clearly, "Thanks for asking, Lucien. My Uncle Dirk died early this morning. My Aunt Friedl called my mom with the news at three this morning."

Lucien felt something in his heart begin to spin. He was not given to prescience and yet, here he was, in the midst of what appeared to be a vision about Dirk Morgentaller's death. As if the vision were fast-forwarded by an unseen hand, he watched himself during his morning's work on a set of eight pine arrow-backs, meticulously overseeing the finishing details that were his trademark. Time continued to speed by. At noon his lunch, usually a welcomed pleasure in the daily round, was tasteless in his mouth. Fascinated, he watched himself chew his tuna on rye, his favorite, without pleasure.

As he sat in the dark on the familiar road — his road — Lucien felt disoriented by the knowledge of another self in another place. A part of him embraced this duality because it meant that no matter what his hands might be doing at work, this other self might be here, on this dark stretch of road leading past the Morgentaller house. This place was important, not only because of Dirk Morgentaller. It was where he'd seen a moose calf amble down the road, all legs and head, on his way to the neighboring hay field. The calf had not been bothered by the sound of Lucien's decelerating engine or by the lights that roved over his long legs and boney rump. The calf remained unconcerned when Lucien's truck heaved noisily over uneven asphalt. The young, foolish creature seemed to travel in a trance, but once, Lucien remembered, a blank face peered over a honey-colored shoulder and then, without any sign of worry or interest, turned away. Remembering the calf's indifference made him wonder if he, Lucien, might not be a real, flesh-and-blood man after all.

Without knowing what he was about, Lucien started his truck, inched it into drive, made the u-turn his heart demanded he make. A quarter of a mile up the road, in the small cut Joe Deptford made to accommodate his grader loads, Lucien Morrow parked. He looked at his watch and then opened the door and stepped out into the snow. An unfamiliar feeling of dread pulled him deep into the hardwood forest. He expected to make noise, reasoned he should have made noise, but his footfalls were silent.

As he walked, Lucien was aware of a Christmas present from Arlene, the flannel scarf around his neck, of the heat trapped there, of his ears cold beneath the dome of his Thomson's cap. He veered more deeply into the woods at the same moment that he understood he couldn't keep what he was doing secret. Everyone in these parts knew him, knew his truck, and it was there, in clear sight, on the shoulder of the road. If anyone came by, they would stop to look for him, sure something was wrong. Despite the threat of an unfamiliar, perplexing shame, Lucien kept on.

He stopped at the clearing marking the edge of the Morgentaller back garden and stared at the two trampled pathways that led to the house, the narrower one to the compost pile, the broader to the woodshed. Surrounding these paths the snow was flawless, without the deer and turkey tracks embroidering the snow around similar pathways in his own back garden. It occurred to him to leave tracks. That way, if Friedl Morgentaller discovered him, he could tell her he needed to use the phone. But he knew he would not be discovered as surely as he knew Dirk Morgentaller had died. Hadn't Charlie Fander told him so?

In his imagination, the widowed Mrs. Morgentaller put on her parka and left the warmth of her bright house to walk the short distance to the tree line. She looked down and discovered Lucien's size eleven boot prints before she called out, "Thank you. Thank you for coming." It seemed to him then that he and the widow had entered into a pact together. He shook his head very slightly to dispel the dazzling idea of an agreement between the recently bereaved woman and the stranger that had taken up residence in his body when he'd first caught sight of the Morgentaller lighted windows.

Lucien stepped onto the path leading from the wood-shed, walked to the house, and then onto the pristine snow bordering the back wall of the house. The first window, whose sill sat only two feet from the ground, opened onto a medium-sized, dimly lit, womb-coloured room. A sewing machine sat on a table in the midst of small squares of fabric. Beyond this room, across a hallway, Mrs. Mor-gentaller — Friedl — stood in an ancient copper tub, the kind Lucien had seen in old westerns. In these movies, the tub, usually placed in the middle of the kitchen floor, was filled with pails of hot water heated on a wood stove. He could see from his place outside the window that Friedl Mor-gentaller's copper tub had been plumbed in. Dirk likely found it for her on a scrounge to one of the same New Hampshire haunts Arlene visited with Lucien, where salvage from old buildings could be had for hauling charg-es.

Friedl was a large woman, and her abundant blonde hair made her appear even larger, piled as it was on top of her head, a style that added to her height and broadened her face. Her skin, at least all he could see of it, bright pink from the heat of her bath, exhaled an opalescent mist. Lucien held his breath when suddenly Friedl reached for a nearby towel. He knew without knowing how he knew that she had been thinking a while about toweling off but had only just worked up the energy to move.

Arlene was a small woman, had always been small, even through the pregnancies and childhoods of their four children. He knew from the various pieces of lingerie and clothing he'd bought for birthdays and Christmases over the years — teddies, lounge pajamas, and matching lace panties and bras — Arlene was a steadfast size four. Naked, her body offered him all the pleasures of womanhood. Clothed it seemed all planes and angles and, he had to

48

admit as he studied Friedl Morgentaller, brutally uninteresting. He estimated Friedl Morgentaller's body would make five, perhaps six, of Arlene's. He estimated the weight of her pendulous breasts with their large pale nipples and when he'd absorbed all he could of their mysteries, focused on the shape of her thighs and the contours of her belly. When she turned her back to dry her legs, he was astonished by the symmetry of her rump.

Lucien viewed the curves and crevices of this unknown woman with perplexity rather than lust or titillation, as if in studying her he might find the heft of sorrow in the secret recesses of her flesh. He studied her hands as she toweled her limbs and torso and felt his heart break at the sight of the shiny red polish on her toenails. As he drank in Friedl Morgentaller, a cat came into the bathroom, a large black cat that stood on hind legs to inspect the contents of the tub the woman stood in, toweling, toweling.

The first sob broke from Lucien's chest without any warning. It was in the air around him, its echo mingling with his visible breath. He put his hand over his mouth, muffling the sobs that welled up from what seemed like a fissure so deep and so alien it could not possibly belong to him. He crouched down in the snow, afraid he might frighten the newly widowed woman. The idea of frightening Friedl Morgentaller horrified him.

Crouching, his tears falling onto the trampled snow, he found himself hoping she would discover him, open her back door, invite him in for coffee. He wanted with all his heart to share her heartache. He waited to be made honorable, his shoulders tense and expectant, for several minutes. When she didn't come to the door, he thought of knocking on it. His sobs grew quieter until they were nothing more than small mewlings that attracted the cat to the inside window sill.

Feeling useless and bereft, Lucien edged away from the Morgentaller house. No longer concerned that his tracks might frighten the widow, he stumbled around the house to the long drive leading to the road. It was still his road, he told himself. It was still the road connecting his garage, his woodshop, his kitchen, his bedroom, to the woods, to the moose, to the deer, to the men and boys in the Thomson's woodworking shop in town. It was only he who'd changed, he told himself. All else remained the same.

Lucien reached the shoulder of the road and began to run, not because of fear or guilt but because the pull back into ordinariness and timeliness had taken hold of him once more. The truck, his truck, whispered to life with a flick of his key. He cinched his seatbelt tight and shifted into drive before he could see, before his tears stopped, before he was himself again. A few miles after his second u-turn of the morning it was all over. The heater warmed his feet, helped him to forget how they'd gotten so cold.

At work, he hung his coat on his customary peg, leaned in with interest when Aubrey began to talk about a film he'd seen the night before. A man had been listening in...it was a German film...he hadn't minded the subtitles. Suddenly, Lucien imagined the large German woman, still naked from her bath, in the room with them. Lucien held his breath and then expelled it with a force that unnerved him and made his fellow workers glance at him curiously.

"Do you ever do secret things?" Lucien asked the men abruptly. Startled, Aubrey took a step away from him. Lucien knew then that none of them were what they seemed, that their routines of gluing and joining and sanding were distractions from the deep lives they did their best to conceal from one another and themselves. Someone dropped a large clamp on the cold cement floor. The noise freed the men to move away from one another into their usual work routines.

In the corner, Charlie Fander mused over an order. Lucien walked to the boy knowing that the morning had given him something he'd never experienced before, something that was connected to the young apprentice. The boy looked up at him and said simply, "My Uncle Dirk died, and my aunt, she's broke up." The boy took a moment to shuffle around in his grief. "Ma says she'll be going back to Germany. It's been lonely here without her sisters. She moved to Vermont for my Uncle. They met when she was here on a visitor's visa way back in the seventies."

Lucien nodded. "Help her," he said, pressing his terrible stare onto the boy's young, bewildered face. "She'll need you to help her pack up...and to remember him." Charlie Fander colored scarlet. "It's something, to help someone who's grieving. It's something." The other men, sensing Lucien's treacherous emotional currents, busied themselves with setting out the tools for the morning's work. Lucien touched the boy's arm. "You like to build?" he asked.

The boy shrugged. "It's something," he answered. And then, as if in the grips of a revelation, he added, "I don't dislike building."

"That's something, too," Lucien said.

The scent of sawn wood and linseed oil soothed the deep fissure in Lucien's heart. He set to work with his usual concentration and pleasure and at five gathered his lunch pail and coat, finally free of the burden of dread he'd felt when he'd crept up on the Morgentaller house earlier that morning. He knew with certainty what was inside the house now.

On his way home, he counted fifteen cars parked outside the Morgentaller property. All the windows blazed at the end of the drive. As he passed, he silently wished Friedl Morgentaller balm for her broken heart. At home, Arlene was in the midst of defrosting a stew they'd cooked together when Larry Olsen claimed his five-point and shared the venison with everybody in their neck of the woods. "I stopped at the Morgentallers this morning," Lucien said, pouring wine. His voice was his own again. He knew Arlene wasn't listening yet. "I stopped because I wanted to see what grief looked like."

He watched his wife's head swivel up from the salad bowl. Her eyes held his. "What do you mean?" Her voice reminded him of a rasp making its first pass on new wood.

Lucien allowed the story to tumble out, watching solemnly as his wife listened, her hands gripping the counter edge as if afraid she might fall if she let go of the familiar, glossy wood. When he was done Arlene drew back her shoulders. It was an old, familiar barometer of trouble coming. "You saw her naked? You peeked in her windows?"

Lucien bowed his head and fought for the courage to see this journey to its end. "It wasn't like that," he said. "I think it was more the losing of him I wanted to see."

Arlene walked out of the room. He was left with the smell of venison, of onions, with the comforting sight of their cooking utensils in easy promiscuity on the counter. "I couldn't help it," he called after her, almost jovial. "It was like nothing I've felt before. The lights have never been on, and then they were, and...I imagined the husband was dead. And it turns out he was."

Arlene returned to the doorway. "You know this dead guy?"

"His nephew. From work."

"Oh," said Arlene, as if this explained everything. And then she asked in a voice that was not quite hers, "What were you thinking when you were looking in her window? I'd hate to think of anybody doing that to me."

Lucien reflected on his morning. "I wasn't thinking," he said after a time. "I was crying." He had begun to cry again. She raised her eyebrows. Arlene Morrow had always counted on Lucien to be the strong one. Even when he put Buster down after the cancer got his second hind leg and the vet told them the dog would have to drag himself about on little wheels if they let him live, he didn't cry. Her face went pale and the counter no longer held her up. She crumpled to the floor. "I know," he said. He stood over her, crying. "I know, Arlene."

Arlene got to her knees and pressed her face against Lucien's legs. "Let's go to the funeral," she whispered. "Look in the paper. Tell me when and I'll take time off. You've had a shock. You need closure. That's what Dr. Phil says. After a shock, you have to have some kind of ritual for closure. That's what a funeral is."

"No," said Lucien, louder than he intended. "I don't want to go to the funeral. I didn't know the man. It wouldn't be right."

"What then?" She took his hands and pulled herself to her feet. Lucien moved away from his wife, sorry he'd made his confession, sorry he'd asked Charlie Fander anything at all. There was something reverent, something insistent and mysterious at work in his soul regarding Friedl Morgentaller. He heaved another great sob knowing he would have to live with this thing from now on, this ability to see beyond the bounds of the physical world into its secret, sorrowful places. He would have to live with the image of the widow toweling off, her cat on the low window sill answering his small, stifled cries.

———

Canadian Jane Buchan has lived in Vermont since 2002. As well as writing fiction and non-fiction, Jane currently teaches writing and research courses at the Community College of Vermont, and in her life coaching practice helps clients build resilience after school and life learning traumas that contribute to high Adverse Childhood Experiences (ACEs) scores. Learn more about Jane at http://www.winterblooms.net.

A WAY WITH WOMEN *

Margaret Pearce

First Engineer John Scarlett showed a discontented face to his cabin mirror. Today was his birthday. It was also the landfall at Thetis, and the whole crew had been granted shore leave. Two things normally worth celebrating.

Except the birthday he was celebrating was his fortieth, and revisiting a planet was depressing. The ten years of his absence was usually twenty to thirty years on their time scale, and looking up old friends and acquaintances was a sharp reminder of the transience of life.

Still, the mirror reflected a fine figure of a man. He straightened his shoulders and tucked in his paunch. There was very little grey in his thick dark hair, and if his eyes were starting to bag, and the lines around his jowls deepen, so what! Lines of experience and maturity gave a man character. Half these smooth-faced kids looked like pansies. At least he looked every inch a totally masculine man.

The rest of the crew were in a riotous holiday mood. Thetis was the ideal place to spend leave. Its reputation had spread through the galaxy. There were no hostile life forms, diseases, or any political instability. The medikits and stunpacks were worn as a formality.

The civilisation had a highly developed technology, but only advanced in a way that made living more pleasant.

* A version of this story was published in CYGNUS CHRONICLER June 1980 and THE MENTOR 72, November 1991 one use only.

There was heat, light, power and sanitation, but no slums or grim rows of factories. The fully automated factories were discreetly underground, and the airy council chambers, hotels, temples, amusement places and private residences were set among well-kept parks and gardens. An ideal climate, magnificent scenery, and an over-abundance of beautiful, hospitable women enhanced its attractions.

John watched the swaying hips of the cute little biologist in front of him. She had a narrow waist and long legs that showed to full advantage in the tight silver uniform. He brooded for a few seconds on her lack of taste in deserting him for the blonde boy who looked as if he hadn't yet started shaving, and then cheered up.

Thetis was one planet where there were plenty more fish in the sea. The women outnumbered the men by a ratio of ten to one. Men were such a novelty even the most miserable specimens of masculinity were rushed, and he was no miserable specimen. He inflated his chest at the thought.

'Getting ready to conquer the planet, Casanova?' jeered the voice behind him.

He looked around at his dumpy second engineer and hid his annoyance behind a patronising smile. Her attempt to beat him to the job of first engineer had been slick, but after all he was the best damn engineer on the space freighter. She was sharp and smart, and ten years younger than him, but she was only a woman, and a dowdy one at that. Women had their place, but not in the engineering profession.

"Enjoy your leave, Carmen," he said, and had the pleasure of seeing her face darken.

In John's one-use-for-women mind, Carmen was definitely surplus on a planet of beautiful women. Come to think of it, she was surplus issue on a freighter light years from nowhere. Pleased with that last thought, he paused on the landing field, trying to decide where to go.

He could look up Llalla of course, but she would have aged twenty years to his ten. He was not a great one for renewing old romances. There was only ten days' leave, and the planet was crammed with so many beautiful women he felt he should share himself out generously.

"Just the man I wanted to see," said the Captain.

John straightened to attention. Not that there was any need to. The Captain was in civvies, and very tasteless civvies at that. He wore high wading boots over stained and dirty cotton trousers, a torn shirt without buttons with an old hand-knitted cardigan over it. His bald head was covered by an old towelling hat threaded through with fish hooks and flies.

"Sir," John muttered in a pained voice.

"I've got a fishing trip lined up," the Captain said. He handed over a thick satchel. "It's the serum that the third temple asked for. Deliver it for me, will you?" It was an order, not a request.

A hovercraft tilting under the weight of several old men wearing the same type of stained and ragged clothing as the Captain swooped down. There was a babble of old men's voices as the Captain climbed in, and the hovercraft spun around, gathering speed as it headed in the direction of the ocean.

John shrugged, and hailed a hovercraft. The young man driving gave him a resentful look when he asked for the third temple, and slid up the partition around the driving area. John ignored the driver. He tried to remember what Llalla had told him about the temples on his last incident-filled leave. It was either her mother or her grandmother who were temple caste. He couldn't remember whether

Llalla had a profession or not. All he remembered was her zest for being hospitable.

Most of the medical profession and all their attendant biologists and technicians were automatically temple caste. Temples were like hospitals and research clinics merged into one. They were still built in high conical bullet shapes modelled on the first disabled space ship that the original settlers used as combined hospital and laboratory. Only now, the high cones that reared over the gracious low buildings scattered around the countryside were built of white stone or shining marble.

The third temple was unmistakable, with its three blue lines of windows high up its smooth sides. The hovercraft drifted up the imposing steps to the wide landing. Two tall women in the regulation sweeping white robes watched him as he stepped down from the hovercraft.

A lot of the temple women were tall, which set off interminable arguments among the crew as to whether height was related to intelligence. The temple women were the physicians, research scientists and technicians.

"First Engineer John Scarlett of the space ship Lucillus," he reported. "I have the serum ordered."

The women inspected him in silence. They were both young with long glossy red-brown hair and luminous grey eyes set in regular features. However, there was a rigid austerity in their faces that detracted from their attractiveness. Their countenances hinted of a regime of celibacy, poverty and obedience. All concepts that made John uncomfortable.

"Take it to Llalla the third," one of the women said at last.

She snapped her fingers. Another young woman came forward. She was just as tall, but there wasn't the same severity in her face. Her mouth dimpled into a smile, and her blue eyes glowed pleasure and admiration. She had a heavy mane of long golden hair.

"Please come with me," she said in a husky voice.

John followed her up to the circular ramp and along the glowing antiseptic corridors. He wondered if it was possible that Llalla the third was the Llalla he knew? If so, he calculated she would be about fifty now.

His guide paused at a door and knocked. It slid open. She winked at John and left. John stepped through into a small office. The black-haired girl sitting in front of the screen looked up. She looked exactly how John remembered Llalla. Perhaps Llalla had passed on her striking good looks to a daughter.

"The serum ordered," he said lamely.

The brown eyes inspected him. Then they lightened to the flashing pools of pure gold in the way John remembered.

"It is you, John? I wondered if you were still with the Lucillus."

John put the satchel down and stared. The long black hair rippled down her back, and her face was smooth and innocent in its young curves. It was Llalla and she still looked twenty! He tried for an uneasy grin. She stood up and flowed into his arms. He kissed her. She was exactly the same as he remembered with the almost physical aura of vitality and energy.

"We're here for a fortnight. Have you some time to spend with me?" he asked with his face in the remembered perfume of her hair.

"It will take some time to clear this lot." She gestured at her screen. "Why don't you go sailing. There's a spare hovercraft at the house if you want to wander around, and I'll catch up with you when I finish."

John nodded and patted her rump. He must have made some impression for her to remember over twenty years his fascination with the small sailing boats. It was where they had originally met after all. They had had a spectacular collision with a tangled mess of ropes and sails, which forced them to the shore before they could disengage.

There was a spring in his step as he left the temple. He nodded cheerfully to the two tall women on duty at the entrance. They looked through him with an untroubled detachment.

Llalla's house was as he remembered, a well-built stone dome nestled into the side of the cliffs overlooking the ocean. The winding track still led down to the little boat-house. He thought it was steeper and further than he remembered, but the same pleasure came back at the sight of the sleek hulls and the carefully folded sails.

He settled to the delights of sailing. After a while his thoughts came back to Llalla. What was the secret of her inexplicable youthfulness? All the people on the planet were young and beautiful. It was one of the wonders of the galaxy. Until this trip, he had never seen anyone old, so it was a mystery where the Captain had dredged up his fishing companions. They were as wrinkled and gap-toothed, with their sparse white and grey hair, as any of their Earth counterparts.

There had been rumours that the colonists of Thetis had a longevity process, but ones unsupported by fact. John scowled as he remembered the endless discussions about the youthful population of Thetis. Was the ageing population euthanised? Maybe the underground factories weren't automated after all, and the oldsters were imprisoned out of sight working them until they died.

Space travellers had little better to do during the long months between planets than to endlessly speculate, exaggerate, and no doubt misinterpret the eerie, odd and unusual customs of the various planets. Most populations had their own collection of distorted rumours and hearsay surrounding some unproven superstition.

It seemed to be a fact that the visible population of Thetis was handsome and in vital good health. So the ageing processes were not as obvious as would be in an environment with problems of hostile life forms, poisonous atmosphere, viruses and incorrect diet.

John leaned over hard as he tacked around. The oldest men seen apart from the Captain's companions were approaching middle age. If there were a longevity process, would women, to him being the vainer sex, take its path earlier in life? It did seem logical to assume that a male would prefer to stabilise the longevity process nearer his prime. What man would want to spend a few hundred years looking like a half-grown, gangly, youth?

Then again, he had just seen some decrepit old men. Where did they fit into the planet's culture? Were they rejects from a longevity process? Was the longevity an accumulated genetic thing because of the favourable environment, or was it a deliberate process? Was there some way he could separate the whispered rumours and speculations from concrete facts?

John sailed back to land and put away the boat and the tricky to rig, orange silk sails. Llalla was still away. He took out the motorized hand glider, and drifted around the scattered buildings. Young men and women were flirting and dancing in the amusement parks. There were a few men around his own age, but no old men or women. It was a planet of young people.

He studied the youthful population enviously. At the back of his mind pounded the remorseless reminder that spacemen crew are grounded at age forty-five. Captains last until sixty-five but they have less physical demands placed on their ageing frames. All the crew had to have quick physical reflexes and agile minds to deal with unpredictable and highly variable dangers. And ageing is a process that is only speeded up by the inevitable high doses of radiation from outer space.

It wasn't fair that soon he would have to step down, or be pushed aside by a younger, and less qualified person. There were worlds he hadn't explored, women he hadn't met, and technology he hadn't mastered. The idea took firm root in his mind. A reprieve from ageing. Was it possible?

The hang glider left the populated areas behind, lifting over the dense forest and jagged mountains. For an hour or so John was mostly flying over a wilderness untouched by development, then the forest thinned to farms and neatly landscaped parks and gardens. The next village was unusual only because it lacked the usual cone-shaped temple.

Figures strolling on the paths looked up. Some boys wrestling on a patch of green lawn stopped what they were doing. Seeing the markings on the hovercraft, they jeered and called out something which he couldn't possibly hear. A cascade of stones thudded on the underside of the metallic craft.

John spun the hang glider in a lazy circle to return. An old man with a fringe of white hair on the edge of his bald skull looked up and spat with a contempt obvious even from a distance. It was all very puzzling because of the planet's unblemished reputation for friendliness. John shrugged the incident aside and set course back to Llalla's dome.

She was now home, the place brought alive by her presence. John looked at her fresh beauty with rather more than simple appreciation. He couldn't submerge his greed for longevity beneath his desire for the company of his friend. He was as sure of his ability to discover the secret as he was sure of his way with women. Fortunately, he didn't have to fish very much to get Llalla talking about the subject.

"Sorry, I couldn't get away earlier. My grandmother died recently, and there is still loads to sort out," Llalla apologised with a complete absence of sentiment.

"Was she as beautiful as you?" John asked.

Llalla laughed. "I don't take after her. She had red hair, big brown eyes and white skin."

"Was she very old?" John asked after a pause.

"About five hundred years, I think," Llalla said with a yawn. "Goodness, I'm tired. We had the vigil for Gran last night plus my clinic today and seeing solicitors. I'll be glad to get some sleep."

"What did she die of?" John tried to keep his voice casual, but it was an effort. He moved away so she wouldn't be aware of his tremor.

Llalla stretched on the bed and shut her eyes. "Just the usual. She decided she had enough, asked permission, and did a ceremonial fade out."

John decided that as excited as he was to know more, he shouldn't over press if he was also going to re-kindle their relationship that evening. But it didn't take him long the next day to return to the subject. He felt the pressure of time in the most immediate of ways, for in just another eight days they would leave the planet. In ten years when the ship touched down again, he would be a retired fifty and grounded on his home planet. He was back on the subject as they prepared to go sailing together.

"Was your grandmother a doctor as well?" he asked.

Llalla tacked the orange sails in a sudden swoop that caused him to strain every muscle to sway around with the hull.

"Engineer," Llalla called back. "Isn't this fun? I haven't been sailing for ages. What do you think of the new sails?"

"Terrific," John yelled back, gritting his teeth at the warning ache of his back.

That night he soaked in the hot mineral spa and Llalla scrubbed his back.

"That's wonderful," he almost groaned. "God! I wish I were like you. Don't you ever get tired, Llalla?"

There was silence. She had stopped scrubbing. John turned to look at her. Was there a grim amusement in her eyes? She lowered them and blushed. John decided it was his imagination and all the steam.

"Would you really like to be like me?" she asked.

"I would love to." He put all the sincerity he could into his voice.

"You're an engineer, first class?"

John nodded and waited. Llalla looked thoughtful. "Now that Llalla the first is gone we need another engineer. The Elders won't let us advertise for recruits, not wanting over much publicity. Anyway, the custom is that the men have to volunteer of their own free will or it doesn't take."

"What happens if it doesn't take?" John demanded, wondering if there was a grimmer reason for so few elderly men in the society.

Llalla evaded this question. "So many of the men," she blushed again, "are refusing the longevity treatment. They never used to. It's all this men's lib."

"Is it a long treatment?" John asked.

"No, but you would have to resign your commission."

John was silent. His career was his life, but without longevity, his career was finished in five years anyway. Space travel was not for geriatrics.

"I'll resign," he said at last, used the cover of reaching for a towel to avoid having to look into her eyes.

He would write an official resignation, show it to her, and then not hand it in. With the longevity process, the world would be his oyster. The clause in his contract that demanded avoidance of other worlds' religions, rites and entanglements, physical, intellectual, emotional and psychical didn't really apply this time.

The ship wouldn't be back for another twenty years by this planet's time scale, and by then anything could have happened. He could even transfer to some other ship that avoided this corner of the galaxy.

An anxious forty-eight hours went by while the temple considered his application. Another day passed as they checked his engineering skills, and gave him interminable IQ tests. It was twenty-four hours after that before the instructions came to proceed to the temple.

"You have handed in your resignation?" Llalla checked anxiously.

"Of course," John lied.

"And you do understand what is involved?" Llalla asked as she escorted him to the operation theatre, deep underground.

"That it's a longevity operation and in return I am contracted to the service of the temple until I choose to fade-out." He kissed her. "It means my love, we're going to be able to spend a hell of a lot more time together."

A faint cloud crossed her face. "If it is still your desire, my love," she answered, and kissed him back with an unexpected passion.

John was bathed and cleansed even including an unpleasant enema, and laid out on an operating table with a nasty resemblance to a sacrificial altar.

"You are volunteering to undergo the longevity process of your own free will?" the masked person beside him asked.

"I am volunteering to undergo the longevity process of my own free will and in return promise to work for the temple until I decide to fade out," he recited as Llalla had coached him.

It seemed to satisfy the circle of gowned and masked listeners. Someone came forward with a hypodermic. He took one last look as the circle of faces, anonymous in masks and theatre gowns and drifted into unconsciousness.

When he woke, he was back at Llalla's dome. He had a thick tongue as though he had been drugged, and a slight soreness in his side. He couldn't see or feel anywhere on his body that he had undergone an operation.

"You all right?" Llalla asked.

"Yeah, but where did they operate?"

"It's all done with a deep injection, no cutting, and they use a keyhole camera through a tiny incision. So no worries. They know exactly where they're going. It's only a ten-minute op."

"Why does my mouth feel so foul?"

"It's the drug to keep you knocked out," Llalla explained as she gave him a colourless drink. "You have to be kept immobilised until the process takes effect, and it's easier to keep you drugged than strap you down for that long."

John took a long drink and immediately felt better, a lot better. His whole body was flooded with a sense of well-being. The soreness was gone, his vision clearer, and his mind felt sharper and more alert.

"After a decent breakfast, what say we go sailing," he suggested.

"There'll be plenty of time later," Llalla promised with a smile. "Right now we have to go back to work. There are some repair jobs waiting for you."

John went with her to the third temple, and learned that it was now his temple. The guardians greeted him with courtesy and escorted him to the lift that dropped with sickening speed below the ground. Once down he was handed over to the tall golden-haired girl.

She dimpled at the sight of him. She waited until the lift closed on the austere faces of the guardians, put her arms around him and kissed him passionately.

"Welcome back," she breathed in her husky voice.

John kissed her back with enthusiasm, but he felt a fraction uneasy as he stared into the sparkling blue eyes level with his own. Very tall females were unusual on his home planet. Still, a man was adaptable.

"What about this repair work" he suggested after a while.

She told him she was also an engineer, and that her name was Derfa. At first he was a bit taken aback by her technical knowledge, until he remembered she could have more years of experience than he had. They worked together in the echoing flood lit caverns on the power generators.

John, immersed in the occupation he loved more than women, looked uncomprehending as Derfa had to repeat her statement—it was time to eat. They caught the lift up, and he emerged blinking in the well-lit temple. It was just on sunset.

"I've lost count of the days," he said to Derfa. "What day is it."

"Tomorrow is the planet rest day," Derfa said cheerfully.

The Captain had planned for the ship to lift before being inconvenienced by the planetary rest day. How many days had he lost? The ship would be blasting off within the hour. And worse, the temple's exit was locked down by a vibrating forcefield preventing him from walking out.

"I've got to see Llalla," he told Derfa.

She pouted, but blew him a kiss and joined the crowds of white-clad females heading towards the communal dining room. John raced up the circular ramp that led to Llalla's office. Although the ship wouldn't blast off for another fifty minutes, all ports would be sealed within the next half-hour. Once sealed they would stay sealed. The Captain was not the sort of person to abort his lift-off for the sake of one crewmember.

"Llalla," he blurted out. "I've got to return to the ship."

Her eyebrows raised. She looked shocked. "You belong here now, John."

"Of course." John's mind was racing as he thought of the forcefield across the temple entrance. Was the forcefield to keep people in or out of the temple? Even when they were turned off, forcefields took minutes before they dropped enough in power to allow one to pass through. "I must give my resignation verbally, otherwise it won't be accepted."

Llalla remained silent.

"Don't you understand, Llalla?" He put all the sincerity he could in his voice. "If I don't, I'll be listed as a deserter, and there'll be criminal charges the next time the ship touches down."

Much to his relief she nodded, and opened a channel on the screen. John thanked providence for the cultural pattern of this society where a man's word was his bond, and a verbal contract in the presence of witnesses was considered almost sacred. It was the one argument the guardians would understand.

"You have left it a bit late, which might have been our fault," the guardian admitted when she lifted the force field. "You have worked a very long shift doing repairs."

"I'll come straight back," John promised earnestly.

"Naturally," a shade of grim amusement crossed the austere face. "You now belong here."

John gave Llalla a last kiss and pelted down the winding ramp, through the archway and hailed a hovercraft. "I've got to make the ship inside ten minutes," he gasped.

The spaceport pulsated to the roar of the engines. John sprinted for the gantry with its lift leading to the one small cargo port still open.

The Captain was bristling with indignation. "Thirty seconds more and you would have been logged as a deserter. Get to your post Mister Scarlett."

John tumbled into the contour couch by his control board. Carmen, the second engineer, gave him a sour smile. "Nearly did it this time, Casanova."

"And you nearly stepped into a pair of boots too big for you," he commented.

The sirens shrilled their warning. The ship lifted. The screens filled with the velvet blackness of space, and the receding green and gold planet hanging like a jewel in it.

Elation welled inside John, adding to his sense of joyous well-being. He got away with it! He now had longevity and his career. When he finished his shift he went to his cabin.

He wasn't tired, but he was sure that the radiant energy surging through him would be noticeable. Of course, it was too early for the treatment to show, but his cheeks were pink and his eyes sparkled with excitement and good health. He threw his crumpled cap into the corner and inspected his hair. Was it his imagination or were the odd streaks of grey fading?

The weeks, and then the months slid by. They made landfall at first one planet and then another. All the time, John felt better and better. The cute biologist left the blond young boy and moved back into his cabin. He needed less sleep and had more energy, his brain seemed clearer and retained information more easily.

His new-found stamina was tested to the utmost when the ship was caught in the swirling tail of meteor dust. The entire crew worked around their shifts with frantic speed. John gloried in the long, sweating, back-breaking hours of work.

Other crew members dropped off one by one, stupid with fatigue. He noticed with glee that even Carmen, his second engineer, had to drag her dumpy body off, and she was one tough female. Eventually the emergency was over and the damage repaired.

"Still as fresh as a daisy," one technician marvelled. "The man even found time to shave."

John grinned and went off to get cleaned up, sleep and feed, in that order. He was whistling absently as he headed back to his cabin after his shower, when his thoughts suddenly went into overdrive. He fingered his smooth chin. When had he last shaved? With so much happening, not just with the meteor dust, but the trouble on the last planet, and the emergency on the planet before that, he had been working and sleeping with very little leisure time to think about anything.

He peered at his face in the mirror. It was a young face, smooth and olive skinned with the pink flushed cheeks of perfect health. His dark eyes sparkled under slanting narrow brows. Narrow! He stroked them with his long fingers. They used to be heavier, and bushier.

He looked at his hands. They were still the same capable hands he always had, but they were smoother and less scarred, and there was no black hair left on the joints of each finger or on the backs of his hands.

Stricken with a terrible suspicion he pulled off his coverall. He stared at it with distaste. He had just scrubbed and showered, but the clean clothes had black hairs all over them. By God! He was moulting!

The mirror reflected his bewildered face and heavily muscled brown body. He looked down at his chest still decorated with a few scanty hairs. Was it muscle or was there a flabby swelling around his nipples?

The door opened. "Heading to bed are you, Honey?" asked his green-eyed cabin mate.

He grabbed his coverall to hide himself. "Out, you bitch," he roared.

He lay on his bunk in shaking terror. Was it because he was overtired, or did the longevity treatment cause loss of body hair? He broke into a cold sweat. Was there a female hormone in the longevity treatment? His hand crept up to finger the soft swelling around his nipple.

He had a sudden memory of the old man at the isolated village, and the Captain's four fishing companions. A few old men among thousands of the population on Thetis. What became of the rest of the men as they grew older?

In the quiet cabin his shaking got worse. His mind tried to evade the conclusion that lurked, waiting in his subconscious. He kept his mind hammering rigidly at the only important point. Was the process reversible?

The months slid past. The voyage of the Lucillus settled into placid monotony. The next planet fall was some time in the next ten days. John's young face was sulky and morose, and although he worked like a demon on duty, he was no longer a gregarious crew mate off duty. After each shift he fled to the sanctuary of his cabin.

"Unpleasant bastard these days," commented the green-eyed biologist who had long since found a more agreeable cabin mate.

"Yeah," agreed the pert nursing sister. "Something must be bugging him. He hasn't made a pass at any of us for months."

Alone in his cabin, John lay on his bed clenching and unclenching his fists. His body was changing. His body hair had rubbed off, and his breasts pushed further and further out. His hips were broadening, and the layer of fat collecting across his buttocks nearly had him weeping.

He could rigidly bind his breasts flat so no one would suspect, but the wider hips were altering his stride. He couldn't help but walk with a willowy swing. Down in the engineering room someone limp-wristed him out of the room to a chorus of snickers. Not only did the very sight of a female body, and there were plenty flaunted around the ship in the tight coveralls, make him physically sick, but his sex organs were shrinking and atrophying.

It was just before planet fall when it happened. He was bent over inspecting the bases of the stabiliser shafts. A passing technician pinched him on the bottom. He swung around and flattened him in outraged fury.

The Captain stood watching, and that was unusual. It was not like the Captain to prowl the ship. There was a nasty gleam in his eyes. "I'll see you in my office, Mister Scarlett," he ordered.

John followed him up, and stood in front of the Captain's desk and listened with disbelief. "You're fired, Mister Scarlett. Carmen is promoted to first engineer."

"A God damned woman in my job," John seethed. "I appeal, Sir." The Captain glared across the desk at him without replying. "I'm entitled to my rights. I haven't broken any regulations."

The Captain tapped his finger at the articles of the Company, set in plastiflex under his desk cover. "You've broken your conditions of contract, clause 10, sub-section 11(a)."

John promptly burst into tears. "I didn't know," he wailed. "And I'm still a better engineer than Carmen. Nothing changes that."

The Captain looked embarrassed and handed him a handkerchief. "It's not sexism, although transvestites attract all sorts of cranks and ratbags, but officially you're temple property, and can't be employed by the Company."

"What will I do?" John sobbed into the Captain's large handkerchief.

"You're contracted to the temple," the Captain repeated, and waved a hand in dismissal.

John lay in his bunk staring at the ceiling. The Captain came in with two orderlies.

"Sorry, son," he said mildly.

The orderlies put on the straitjacket. John fought, but they knew what they were doing. They pushed an injection into him, and went out, closing the door softly.

"What was that for, Sir?" John snarled, straining against the canvas folds and resisting the temptation to start weeping again.

"The logical thing in your condition is suicide."

"Yeah," John agreed sadly.

"The temple guardians will claim damages against the Company, if you do. You are our responsibility until I can get you shipped back to Thetis in one piece."

"In one piece," John howled.

"I'll get some tests done," the Captain soothed.

The Captain visited a few weeks later. John's hair had grown. It was a glossy tousled black, curling around his ears and neck. His huge dark eyes were haunted and desperate. He blinked the tears away from the long black lashes and tried to grin. It came out as a tremulous dimpled smile.

The Captain shifted uneasily and avoided looking at the deep breasts straining against the straitjacket. "It's not reversible. Biologically you're a male, but they've implanted something. A parasitic tissue flooding something through your system. Your body is fooled into thinking you're a nubile female, hormones, glands and cells keep adapting to the messages they are getting. It's what reversing the ageing. Interesting, really, the longevity is a female process, and a male body adjusts by turning female."

"Operate," John begged through dry lips.

The Captain shook his head. "By the time we trace and cut out whatever is growing right through your innards, you wouldn't survive. You're not the first to desert on Thetis, you know."

"I don't want to survive," John whispered.

The Captain shrugged and left the cabin. He was a humane man, but he was also the Company servant. The ex John Scarlett, first engineer would be kept under sedation until he was delivered back to Thetis. The Guardians would probably brainwash him into acceptance of his femininity. They had their techniques. After all, they did it all the time.

The Captain's mind lingered on his fishing companions on Thetis. Four argumentative fishermen of integrity. The Captain wondered how the others like them on Thetis were managing. More and more men were prepared to ignore longevity with its fifty per cent risk of death, and to accept the option of remaining male and ageing, slowly, but nevertheless ageing.

He strolled back to his office to make out his usual disapproving report on Thetis. Not that the Company would be persuaded out of its profitable trade because of the occasional drain of highly qualified crew members. As the Guardians smugly pointed out, the men had always "of their own free will, volunteered for the process."

The Captain sat down and glared at his inoffensive voice-activated secretary. Hundreds of spacemen enjoyed the hospitality of Thetis without being affected by contact. How did the Guardians manage to get the highly-qualified spacemen they required so effortlessly, and without having a single fatality among them?

Was it coincidence that it was only the crew members who fancied that they had a way with women who were seduced into deserting and defecting? Did they have a latent feminine streak that attracted and accelerated the safe process of transition, or were the highly qualified more carefully looked after?

The Captain shrugged. It was something he would never be certain about. He had managed to escape Thetis at seventeen. Fortunately he had never been cursed with an uncontrollable male drive, or been the sort that women were drawn to. He had found the female dominated society unpredictable and not that attractive anyway. His pleasures were fishing with the friends of his childhood.

He started dictating his report. In Thetis, a way with women too often led into the ultimate in empathy, the inevitable transformation into a female with a way with men.

————

Margaret took to writing (mostly fantasy) instead of drink when raising children. She has had children's and teenage novels published, three romances released with Robert Hale, and several more published as ebooks. She lives in Australia, and currently lurks in an underground flat in the Dandenongs – still writing.

DIAGNOSIS

Dixiane Hallaj

El Patrón looked around his bedroom. *So it's come to this. The limits of my world—bounded on the east by velvet curtains, on the north by French doors to the veranda. My eyes can barely see the outline of my mountain beyond the fields.* His grin transformed his face into the older version of the handsome green-eyed portrait that hung over his bed.

His whisper was barely more than a breath. "Never mind, I'll have the last move in the game. I'll reach out from beyond the grave and ride on the west wind to murmur in your ear, 'Checkmate, Jacoba, my love.'" The smile morphed into a grimace of pain, and his hands moved to press against his upper abdomen. Cancer. He understood the word and the sickness. He understood the pain that came with it. Cancer had taken his beloved Virginia from him, after a lingering, pain-filled decline. The wave of pain subsided, and he rang the bell on the bedside table.

Juan's wife appeared before the vibrations died away. "Sí, Patrón. What is your wish?"

He smiled at the formality. Her name slipped his mind, but he valued her bravery. She was the only woman from the village willing to come and stay in the house. His eyes closed momentarily as an echo of the pain threatened. After all these years, the villagers still thought Jacoba was a devil-spawned witch. Maybe they were right. Jacoba had changed little over the years. Her dark beauty had matured, and the body that had once fired his passion beyond control was still the envy of women half her age. Her perfect skin had never been forced to stretch over the burgeoning life of a child; her hands had never roughened with work. If only she had…

"Patrón."

The woman was still standing patiently, waiting for him. "Sorry, Carmen." To his surprise, the name slipped off his tongue as easily as his own. "Could you light the lamps?" He watched her go through the process of removing the glass chimneys, examining the wicks and the kerosene level, and putting the three lamps together to be lit on a single match. Economy was as much a part of her personality as kindness. "Thank you. Please, sit down." He gestured to the chair beside the bed, and waited until she perched on the edge of the seat. "I want to thank you for all you're doing for me."

"Really, Patrón, it is nothing. I received your thanks many times over in the many years since you came. You and your lady wife saved many lives in the village, including that of my husband. We all owe you."

His lady wife. Not Jacoba, but Virginia. The distinction and the underlying criticism used to anger him. Now it pleased him. It still surprised him when wisdom and superstition coexisted. Yes, his lady wife had done a lot to help the women of the village. A small movement from Carmen brought his thoughts back to the present.

"Some things need to be said while there is time. Soon I will need even greater care, and I will be unable to thank you for your kindness." Carmen bowed her head in silent acknowledgement. For a moment he saw the woman with jet black hair that greeted the carriage when he and Virginia first arrived on the plantation.

Already "comfortably plump," Carmen had taken one look at Virginia, pale and exhausted from the arduous day-long ride from the city, and ordered the driver to go straight to the village, quelling all objections with a single look. She'd settled Virginia in her own bed with a cup of cacao and left her in the care of a neighbor, sending another neighbor to bring the priest to give her spiritual comfort, before returning to the plantation house to supervise the unloading of the baggage and the cleaning.

El Patrón smiled at the top of Carmen's head, now shot with white. They would never have survived the first six months in the New World without Carmen and Juan. But he took credit for what he did for them as well. His village was still the envy of the entire region. Young men from around the country would come for work, hoping to marry into the village, often bringing a sister with them. It was good that new young people came, because the village youngsters were all sent to school, and many pursued careers in the city. Virginia had been adamant that the children get an education. Even the girls were taught to read and write and do arithmetic. Virginia also taught them about sanitation and nutrition.

"Will there be anything else, Patrón?"

"No, thank you. Just ask Juan and the priest to come to me at first light tomorrow." Carmen bobbed her head and moved toward the door. "And," he raised his voice slightly, stopping her mid-stride.

"Sí?" She turned with a smile on her face.

"Could you please ask my wife to come here?"

"Of course." The smile wavered for a moment.

Left alone, he made his way from the bed to the small

desk of polished mahogany. His legs wobbled under him, but he managed. Days with no appetite and little solid food took their toll. Once seated, he ran his hand over the carving of wild roses that graced the drawer fronts. The desk looked out of place, too delicate for the heavy curtains and the massive four poster bed. Jacoba had wanted to move it to a guest room, saying that a man's attention should be on the woman who shared his bed, not on writing and work. She'd lost that battle years ago, on many fronts.

"Do you want something, love of my life?"

"Yes, dear, I want to talk to you about the future. You've been an absolute angel since I've been ill. You've done so much for me. Carmen tells me you prepare all my meals with your own hands. This is so unlike you."

"No, it isn't unlike me. I've always wanted the best for you. You are my life, and you have always been my focus. I'm preparing all your meals because I'm convinced that my mother's special recipe will make you better. She made me swear never to reveal it, but it works. I know because it did wonders for her."

"Thank you, Sweetheart. Your solicitous attention is touching." He pasted what he hoped was a sincere smile on his face. "I'm approaching the end of my time on this earth—"

"No, don't say that! My mother's special knowledge will make a new man of you. You won't recognize yourself."

This time his smile was genuine. Once he was safely tucked away in his coffin, he certainly wouldn't recognize himself. "Be that as it may, I want to talk to you about arrangements for…later."

"What did you want to tell me?"

"I know we've had our differences in the past, but

you've come through when I need you." He looked down at his hands. "It's time to heal old wounds."

"Please, don't bring up old arguments. Do we have to talk about it now? I'd rather talk about something more pleasant."

"All right. I won't talk about it again. I'll just say that I am overlooking whatever happened. Perhaps the girls were—"

"I said I didn't want to talk about it. I want to concentrate on you. Not on what is now ancient history. So your precious darlings rebelled against your tyranny. It happened a long time ago."

His jaw tightened in anger. Jacoba had been the epitome of the wicked step-mother, but he'd been too besotted with her beauty to notice—until it was too late. "I thought you didn't want to talk about it...or did that mean you didn't want to listen about it?"

"I—"

"You would do well to listen before I change my mind." He took a deep breath to calm his anger and the pain hit him again. He clutched his stomach and closed his eyes, concentrating on keeping his expression as neutral as possible. His pride strengthened his will. At some point he would be unable to control himself, but he was determined to delay that as long as possible. Yes, he had to arrange everything while he was still in control.

"Are you all right? Can I do anything?"

"Yes, be an angel and get me some soup and your wonderful hot cacao."

How could the wound still be so raw and tender after all these years? It was better just to write the document and not talk about it. He pulled out paper and pen. The new fountain pen had arrived from Germany only months earlier, and it still gave him pleasure to write with it. Even a dying man is allowed small pleasures. As the pen lightly touched the paper, he thought briefly of his old tutor. Already white-haired and old beyond his childish imagination, the man had wielded a merciless ruler that left Enrique's knuckles bruised and sore for months until his handwriting met the exacting requirements of aristocratic penmanship. Fountain pens were indeed a godsend for someone who suffered the learning process using quill pens. Enough reminiscing. He had work to do and very little energy left with which to do it.

To Whom It May Concern:
This is the last will and testament of Enrique Herrera. I hereby leave my house, my land, and my worldly possessions to my wife, Jacoba Jardinero Herrera, with the following caveats:
1. Jacoba must reside on the property for at least five years after my death, and cannot sell it to anyone outside the family during that period.
2. Jacoba must personally oversee the operations of the property. Should she choose to reside elsewhere after the five years of residence, she must return every six months or less to inspect the property. Should she fail to bear this responsibility for any reason whatsoever, the terms of my previous Will and Testament will be implemented.

He was still blotting the last sentence when Jacoba's footsteps sounded outside the door.

"Thank you, my dear." He cleared a space for the soup. "You will enjoy reading this." He handed Jacoba the will. "I'll sign it in front of the priest and Juan in the morning." He turned his head slightly as he picked up his spoon and watched Jacoba's reflection in the French doors. There was no mistaking the triumphant grin, although he was sure the red glow of her eyes was merely the reflection of the lamp light.

Enrique barely managed not to spill his soup when Jacoba's arms snaked around his neck, and she whispered in his ear. "Darling, you are so good to me. You know this is my home. The house means so much to me, I could never leave it. I'm so very grateful that your children won't be able to kick me out of it when...I mean *if*...anything happens to you."

He smiled up at her. "You deserve everything you get, Jacoba. You've done a lot since you moved in." Yes, you've done a lot—a lot to splinter this family beyond repair. He pushed his bowl away and leaned on the desk to rise.

"You haven't taken half your soup. Can't you manage a little more?" Jacoba reached for the spoon and held it out for him to take another bite.

"I can still get a spoon to my own lips, thank you, but now I have other needs. Please leave me to attend to them."

"May I leave the cacao?"

"Yes, please do." Was he imagining the smirk in her smile? "And send someone to clean later."

"It is my pleasure to serve *all* your needs."

He disregarded her outstretched hand as he slowly stood, ignoring the cramping in his bowels while fearing an onslaught of the greater pain. He motioned her away.

"Promise you'll drink your cacao?"

He nodded, concentrating on appearing calm until the door closed behind her. Of course she would come to empty the chamber pot herself. She didn't want the servants to see the bloody mess and escalate the rumors that must be flying around the plantation.

He gagged as he slid the chamber pot under the bed. He took three deep steadying breaths and moved to the wardrobe. He had time. She wouldn't return until she thought he was asleep. His hand fumbled in the dark interior of the wardrobe. Where was it? He couldn't remember the last time he used the precious vacuum flask. He'd heard they were becoming common now, but when he'd had his shipped from Europe, it was a thing of wonder. He remembered the taste of strong coffee, still hot from the miracle of the vacuum flask. The warmth spread from his body to his soul, sitting astride his beloved stallion high on his mountain. He pictured the endless expanse of fields, and his body ached with the remembrance of strength.

He shook the cobwebs out of his head. His mind had been straying more and more lately. He must keep alert until everything was arranged. He poured the cacao into the vacuum flask, tightened the cap, and replaced it on the back of the shelf.

He sat again at the desk and quickly penned a letter to his attorney.

Mr. Perez,

My doting wife has been solicitous in the extreme for the duration of my final illness. She has made me coffee every morning and hot cacao every night with her own hands, not allowing the cook to witness the "special recipe" handed down through her family. The package with my signature across the seal contains a cup of her cacao. In the event of my death, please hand the contents of the package over to the police to be analyzed. I strongly suspect arsenic.

Why do I drink the concoctions if I think I am being poisoned? Arsenic is not a pleasant death, but it is quicker than the alternative. Cancer can be a long, unpleasant journey. My medical training and my life experience tells me I am on that journey. I recognize in myself the same symptoms I saw in my beloved Virginia. I suffer as she suffered, but without her bravery to endure.

My wife Jacoba is, as I tell her constantly, an angel, albeit the Angel of Death. The fact of my illness, which she does not suspect, does not lessen the severity of her crime. I count on you for justice.

Thank you, old friend, for this one last favor.

Your friend in death as in life,
Enrique Herrera

Dawn came, and with it new waves of misery. He had lain awake for so many hours that he wasn't sure if he fell asleep or just lost consciousness with exhaustion. He kept his eyes closed, hoping to recapture the oblivion for a few more minutes. Whispers brought his mind to full alert status, but his lids didn't even flutter.

"Perhaps we should return later."

"No, Padre, El Patrón asked us to come at first light. We shall be here when he wakes."

"But today is market day. You have duties."

"Yes, and this is one of them—and Mass can be a little late today, can't it?"

"Yes, of course." There was a creak of leather and wood. Probably the priest shifting in his seat. Enrique tried to sink into the ensuing silence.

"Did you bring the Sacraments, Padre?"

"Hmm?"

"He may want communion or last rites."

"Do you think it's come to that?"

"Perhaps. I sent for Lola."

"What?"

"Shhh." The whispers became softer. Enrique's heart thumped in his chest, and he strained to hear.

"Is she coming?" The Padre's question echoed his own.

"Perhaps. Who knows if I greased the right hands to get the message through? Only God can answer that."

"When will she get here?"

"Again, only God knows. It could be as early as today, or it might be next week, or never." Enrique struggled to quell unwarranted hope. "You could pray while you wait." Enrique didn't have to open his eyes to see the smile on Juan's face. The soft rattle of rosary beads almost brought out his own smile. This priest was young and fresh out of seminary. He allowed his eyelids to flutter.

"Buenos días, Patrón."

"Buenos días, Juan, Padre." He struggled to sit and Juan pulled him up with a strong arm around his shoulders and stuffed pillows behind his back. "Thank you both for coming. Sorry I'm late to the meeting." Juan smiled at his feeble joke.

"We are at your service, Patrón." The priest may have dedicated himself to the service of God, but he knew who put the bread on his table.

"Juan, please help me to my desk." Why did the pride that did not allow him to accept Jacoba's assistance yesterday not bother him with Juan? "I asked you here to witness my signature, and to swear that I am not under duress as I sign a document." He sat and took the paper from the desk drawer. "I have changed my will, and I need witnesses." He leaned his left arm across the top of the paper and scrawled his name at the bottom. To their credit, neither man seemed to be trying to read the text while signing their names.

"Would you like communion today?" asked the priest as he handed back the pen.

"No, thank you, Padre. I know your flock is waiting for

morning Mass. I will send for you when I need you again. Juan and I still have a few business matters to discuss." The priest bowed and left.

"Juan, in the back of the second shelf of the wardrobe, you'll find my vacuum flask. It is a gift for Señor Perez. Please take it along with the will and another letter that should be opened before he reads the will."

"Please, Patrón, do not speak of your death."

"Let's not fool ourselves. We both know that I have days at most. I grow weaker by the hour, and it becomes more and more difficult to keep my focus. My mind wanders and drifts. I cannot leave this room, and soon, I will be unable to manage my own biological needs and be totally helpless—a body with no ability to move or even speak."

Juan made the sign of the cross. "May God forbid it."

"Thank you, Juan, but I don't expect God to work a miracle for me." No, he would not linger with the cancer—neither would he allow Jacoba to go unscathed. He sealed an envelope with the letter and the signed will, scrawling the lawyer's name on the front. "Now be on your way before the day's produce becomes too wilted to sell." The pain was escalating. "Please tell my wife I am ready for my breakfast…and her special coffee." He was barely aware of Juan helping him back to bed. The pain was intense. No, not intense, it was overwhelming. The pain made his ears ring with its roar; his body trembled in the winds of its fury. It filled his being, leaving no room for thought or memories.

* * *

Enrique's eyelids opened to daylight. His first thought was relief that he was still alive and the pain crouched quietly within him, perhaps as exhausted by its recent rampage as he was. He took pleasure in drawing breath. How long had he been sleeping, if indeed it was merely sleep? Soft voices murmured outside his door. His heart quickened with the memory of an earlier conversation. Could it be Lola?

His mind's eye pictured a girl, dwarfed by the huge desk in the office, bent over the complicated books he had devised to track the many aspects of running the vast plantation. A thought fragment came with the image—an echo of regret that her quick mind was housed in the body of a petite woman that few men could take seriously. Then the fragment dissolved as he deliberately replaced it with other visions of the two of them planning some new venture.

Impatient to know if she had indeed come in his last hours, he tried to call out. His voice refused his command, and he coughed weakly. It was enough. The door opened and his heart sank.

"My love, you're awake. Let me help you. I was just going to take your breakfast back to the kitchen."

Good. It was still morning. "No, I'll have it now, if you please."

Jacoba picked up the coffee cup and offered it. "Start with some coffee, and you'll feel better."

His stomach roiled at the thought. Now that the pain was small and sleepy, hope for a few minutes with someone dear to him blossomed into a fragile thought. "Perhaps I could eat a small piece of bread with honey. Then I can enjoy my coffee more."

A shadow passed over Jacoba's face. He wouldn't have seen it if he hadn't been watching closely. "Of course, dear. It's marvelous to see you express interest in food again. I'm sure you're getting better. I'll go to the kitchen and get it for you."

As soon as the door closed behind her, he got out of bed. Holding on for support, he managed to relieve himself.

Before sliding the pot under the bed, he added the coffee to the mess. He turned to put the empty cup on the tray and clutched the bedclothes as the room spun around him.

"Wait! I'm coming!" Jacoba's voice. Had she seen him empty the cup?

"I'm..." The croak surprised him. His mind was clear, but his body was so weak. One of her arms went around him and she supported his weight with her body. She removed the cup with her free hand and placed it on the tray. The room had steadied, and he managed to climb back in bed with a little assistance.

Jacoba was beaming when she settled him with his tray of bread and honey on his lap. "I'm glad you changed your mind about having coffee first." His smile was one of relief.

The day passed with naps punctuated by bouts of pain. The night differed only by the different form of illumination. Surprisingly, Carmen was still there whenever he needed to get up. She helped him situate himself and went into the hallway to give him privacy, reappearing to help him back to bed. His gratitude went unspoken.

* * *

Sunlight leaked around the velvet curtains. Carmen nodded in her chair, her feet propped on the chair from his desk. He struggled to sit upright, and her eyes opened. Instantly she was on her feet, propping his back with pillows.

"Carmen..." He wanted to tell her he didn't remember anything since breakfast yesterday — at least he hoped it was yesterday. He wanted to ask if she had been there all night, but all that came out was a formless whisper. She handed him a glass of water, then steadied his hand with her own as he brought the glass to his lips.

She answered his unasked question. "My place is here

now. Juan insists, and I dare not go against his wishes."

"But..." Enrique knew there wasn't a force on earth that could make Carmen quail. He accepted her gift with a nod, and puzzled over the implications.

"Try this." She held a spoon to his mouth. "Bread soaked in milk and honey. Try to swallow." He managed a couple of swallows before being wracked by cough. Exhausted, he drifted toward sleep. The pain paced within him, alternately growling softly and roaring threateningly. Strange, the pain had not raged its full strength on him again, or perhaps he had slipped into unconsciousness to avoid it.

* * *

The pain woke him to lamp light. Without the strength to scream, he groaned. The pain-dragon bathed him in flame. Muscles contracted without his control. Visions floated before him, blurred and ghost-like.

"Carmen?" A thin whisper escaped.

"*Sí, Patrón.*" Strong arms lifted him off the bed. The smell! Oh, God the stench!

"Just lower him into the tub. If we can't get the nightshirt off, we'll cut it off." A voice somehow familiar. The voice of a ghost. "Tell Pilar to take all this bedding and boil it." Movement around him. Ghosts moving about in the dim light.

"No, Señora, you mustn't open the windows. He will catch a chill."

"He will catch worse than that breathing this air. When was the last time he was bathed? When was the last time his windows were opened?" More movement, more ghosts, but now they had names—all except the little one. Could it be? He struggled to speak, to hold out his hand. His body refused to obey. It was a dream. Yes, that's why he couldn't move. Nightmares were often like that. He called the dragon to wake him, but the dragon didn't obey.

* * *

The taste of honey filled his mouth and birdsong filled the air. So he made it to Heaven after all! God willing, he would be reunited with his Virginia. The dragon had come and gone. With great effort he forced his eyelids to open a slit. Through the curtain of lashes he saw nothing but white fluffy clouds. Satisfied, he relaxed and slept.

* * *

"Señora! Señora!" The harsh sound brought almost unbearable disappointment, followed closely by curiosity. What was real? What was dream?

"Shhhhh. You'll wake him." The sound of broken glass forced him to open his eyes.

Bright sunlight made it hard to focus. Perhaps it was still a dream. Lola stood frozen, looking down at the floor. Juan's hand was raised as though to strike her.

"Juan! What have you done?"

"It's the coffee!" Juan's shout brought Lola into action, but Enrique's mind was faster.

"No!" The two turned to him, distracted from their own paths.

"Papa! You spoke! You're awake." Spilled coffee ignored or forgotten, she rushed to put her arms around Enrique's neck.

"You mustn't let him speak," he whispered into her ear. "I can't know, on pain of eternal damnation."

Lola stood, barely taller than his head as it lay on the mound of white pillows. Her eyes sparkled with tears. "Papa. I'm so happy to see you awake—even if you are still a little delirious."

"You came."

"Yes, I came. I've been here for two days, hoping for this

moment." She leaned over and hugged him again.

"Patrón, I must speak."

"You disobeyed me, Juan. I forbid you to speak in this room, or within my hearing." The voice was thin and quivered with his effort, but the air of authority was still there.

"Juan, don't upset him. Go to the kitchen and ask Pilar to make me another cup of coffee. Please, I need a few minutes alone with my father."

Juan nodded and spun on his heel, but his face was a thunder cloud of anger and frustration.

Lola did not speak until she heard his footsteps retreat. "Papa, you have to know —"

"Don't speak of it." He hoped she could hear the desperation in his voice. "There are things you do not know. No one knows." He paused for several breaths. Talking took so much effort. He only hoped he could say what he needed to say. "Lola, I will die soon. God in His wisdom has struck both your parents with the incurable curse of cancer. I can die quickly, or I can linger for painful months, losing more and more of my humanity as the agony reduces me to a mindless rotting hulk."

"No, Papa. Don't talk like that."

"I don't have the strength to argue. Barely the strength to talk. I held on in the hope that I could see you one last time." He watched the tears move down her face. "It will all work out. I'll die soon. Maybe today, maybe tomorrow. There is no turning back, but without knowledge, I will remain blameless. I have made my confession. I repent the wrongs I have done in life." He paused as much to catch his breath as to send a silent prayer. "I dreamed I was in Heaven."

"Papa—" He stopped her with a gesture.

"If Juan tells me anything that turns my suspicion to knowledge, I will suffer eternal damnation for suicide. As it is, I have only suspicion. Don't worry. If my suspicions are correct, justice will be served." The outburst exhausted him. He had more to say, but no more strength to say it.

Lola put her arms around his shoulders and whispered in his ear. "It's too late, Papa. In your heart of hearts you know that. The truth, once loosed, cannot be reburied."

Anger gave him new energy. "Juan, after all these years, disobeyed my last request."

"I did not disobey you." Juan was standing in the doorway with a tray holding three coffee cups.

"I said that letter should be read after I was dead."

"No, you said it should be read before the will. The will has not yet been read."

Enrique searched his mind, but the memory of his words was drowned by the memory of the dragon's roar. "My meaning was clear."

An astonishing sound echoed through the old house. One that hadn't been heard in many years — genuine laughter. "You men have played chess together far too long. Subtlety was never Jacoba's strong suit, Juan. Carmen finished Papa's coffee one day to stay awake, and she was sick. That's when she started staying around the clock — to make sure the coffee and cacao never got to Papa." Fresh laughter cut off her words. "Oh, Juan, the expression on your face is priceless. You thought it was your idea, didn't you?"

"Aha!" In spite of his anger, Enrique's lips twitched with the urge to smile.

"And you, Papa. I can't believe you really think you can get into Heaven on a technicality!"

"You go too far, Lola. One's immortal soul is not a joke. Remember, I am still your father."

The laughter left her lips and her eyes were very serious. "No, Papa. Right now I am the nurse and you are the patient. You will listen."

"I am literally at your mercy, a prisoner and victim of my disease." He was pleased that his voice did not whine, but the bitterness was unmistakable.

"You listened as your body told you many things. You saw certain signs and you thought "cancer." You saw other signs and you thought "poison." Yet in your mind one was fact and the other suspicion."

"And now they are both fact." The whisper rode on a wave of sadness.

"No, Papa. Now they are reversed."

"But I have already drunk too much, and you have forced me to drink also from the well of truth. I will die either way, but now it is without hope of salvation."

"Nonsense. Now you're going to fight like you never fought before. You're going to prove your will to live."

"It would take a miracle."

She kissed his cheek. "A miracle or a misdiagnosis— either would work."

———

Dixiane Hallaj lives quietly in Northern Virginia with her husband of 54 years and their cat named Dog. This story is an off-shoot (not an excerpt) of the story of her grandmother on which she based her novel, It's Just Lola. *Find Dixie on her blog,* DixieHelpsWriters.wordpress.com *where she posts every two weeks, or visit her on* facebook.com/DixianeHallajAuthorPage.

93

DORMIR NELLA PACE CELESTE

Maria Elizabeth McVoy

Capitolo Primo: La Morte di Nonno il Grande Animatore

It was a Christmas of somber celebration, for the Great Entertainer was dead. He had died as *la Vigilia di Natale* became *Natale* during the midnight Mass. As his entire village gathered to worship the birth of *Gesù bambino*, Giuseppe Di Angelis—called *Nonno* by all who knew him, for he was a grandfather many times over and easily the eldest man in ten villages—lay abed in his garret room. The beautifully carved marionettes that were his livelihood, and his joy, smiled down upon him from the walls respectfully. *Nonno* gasped his last breath, as in Bethlehem, so many hundred years previous, a very special baby boy announced His arrival with His first small cry.

The village had wondered when *Nonno* retired so quickly after the *Festa dei Sette Pesci* without even pausing for a cordial of *anisette*. They whispered concernedly among themselves as they lit their Yule log, each in his own hearth (the logs would burn constantly and slowly until the eve of the new year), and headed out into the cool, starlit night to Christmas Mass. As the Mass began, alight in candles, the Padre himself said a quiet prayer for the unusually absent *Nonno*. If the legends were true and the *Madonna* visited the homes of the humble to warm her newborn *bambino* by the

Yule log, that when she visited the home of *Nonno* the Great Entertainer she would offer him her blessing. Afterwards some would say the *Madonna* and *Gesù Bambino* had taken their rest at the home of *Nonno* and when they left, he joined them.

After midnight Mass, *Nonno's* great-grandson, Sergio, found him lying peacefully with a smile upon his lips, fingers eternally intertwined in prayer. But it was the beautifully carved marionettes that seemed cold without their master.

In the days that followed, each member of *Nonno's* family picked up the dolls and manipulated them as each had been taught by *Nonno* at one time or another. However, none could transcend the puppets into the characters they had become on the special stage *Nonno* had built outside the doors to their old stone cathedral. Tradition held that to bury a man with his most prized possessions would placate his soul into remaining quiet. Such was the belief of *Nonno's* mourners. But Sergio could not bear to commit the wooden bodies of those dolls to the earth, not when there was a chance that one day they could be re-born in the hands of a new puppet master.

When they returned from the funeral on the eve of *La Festa dell'Epifania*, *Nonno's* youngest Great-Great-Grandson Giuseppe laid out his shoes for *La Befana* to fill with toys and sweets in her eternal search for *Gesù Bambino*. Sergio quietly slipped away to the garret and packed the puppets away in a deep blue chest painted with golden suns, moons, and stars.

The first exquisitely made puppet that Sergio lifted, and placed neatly on the bottom of the chest, was the Shy Gentleman. He was dressed in dove-grey morning dress and a matching hat with a minute gold pocket watch. In

95

Nonno's hands, he would have been nervously, or hopefully, checking the time, and perhaps then lifting his head to gaze at his beloved. The Shy Gentleman was quiet and reserved, but also with great dreams of brave endeavor. In many a pantomime, the puppet would find his courage either to win his love or defeat the villain.

Next came the Proud Lady in her blue silk evening frock and tiny matched shoes, with her hair pinned up and red-gold curls cascading over her ivory shoulders. A little silver mirror was clutched in her small white-gloved fingers, so that she might admire her reflection or cast her eyes behind her to secretly regard her admirers. She was haughty and vain, but not completely without compassion. She was simply a creature that had been too long held as perfection to realize her own flaws, and thus they often took her unawares within the course of a play. Sergio tucked her in beside the Shy Gentleman, feeling that they belonged together through the years it might be—if ever—before someone came who could master *Nonno's* puppets.

Next came the Plump Servant Girl, round and apple-cheeked in a striped apron over a homespun dress; her dark hair pulled neatly into a knot under her little white cap. In one hand she carried a grand covered tray, which had made her a favorite with all children, for when she lifted the dome there was always an array of sweets, one for each child—at Christmas there might be small slices of *panettone, torrone,* or *panforte*. Sergio (and probably every young lad in the village) had been in love with the Plump Servant Girl in his youth. No doubt, he mused, it was in no small part to this cheerful, generous doll that the woman he chose for his wife was marvelous in the kitchen and had the pleasantly rounded figure that went with being a lover of her own cooking.

In every great theatrical performance, even one as small

as *Nonno's* opera of puppets, there must be a villain. *Nonno's* villain was the Wicked Magician, clothed all in black with a long cape, a thin, dark mustache, and a hat upon his head with a vivid emerald-green *Drago* curled in place of a hatband. The *Drago* boasted its own strings. As the Wicked Magician would scheme upon the stage the *Drago* seemed to unwind, unfold its paper-thin wings, and whisper into the magician's ear. Although none had a doubt that the Wicked Magician always intended mischief upon the other dolls, the audience was never quite certain about the *Piccolo Drago Verde*. For it could always be seen that whatever trouble befell the puppets because of the Wicked Magician's meddling, in the end all was better than had there been no meddling whatsoever. Sergio was superstitiously careful tucking away the Wicked Magician, careful not to bend the delicate wings of the *Piccolo Drago Verde*. He didn't doubt the *Drago's* ultimate goodness, but he had seen enough of *Nonno's* plays to respect that the path to a happy ending was often as arduous as possible when guided by the undeniably mischievous *Drago*.

The final puppet was the Harlequin, hiding his long-nosed face behind a plain black mask, resplendent in diamond patterned tights of red, gold, green, blue, and purple. He was the unpredictable character—sometimes in competition with the Shy Gentleman for the Proud Lady's hand, sometimes a thief stealing the children's treats from the Plump Servant Girl (or stealing a kiss in exchange for return of the treats), or an unwitting pawn in the wicked magician's plans—never malicious, but always the fool. There was a wisdom to his character that the other puppets lacked, an ability to see the farce within any scenario and to understand it better through seeming irreverence. The Harlequin was possibly the most difficult puppet to manipulate. On those occasions when Sergio had tried, he could never capture that sense of farcical wisdom inherent in the character, but only managed to show the veneer of a foolish clown.

Sergio closed the chest upon the five enchanting dolls. He grieved for the loss of the puppets as deeply as he grieved for the death of *Nonno*.

When the period of mourning was over, Sergio, and the rest of the village, ceased to speak of the Great Entertainer for fear that their words would summon him back from his final rest. But, to the end of his long days, Sergio never ceased to hope that one-day *Nonno's* almost-forgotten puppets would entertain again.

Capitolo Secondo: La Vigilia di Natale

Nonno Giuseppe climbed the rickety stairs to the garret bedchamber with a pile of bed linens balanced on one hand and the other carefully gripped the banister, lest he slip on the steep, old staircase. The room was very different than the way he remembered it from his young boyhood when his namesake, the Great Entertainer, had lived. Now it housed not one narrow bed, but several like a large nursery, each with a chest at the foot for clothing or keepsakes. Gone was the workbench where the Great Entertainer had made his wondrous dolls and mended them when they needed repair. But in the corner, under the pegs where the dolls had once hung, the now-faded blue chest still sat with its golden sun, moon and stars faintly glimmering. Inside, lovingly preserved — and secretly played with for many years by a much younger Giuseppe — were the five marionettes. After sheeting each bed in turn for his great-grandchildren, whom he had not seen since they were probably too small to remember, *Nonno* Giuseppe's gnarled fingers stroked the lid of the faded-blue chest lovingly, and whispered a silent salutation before returning down the stairs.

The house was in an absolute uproar of preparation for *la Vigilia di Natale* and the traditional *Festa dei Sette Pesci*. *Nonna* Aurelia was ruling the kitchen with two daughters and three granddaughters as her helpers. Already Giuseppe could smell the *Baccalà*, and *Capitone*. There would be octopus casserole also, fresh baby sardines in lemon marinade, linguini with a spicy crab sauce, stuffed calamari in tomato sauce, and *Insalata di mare*. His sons-in-law were bringing up barrels of wine for the banquet. Already every table in the house — and several that he was fairly certain were borrowed — had been set end-to-end along the hall and covered with a long white cloth, which somehow each year managed to cover the length of all the tables. Tall, white tapers were spaced out along the table and chairs clustered around, enough for everyone in the family and a few extra for any unexpected guests. Superstition held that Mary and Joseph still traveled on Eve of *Natale* and sought a meal or lodging; in their village there were always extra chairs at every table and extra beds for weary travelers to rest, but especially on that sacred night.

The thick wooden door vibrated with heavy knocking that could only be *Nonno* Giuseppe's grandson, wife, and two young children over from the new world. He smiled tolerantly as he went to answer the door; young Antonio had never taken to heart that he need not wait like a stranger at the door to his ancestral home.

"Merry Christmas!" chorused the children who were surely much too tall to be his great-grandchildren. And then in less certain, but precise, syllables *"Buon Natale."*

"Buon Natale," he greeted them warmly hugging them

both—they were so thin, didn't their mother feed them enough?

"*Buon Natale, Nonno* Giuseppe!" Antonio greeted as he kissed his grandfather warmly on both cheeks. "You remember my wife, Margaret."

Margaret's violet eyes danced with laughter, as if she could hear him thinking she underfed her children. *Nonno* Giuseppe could feel the smile in her lips as she kissed him on both cheeks.

Antonio headed straight to the kitchen and greeted *Nonna* Aurelia to be given a floury kiss before being shooed away; they were, as ever, in dire danger of not being ready in time for the evening banquet. Margaret swiftly knotted an apron around her too-thin waist and took over kneading the *panettone* dough, chattering to her sisters-in-law in heavily accented phrases.

Little Alessandra and Benito scurried up the rickety stairs to the garret to stay out from underfoot until the evening banquet. They were the only children in the garret that year, but they were used to having only one another as playmates and the garret, like many family attics, was a treasure trove for imaginative minds. Though they had visited *Nonno* Giuseppe before, they had somehow never yet discovered the faded-blue chest in the corner. Perhaps there was some magic abroad that Christmas Eve night that finally drew them to the old, faded chest with its enticing gold images of the heavens: a sound perhaps, or a mis-placed shadow, or perhaps, as *Nonno* Giuseppe believed, the Great Entertainer still kept company with his creations awaiting a successor.

However it came to their attention, Alessandra and Beni-to discovered the old, faded chest: "Oh my..." they both uttered in unison as they lifted the dusty lid. The first thing they saw was the bright emerald green of the *Drago* partially unwound from what they would presently discover was the Wicked Magician's hat. It seemed to peer at them through half-lidded eyes, at once both tantalizing and untamed. They paused and looked about themselves nervously, peering behind furniture and down the steep, rickety stairs. This could not be a forgotten chest of toys. And though no one had ever mentioned *Nonno* the Great Entertainer to them by name (superstition still thrived through the generations), they knew that these were the products of a master craftsman. They could not close the chest or look away from those alluringly challenging serpentine eyes.

Alessandra carefully lifted out the *Piccolo Drago Verde* and his hat and the Wicked Magician underneath (somehow, it seemed to her less like a Wicked Magician with a *Drago* on his hat and more like a *Drago* with a Wicked Magician *under* his hat). She fumbled clumsily with the rods and strings for a moment before it all seemed to come together. With minimal movement of her fingers, the Wicked Magician stretched out his limbs and rubbed his hands together with the pent-up schemes of seven decades and, finally, cocked his ear to the whispering voice of the *Piccolo Drago Verde*, who naturally had a brilliant plan as to how they should exercise their newly found freedom.

Benito, as carefully as his sister, lifted out the brightly colored form of the Harlequin. Effortlessly the doll stood up, brushed off his brightly patterned stockings, and straightened his little black mask over his long nose. He then fell into a graceful, if exaggeratedly deep, bow to the *Piccolo Drago Verde*. The Wicked Magician scowled and crossed his arms in a huff.

Over the heads of the marionettes, Alessandra and Benito's eyes met, dancing with pleasure.

As the adults bustled about the lower levels of the house cooking, and baking, drawing wine, and decorating, up in the garret the children, and the puppets of the Great Entertainer, began their own very special preparations.

* * *

That evening at the *Festa dei Sette Pesci*, *Nonno* Giuseppe found himself glancing often at his great-grandchildren to enjoy the secret smiles they shared. There was a restless expectancy in the air he had not felt for many Christmases past, not since he had been a very small boy.

The seven courses of the banquet went quickly, filled with toasts and praise for *Nonna* Aurelia and her kitchen staff. Soon it was nearly midnight and *Nonno* Giuseppe lit the Yule log in the hearth; he remembered another *Vigilia di Natale* when some villagers had sworn the *Madonna* and *Bambino* visited the hearth of *Nonno* the Great Entertainer. The winter wind swirled down the chimney, toying with the flame and casting strange shadows over the walls. The room seemed to grow—or *Nonno* Giuseppe seemed to shrink—and perhaps, for just a moment, it was the same fire all those years ago, lit to warm a mother and newborn child as they came to guide away the soul of a great man. The moment passed and the room was again its usual size. *Nonno* Giuseppe considered if it was not so much a question as to whether the soul of *Nonno* the Great Entertainer had left with *La Madonna* and *Gesù Bambino*, or had remained to haunt the village. Perhaps it was rather that time itself was not always a constant march toward the future, but sometimes folded and overlapped. Moments in the past might be tied to moments in the future, until the time was ripe for miracles to be fulfilled.

Capitolo Terzo: Natale

Nonno Giuseppe followed his family into the star-lit night, smiling wistfully at his great-grandchildren with their scarf-wrapped heads huddled together, as they conspired in a most intriguing manner. The bells in the old stone church called them all to Mass, drawing them away from their warm hearths. Family by family, they gathered in the streets, clasping hands and kissing cheeks as they wound their way down to the old church.

Before and to the left of the doors of the church — thrown wide and welcoming with warm candlelight — stood the Great Entertainer's stage. It was not so very large a structure (for all his greatness as a man and an entertainer, Giuseppe Di Angelis had not cut a very large figure) carved from wood, polish dulled from so many decades of wind and rain, but swept clean of dust, cobwebs, and mud from the feet of exploring children. There were steps leading to a small platform behind where the Great Entertainer had stood to manipulate his puppets, with only his warm eyes showing over the sloping roof of the doll-sized stage. To the right and left of the puppet stage, were carved half moons: one frowning and one smiling, like the two halves of the ancient god Janus, in eternal discord. And at the peak of the roof was a great smiling sun, its rays reaching out in all directions to the darkest corners of the world. Once-deep-blue curtains — now sun-bleached and frayed at the hem — were drawn across the tiny stage, the embroidered suns, moons and stars just a discernable glimmer of gold. Again *Nonno* Giuseppe seemed to have one of those moments where he was not at all certain of his place in time. He could see the same stage on another *Natale* seven decades previous — polished to a bright shine with deep blue curtains and gold embroidery that caught the starlight and sparkled with magic — awaiting daylight for the morning performance by *Nonno*. He was once more Guiseppe, the youngest great-great-grandson of the Great Entertainer.

Alessandra and Benito each took a hand of their distracted great-grandfather and led him into the warmth of the church, without a glance at the stage, lest any onlookers divine their newly hatched plans.

If the *Madonna* and *Bambino* warmed themselves by the Yule log that *Natale*, they left no evidence of their passing. And if *Nonno* the Great Entertainer visited with them, he too left no sign. But who could say they didn't? What could be seen was the warmth of *Natale* in Alessandra and Benito's hearts, their minds already dreaming, as they climbed the rickety stairs to the old garret and curled up to sleep. Between their beds, out of sight of anyone standing in the doorway, sat the five puppets of the Great Entertainer, free at last...awaiting dawn.

* * *

Natale dawned cool and crisp with that rare promise of snow. Alessandra and Benito crept down the rickety stairs from the garret, boots in hand with the blue trunk balanced between them, placing stockinged feet on the inner edge of the stairs where they were less likely to creak and wake the household.

Soon *Nonna* Aurelia would descend to the kitchen to prepare the midday feast: turkey stuffed with chestnuts, roast lamb, lasagna, glazed onions, zucchini, tomatoes au gratin, and, of course, a grand variety of desserts. But first she, and most of the village, would gather at the old stone church with its large outdoor *presepio* — some wondered if it was carved by the Great Entertainer himself — to wish *Gesù Bambino* a happy birthday.

Antonio had often told his children of his childhood

Christmases in the village. He described the long celebration of *Gesù Bambino's* birth from the Novena to the Epiphany. On the Novena *Piferari* would come down from the hills playing carols on their traditional *zampogna*. The children, he himself in his day, wrote poems and traveled house-to-house reciting them. And on the twelfth night of Christmas *La Befana* brought gifts and sweets to all good children, as the Magi brought gifts to *Gesù Bambino*.

Alessandra and Benito were wistful of their father's childhood traditions. Caroling with their friends on Christmas Eve was just not the same. They who loved to write little plays and poems, to stand on their makeshift stage—the landing of their home's main stair, with bed sheet drawn across for the curtain—and perform for their parents.

And so, as the house began, to wake, Alessandra and Benito slipped into the streets. Their boots barely made a sound against the cobblestones as they hurried to the old stone church with the precious chest cradled between them.

Capitolo Quarto: L'Opera deî Pupi

Nonno Giuseppe awoke that morning feeling younger than he had in so many decades. He kissed *Nonna* Auriela's neck as she twisted her once dark—now silver—locks into a complicated chignon and giggled, as if she were a young girl again. They dressed in their finest, as if it were their wedding day, and arm-in-arm walked down to the old stone cathedral as blithe as a courting couple. They passed the wooden Magi, who were still making their way slowly down the street with their camels: a pilgrimage that would not arrive at the manger scene until *l'Epifania*. Finally, they paused reverently before the *presepio*, and gazed upon the wise, placid features of *Gesù Bambino*. All the beautifully carved figures of those gathered to pay Him homage clustered around in a jostling clutter, anxious to worship the newborn King. As always, the stable's animals stood closest, as legend told they warmed the newborn *bambino* with their breath. As the *Piferari* took up their *zampogna* in a merry tune, *Nonno* Giuseppe took his wife's hands and spun her about in a dance that neither had lifted their feet to since their youth. The villagers clapped in time and laughed; some kicked up their heels as well and joined the dance.

When the boisterous tune ended and a softer, more reverent, carol commenced there came small voices—such as had not been heard in seven decades—arguing behind the faded gold-embroidered curtains of the puppet stage. As if every man and woman again become children, they gathered at the foot of the stage and gazed at the tantalizing movement of the curtains, as if the diminutive actors were struggling behind it.

"Move over," called a laughing tenor. "I want to see."

"Don't be rude," admonished a warm female alto. "Ladies and Gentlemen first before the likes of us."

"Oh, you'll always be first with me," returned the tenor, an amorous tone in his voice. A slight scuffle followed and the crowd craned their necks to catch a glimpse as the curtains fluttered with movement.

"What goes on here?" came an imperious soprano.

"Ahem," coughed the not quite reserved tenor.

"My Lady, we thought perhaps an audience had gathered," responded the alto dutifully. A sharp brush against the curtains, and a muffled grunt, suggested that the tenor might have tried to give another explanation before being cuffed into silence.

"An audience?" came a silky baritone, dripping with

charm and innuendo. "Shall I check, my Lady?"

"Indeed, please," the soprano responded, in a fluster.

Finally, a small hand drew aside the edge of the curtain and the *Piccolo Drago Verde* peeked out, followed by the eyes and nose of the Wicked Magician. Below at stage level, the Harlequin's masked face appeared also, not to be outdone, wiggling his ears and producing child-like giggles from the entire crowd and a swift kick in the rear from the Wicked Magician. The Harlequin tumbled in front of the curtain as the Wicked Magician retreated to report on the crowd. *Nonno* Giuseppe, and a few others, noted that the *Piccolo Drago Verde* continued to peak through the curtain and survey the crowd.

Undaunted, the Harlequin bounded to his feet and struck a pose, minute hands on his narrow hips and shoulders squared. In the fine tradition begun by Giacomo da Lentini, under Frederick II, he began to speak:

"Evening to morning the days pass me by,
Until time stands still and my days are spent.
In those precious hours before I die,
As my dearest weep freely and lament,
I regard my life and wonder whereby
Shall I be recalled? As a malcontent,
Despondent, my plans completely awry,
Facing eternity in damned torment?

"May I ever reply, 'not I,' for my deeds
Shall represent me in tales long after
My demise. Stories of my creative
Devise shall be available to read
And I shall live ever in the laughter
Of children, my own, foreign and native."

A stillness fell over the crowd, as if they had been visited by a ghost. The older members of the village, those who had been children in the days of the Great Entertainer, were contemplative. They recalled the plays watched over and over, as with the songs of troubadours, until the crowd could recite along with the puppets, tales that had not been spoken for over half a century except in the dark quiet of their homes to lull a restless child to sleep. Tales that had too long been only fading memories.

The Harlequin held his pose a moment and then swept himself into an elaborate bow, breaking the spell upon the crowd. As he became again erect, the curtains behind swirled open with a flourish and the play began. It was not a play any of the crowd had ever heard before, but it was the familiar characters in their familiar roles: the Shy Gentleman in distant pursuit of the Proud Lady; the Harlequin stealing sweets and carelessly bestowing compliments and dispensing wisdom within practical jokes; the Wicked Magician creating mischief; and the *Piccolo Drago Verde* whispering and guiding the puppets to an unexpectedly happy ending.

All the puppets took deep bows upon the stage. The Plump Servant Girl passed about her silver tray, filled not with the customary sweets, but with little scrolls of paper, bound with blue ribbons, baring couplets of good fortune for the bearer; there were, somehow, just enough scrolls for each member of the crowd to bear one home.

When Alessandra and Benito — having coaxed the very excited puppets back into the faded-blue trunk — descended the platform behind the tiny stage, they were enveloped in the embrace of their great-grandfather. *Nonno* Giuseppe had no words to express the joy that they had brought to him, to the village, and to a Great Entertainer restless in death because his creations had been so long neglected.

Filled with the wonder of having witnessed a miracle, the crowd dispersed, to celebrate *Natale* each with his own family. But for the first time in seven decades the name of *Nonno* the Great Entertainer was uttered aloud. That day his stories were recalled and relayed, to gratifying peals of laughter.

* * *

In the days that followed, in pairs and threes, the elders of the village came to the home of *Nonno* Giuseppe and recited the plays of the Great Entertainer as they remembered them. Antonio sat in the corner with a leather-bound book in his lap and recorded the tales as they were told, so that they would never be lost again. Alessandra and Benito sat by the fireplace, with the puppets reclined beside them, and listened intently.

Perhaps it was a whisper of ghostly breath, or perhaps it was only a draft of air down the chimney, but every once in a while the *Piccolo Drago Verde* would seem to ruffle his paper-thin wings.

Capitolo Quinto: La Festa dell'Epifania

The Yule logs burned in the village, and in the dwelling of the Great Entertainer, until the year turned from old to new and then the blazing fires burned low and became ash. Each evening Alessandra and Benito—and the puppets, who did not themselves recall the words that had made them beloved of the village—studied the Great Entertainer's Operas of Puppets in their father's precise script.

All too soon it was *La Vigilia dell'Epifania*, the night the Magi brought gifts to *Gesù Bambino*, and just two days before Alessandra and Benito and their parents must return home. They had a great performance planned for the morning, after Mass, a play that had been relayed by several elders as being *Nonno* the Great Entertainer's favorite for *La Festa dell'Epifania. Nonna* Aurelia had made sweets, cut small, for the Plump Servant Girl to carry in her silver tray and distribute to the children of the village.

Alessandra and Benito were so distracted by their plans they nearly forgot the village tradition of laying out shoes for *La Befana.* They recalled just as they were tucking the puppets into one of the spare beds and scurried downstairs to lay their shoes by the dying embers of the fireplace.

Legend reflected that the Magi, in their search for *Gesù Bambino,* stopped at the home of an old woman — a good witch, who kept the cleanest house in her village — to ask directions. *La Befana* did not know where *Gesù Bambino* was to be found, but gave the Magi a good meal and place to rest. When they left to continue their search, the Magi invited *La Befana* to join them. She refused, for she had much housework to complete. But after a time she regretted her decision. She gathered the toys that had once belonged to her own son and set out in search of the Magi and *Gesù Bambino. La Befana* never found *Gesù Bambino,* but each Epiphany she searched for Him at each home she passed on her broom. She slid down the chimney and left toys and sweets for all good boys and girls and swept clean the house before she departed.

The children always loved the image of the kindly witch who planned to give beloved toys, and not the rather confusing gifts of the Magi — what would a child do with gold, frankincense, and myrrh? They imagined an Epiphany in which *La Befana* joined the Magi, and *Gesù Bambino* received mortal gifts that any small child would enjoy.

As any children the evening before gifts are received, Alessandra and Benito spent a restless night whispering across the garret, mistaking every burst of wind and scraping branch along roof for the sound of *La Befana's* arrival. They didn't dare check, for their father had warned that those who witnessed *La Befana* leaving her gifts received a smack from her broom. Sometimes it seemed there were more voices up in that garret than just those of the children, but that too could have just been the wind howling down the chimney.

Come morning, Alessandra and Benito were first down the stairs, heedless of the creaking floorboards. And there, in the shoes of each were the gifts *La Befana* had brought them: a brown paper-wrapped package of baked sweets filled with nuts and a deep-blue velvet sack embroidered in gold with suns, moons, and stars.

Alessandra opened her sack and there was a marionette, lovingly carved, of a fine Medieval Lady in a gown of purple with her hair coiled and pinned upon her head and, delicate as a tiny butterfly, upon the coils sat the tiniest golden *drago* with deep purple eyes — a lovely gilt ornament until the second set of strings brought the *drago* to life. As Alessandra delicately manipulated the strings to bring the *Drago Dorato* and Lady to life, she glowed with pleasure.

Beside his sister, Benito opened his sack and grinned with delight as he pulled out a Medieval Rake resplendent in silk of red and gold, with an ankle length cape of red velvet and a golden sword belted at his waist; the sword could actually be drawn by the doll through a clever manipulation of strings, which Benito employed almost immediately. Nearly overlooked in the hood of the Medieval Rake's cape hid another *Drago*, this the same deep red as the cloak. He peered out with mischievous golden eyes that seemed to wink at *Nonno* Giuseppe standing in the doorway, or perhaps it was only flicker of the firelight in the gold.

* * *

It nearly took the intervention of *Nonna* Aurelia to get Alessandra and Benito dressed for Mass that morning, so loath were they leave their new toys. In the end they were permitted to bring the puppets to the church, where the dolls stood and sat in cadence with the villagers; only the *Piccolo Dragos* restlessly shifted on their perches.

Afterwards, their new dolls were entrusted to *Nonno* Giuseppe — so that the fledgling actors could learn from watching the Great Entertainer's puppets, how to perform. Alessandra and Benito climbed onto the platform behind the small stage which had been polished during the twelve days of *Natale* to a bright shine. The faded curtains were replaced with ones of the deepest blue of the midnight sky and embroidered in shinning gold with suns, moons, and stars that caught the light and sparkled with every movement. The entire village gathered to watch the Great Entertainer's puppets perform a play that none had seen in seven decades. It was whispered that during the performance the wind that so often teased the curtains of the stage, and ruffled the wings of the *Piccolo Drago Verde,* was unusually still.

* * *

When the time came for Alessandra and Benito to return to the New World with their parents, the Medieval Lady and the Medieval Rake went with them — *Piccolo Dragos* whispering suggestions all the while. As they played with their dolls and made up their own operas, they recorded them in a notebook their father purchased for them, so their tales would always be remembered.

The puppets of the Great Entertainer and the leather-bound book of his plays remained in the garret of *Nonno* Giuseppe's dwelling and awaited the return of the Great

Entertainer's successors (whose parents had promised to bring them to visit again come the summer months — a time to which all the village looked forward with barely concealed anticipation).

It was said by the villagers — who were no longer afraid to speak the name of their beloved *Nonno* — that the soul of the Great Entertainer slept at last, with the peace of one who is blessed under heaven.

La Fine

———

Maria Elizabeth McVoy is a third generation Italian-American. Some of her fondest Christmas memories are of family dinners with the dining room table covered in a white cloth and lit by red tapers, eating her mother's homemade panettone. She lives in Virginia with her husband — also a third generation Italian-American — their two children, Michael and Rosina, and her very own Piccolo Drago Verde (Virgola Mostro) who helps edit her rough drafts by devouring wayward punctuation.

ROMIEL'S STORY: A MILLENNIUM BEFORE NOAH

Richard Bunning

PROLOGUE – GENESIS

In the times between Adam and Eve and the Great Flood many races of hominid shared the Earth. Bipedal creatures had spread away from the lands of Eden, across the Savannahs of Africa and from there to inhabit every continent. Some groups prospered and some didn't, but however harsh life was for individuals, most populations found their niches. That was until the deluge that flooded the lands when many populations were entirely lost. Only those lucky creatures on Noah's Ark and the fishes of the seas, avoiding the worst of fortunes. However, this story is set in those earlier times, before Nature cleansed the Earth.

Given eons, evolution can produce any sort of biological creature, and in the long age between mankind's first ancestors and Noah, evolution was fast and furious. But there was more than simple nature, more than the regular rhythm of genetic change mixing the potion in our genetic pool; nature had help, or more correctly, interference.

This intrusion into life on Earth came from the then most advanced creatures in the solar system, the Angelic Host. These visitors enhanced the development of one race in particular, that branch of hominid that was to become modern man. The interference started early, when the most advanced apes were still managing little more than swinging games through trees; and ended by leaving us with the first great philosophers, magistrates and mathematicians of our species. The ones interfering, called Watchers in many ancient texts, came from the not-yet-red coloured planet, Mars. Mars itself, scarred by industrialisation, was becoming increasingly unable to sustain biological life.

As we gaze at our world today, we can't help but see that we are following the very same path to destruction as the Martians took a few all too brief millennia ago. Those at the top of the intelligence tree see themselves as superior, and so inevitably either as gods themselves, or more likely given that they are mortal, as at least the special concern of the 'Immortal Almighty'.

The battles over who and what the Almighty is are familiar enough to all of us. Religious strife follows us into even the most recent second of the present. The God questions played out to the bitter end of life on planet Mars, as it often threatens to do on Earth. On Mars the last manifestation of spirituality encompassed a split into just two final 'truths', that of the Orthodox and that of the Fallen. This schism is the key to the activities of the Martians directly affected the course of our own histories.

The Orthodox insisted that the Earth was a treasure to be left untouched, free of Martian influence, left to the processes of nature. They believed that Martians should only be allowed to live within the Earth's ecosystem and exploit its resources if they didn't interfere with the evolution of mankind; if they lived as in a self-contained 'village' within a nature reserve. The Fallen had no such qualms about intervention. They broke orthodox religious law by invading, and manipulating, life on Earth for their own nefarious ends. They fell on mankind like a dark shadow, enveloping, smothering and enslaving all the tribes of mankind. The invaders were small in numbers, but nevertheless devastating, as the Fallen bred with humans, to create their own far from angelic races.

The Two Hundred, Fallen Angels, did all manner of experiments on the great apes. Ever more exotic hominid creatures were 'engineered'; causing what would prove to be irreversible biological changes. As one can read in the Book of Enoch, modern people are, in part, the descendants of certain Angels. A species that ensured their own genetic survival by imparting some of what makes Homo sapiens. They bred a creature, part Martian and part hominid, more intelligent than all other ape species. Just possibly, if there rests any truth in modern reports of visitations from space and distant time, then Watchers may not yet have finished with the Earth.

The Anakim were the early creatures, the men, that came into being through the Fallen Angels' engineering. The Anakim were never a homogenous race, but were rather the product of a long-running and open breeding programme. Scriptures describe them as 'giant' hominids, who were far closer in form to the Martians than is modern man. They had a huge influence on antiquity; for example, it was the Anakim that built the Empire of Atlantis. Our hero, Enoch, was an Anakim scribe, taught to write by Martians, including Baraquiel, Arakiel and Sariel. These were powerful creatures, but the strongest of the Angels was Azazel, the mighty general that all others paid homage to.

There have been many that have doubted the veracity of the Book of Enoch, as there still are. But even those that belief there is some truth in its words ask many difficult questions. One that has persisted, is whether any of the Martian Angels had wings? Or did our storytellers, latter in time, by then unable to comprehend the building of flying machines, add the mechanics of birds?

Perhaps some Godly ambassadors did or do have wings, and perhaps not. But all those that have a place in this history have no such limbs. It is error and fantasy amongst generation upon generation of copyists and translators that's been responsible for introduced such misconceptions. The Martians were wingless creatures, without even a single fluttering feather. That Angels fly, or at least did in these times, is already clear—by travelling as we do, in purpose built vehicles.

As time passed, and bloodlines diluted, the Anakim became increasingly indistinguishable from modern man. But families of 'giants' persisted down the centuries. Amongst the last regularly recorded are in the history of ancient Greece: Achilles, Hector, Priam, Ajax and their kith and kin. Even though, generally speaking, by then they were more man than giant, they were still a race apart from their more human subjects.

Many of the Anakim became unhappy under the yoke of the Fallen, despite, or perhaps because of, owing their very existence to them. The wish was often expressed that the Fallen should have never revolted against the religiously orthodox majority on Mars. By the time of this story, many were eager to throw in their lot with what was left of civilisation on Mars itself. The cogs of revolution were turning. Resistance was growing in the City of Angels, and the de facto leader of the rebellious was Enoch.

Enoch, wrote as subversively as he dared. He recorded not just political discontent, but the cruel breeding programmes that had produced all manner of challenged creatures, from orcs, to hobgoblins, and from ogres to imps. Many of the experimental lifeforms of that time would go on to find their own parts in the "mythological history" of the Earth. Those are other histories.

* * *

Enoch was already an old man, being three hundred and sixty-five years of age as this story unfolds. The longevity of the ancient Anakim seems unbelievable to us today, but I feel no pressure to question the counts of longevity as they appear in scripture. Enoch worked as a chief scribe in the offices of the Fallen; giving him access to many of those in positions of power including the most senior of the Two Hundred. Enoch was almost unique among the Anakim, having had the privilege of visiting Mars and communicating with some of the Host. The scriptures tell us in some detail about Enoch's report of his fantastical journey. Enoch was the greatest 'man' of this age, but our hero during this story's brief days was Romiel, a copyist scribe working directly for Enoch. Romiel was diminutive, almost more human looking than a typically tall and elegant Anakim. He hardly stood two metres tall even balanced on his tiptoes. Scripture records some details of Enoch's ancestors, but we know nothing of Romiel's immediate family. He may not have had one as such, as many Anakim were created in the test tubes of scientific laboratories.

Romiel, like Enoch himself, had long struggled to accept the brutal leadership of the Martian colonisers of Earth. His wish for an independent life was only reinforced after he set eyes on the beautiful Jeseka, Enoch's daughter. Romiel started dreaming of a life for them together, free of the yoke of the Fallen. Romiel regularly considered the thin possibilities of escaping the "mountain of the leader", Mount Hermon. Enoch knew of Romiel's designs on his daughter and, though concerned for her wellbeing, didn't entirely disapprove of the young scribe's interest. In fact, it wouldn't be long before he came to positively support

Romiel's ardent ambitions.

ACT I – ESCAPE, CAPTURE, AND CONSTERNATION

Romiel plunges down from the City. With the first light of dawn Romiel descends from the high walls of the space-port, on the Eastern outskirts of Hermon. He departs desperately clinging to the shoulders of a mighty winged-lion. In truth, this flying "monster" is more akin to a huge flying squirrel, than anything truly similar to either the king of cats or the bird winged lions of many, including Persian, mythologies. All the skill in flight this beast could achieve it does, which means a run and glide off the defensive walls of the City, down onto the plain below. Romiel precariously hangs onto the reluctant lion, crudely directing the trajectory of the flight by pulling at its shoulders, left and right. After a flight of a couple of terrifying minutes Romiel is relieved to make a relatively safe, if exceedingly bumpy landfall.

For Romiel, this is a leap of faith greater than merely trusting his safety to an all but wild beast. He is trusting Enoch's assertion that he is an expected emissary to the orthodox Martian Host. He has only the vaguest of ideas about what his mission is meant to entail. Enoch's assertion that the less one knows, the less one can reveal if captured, has done nothing to assuage Romiel's anxiety. Romiel plunges into the unknown with the reckless abandon of youth and the belief that being under the protection of the orthodox Martians will be an infinitely better fate than remaining enslaved, and possible fodder for experimentation, in the hands of the Fallen. And of course, there is always the dream of escaping to the stars, to better worlds entirely.

As Romiel lifted his head from the bush that absorbed his remaining momentum, he finds himself staring at half a dozen spear points. These are poised so close that he can see the smeared stains of previous victims on their crude forms. On looking slightly further from the points of deep preoccupation, he is shocked to see the surrounding group of vicious-looking ogres. Just to emphasise his precarious position, he can't help but notice that several of the warriors carry hominid skulls as trophies, tied around their torsos. In the distance, he glimpses the lion making all due haste to get away. Romiel's plight has been followed from the City's walls, by eyes now peering through a spy-glass at the proceedings below. Samuel, a gossip if ever there was one, is sure to convey all he has seen to Enoch, and perhaps, less beneficially, to others.

Romiel had informed Jeseka, at their last tearful meeting the evening before, that should she not hear from him, within forty days and forty nights, she is to assume him dead and get on with her life. Jeseka knows that she could never forget or rest from searching until the very moment she touched his body, alive or dead. It had taken all her will to obey her father, and so not pressure Romiel to take her with him on his precarious journey.

As he is unceremoniously pulled to his feet, Romiel fully expects to be immediately served up as a breakfast snack. But for the moment, he is spared and prodded hastily towards the cover of the forest. The ogres are seemingly less than starving, and appear to be enjoying some sport in just intimidating him while keeping him physically intact, so able to carry his own weight towards whatever fate waits. They look to already have enough to carry, with the limbs and carcasses of several creatures balanced on stooped shoulders. The ogres move silently back into the depths of the forest with Romiel and march on without a moments respite. Occasionally one or another prods or pushes Romiel, so discourage him from lingering. They march perhaps twenty kilometres, dodging around trees and pushing through sometimes thick vegetation. Romiel is now relieved that Jeseka isn't with him. As the hours pass, he tries to fathom a reason for this tribe to have been operating so close to the City. What, he asks himself, happened to the rather more civilised reception committee of his imagination? But most of his time is spent simply trying to keep ahead of prodding spears. Just keeping up with the naturally faster ogres is proving to be anything but easy.

Romiel is exhausted by the time they reach caves, which are clearly the ogres' home base. He is immediately shoved into a bamboo cage and hoisted high above the ground. This leaves him momentarily spinning with the twisting of the rope, halfway between a huge tree's massive bower and the rocky ground. As the hours pass and night falls, the already cold temperature rapidly tumbles. Poorly clothed for the conditions, Romiel isn't sure whether thirst or cold will kill him first. Either seems preferable to being eaten, and likely still alive for some time beyond first bite. He tries to distract his macabre thoughts by thinking further about what might have motivated the ogres' actions. A thousand possibilities cross his mind, but none seems satisfactory.

* * *

Since the Anakim are not so much a race as the product of an ongoing breeding experiment, the individual appearances vary greatly. As said, Romiel has a superficial appearance that isn't so different from that of modern man. However, Enoch has much more the appearance of a Martian. His wife, Edna, and to a lesser extend their daughter, Jeseka, are different again. Both are more 'neanderthal' in appearance. Jessica is very bright, and certainly physically stronger than Romiel. She stands half a metre taller, and is heavier in the shoulder. She is also extremely hirsute compared to Romiel. She is hairy enough that it is heat rather than cold that generally most troubles her. She is always very modestly and fashionably dressed, being very much the sort of girl that favours pinks and frills. Jeseka is well proportioned, despite her heaviness, with a silhouette that even many modern girls would be envious of. She is fast and agile, if rather heavy on her feet.

Enoch, his wife, Edna, and Jeseka, the only one of their children yet to establish an independent life, sit down to dinner. Edna serves, as Enoch hides behind a scroll of seemingly vital reading. Jeseka can't help but raise her concerns for her beau. "I hope Romiel has found somewhere to shelter for the night. I fear for him alone in the forest, a reluctant warrior at best."

Edna replies, "Don't worry yourself dear, I am sure he'll be fine. There's no use in fretting. Find some distraction or other, because it might be a long time before we have news. Anyway, no news is better than evil news, or at least so the saying goes."

"But Romiel's alone among the wild heathens and the trolls. Who will watch his back?"

"God will, my love."

"If God isn't too busy disciplining his Angels?"

Enoch scowls over his scroll. "Don't you go taking God's name in vain, my girl. We have little enough belief here on Earth without my family wavering. Years ago, when I was in peril, God came to my aid. I was immersed in bright lights as though before a holy vision, and then even at my hour of greatest peril..."

"Yea, we know father. And an Angel of the Lord came down, and a light shone over the sinners standing with swords drawn to do you harm. And with a rushing wind, as though before a tempest, this dragon like vessel drew you up and journeyed across the sky into the firmament of the heavens. And behold you visited the true planet of the Angels."

"By the stars, you remember my stories well, my sweet daughter. Rest assured that Romiel will be fine. The Lord works in mysterious ways."

"And so do you, dear Father."

"Yes, yes. Let it be known only by us that there are forces from abroad, ready, poised to take the City. The Host, is encamped in the forest around the mountain waiting only for my signal. Not only is our army mighty, but God is the most powerful of allies. The very walls of Hermon are sure to fall."

Unfortunately, at this moment, on the other side of the door, an old servant is listening. This half-crippled and dwarfish creature, saved from being cast into the wild only through Enoch's kindness, should be the most loyal of employees. But that is far from being the case.

Jeseka hears a dragging foot retreating up the passageway. "I think Jasper has been listening again. Why do you keep him as a servant? He can't see when something needs cleaning, and with his twisted back and bad leg, it takes forever for him to do anything."

"Be kind, Jeseka. Who else would feed him?"

"Well at least make him bathe. How can I feel kind when his smell sickens me?" She scowls at her father. "At least discipline him for eavesdropping on our conversations."

"No, Jeseka, let him go. It is beneficial that he passes on some essence of our supposed good fortunes. I was aware of his presence."

Jeseka is suddenly angry, "You mean you are scheming,

risking Romiel as some sort of sacrificial goat. Nothing is ever straight forward with you, is it Father?"

"Don't worry. Yes I have schemes, but also, I have done all I can to ensure Romiel's safety. After all, he isn't just important to my dear daughter, he is important to our desperate cause. The Fallen must believe a large invasion is in progress."

"So there isn't an invasion?"

"There are forces here to rescue us."

Jeseka is far from reassured, but recognises that doubting her father's intentions can do the situation no good. She bites her tongue and excuses herself from the table.

* * *

To his surprise Romiel survives the night in the company of ogres. Though bruised and short of sleep, he is pleased to have the cage lowered to the ground and be passed a coconut shell full of water. Then this small pleasure turned to surprise when not much later he is released from the cage, not to be prepared as a feast, but only to be marched still further, over rocky hills and down into the middle of a wide valley. They stop as the leader of the party holds one massive hand over his hanging brow, and looks up, possibly measuring the position of the sun. Then from a distance a roar is suddenly to be heard, which grows quickly louder, and before Romiel can gather his wits, a craft has swooped in, reversed its engines, and landed. Even more amazingly, the ogres don't run in terror. Indeed, they display a state of nonchalant expectation.

A minute later a tall Martian emerges and stands before them. Romiel is most surprised when the arrival address all his words directly to him. "Enoch promised you would be here, and so you are. Come, come, Romiel, we have a lot to plan and no abundance of time." As the Martian talks, supplies are being brought from the ship and stacked.

Romiel guesses that they are by way of payment. This seems to be confirmed as one by one the ogres lift the crates and head back up the hill towards their caves.

Romiel is urged to follow the Martian into the craft, and as he does the doors almost immediately close behind them.

"Come Romiel, to the left there, quarters are prepared for you. Eat, refresh yourself, and after you have rested I'll call to take you for an audience with our pilot."

ACT II – SCHEMES, PLANS, AND SKIRMISHES

As Enoch planned, Azazel, the natural leader of the Fallen, is undone by his own expectations. Already certain that an invasion is coming, the report from the eager-to-better-himself Jasper seems to give his suppositions substance. Azazel quickly gives out orders to assemble the Fallen's strongest forces, and for their dispatch to track down invading legions. The supposed major invasion is given further credibility as regular skirmishes are soon being reported. Enoch has planned a series of diversionary attacks that are now being implemented. These only serve to draw out further forces from Hermon's defences. Most of the incidents, are small scale intrusions by Methuselah, and Enoch's other sons, Regim and Gaidad, and a few dozen other troop leaders. Azazel has no way of knowing that the enemy are actually very thin on the ground. No sooner have his forces made fleeting contact than the attackers melt away. Azazel, always prepared for war, and never even trusting his closest allies, becomes increasingly con-vinced that failure to track down the enemy can only be because he has traitors in his camp. Soon not even the Fallen themselves are above his suspicions.

* * *

Enoch's plan is working to perfection. Before long, with the City barely garrisoned, his people will have a chance to slip away into the forests. Once assembled in the wilderness, the righteous should be whisked away on the Host's craft, while Azazel's main forces are still scattered, charging back and forth across ever more distant territories. But there is one spy in the camp that could yet see most of Enoch's plans turned to dust. Samael, his close friend, is bound by fear for his life and that of his family, to the will of the Admiral of the City's fleet, Asaradel. As the Angel threatens him and yet promises rewards for information, Samael is soon offering to spy on his friend.

Everyone needs a confident from time to time, and Samael, the next most senior in Enoch's group is his. Enoch has long valued the friendship of one that doesn't necessarily see the world through similar eyes, of one that is happy to drink at the altar of the Fallen, of a confidant to test his own beliefs against. So it is normal that when his friend appears Enoch is keen to gossip. During their chitchat the strange flight of the lion, earlier witnessed by Samael, is soon under discussion. When Samuel mentions the incident, Enoch becomes suddenly and surprising alert. Enoch, usually quiet and reflective, hiding his raw emotions, seems positively exuberant. Extraordinary though the story is, Samael wonders what in particular gives cause for Enoch's strong response? Samael begins to circle the subject and listen, and gradually puts two and two together. He realises that the passenger on the lion was most likely Romiel. And that being the case, such information might save his family's skins, if, unfortunately, at the cost of stretching Enoch's. Romiel had long seen a certain duplicity in Samuel's character, and guessed that under pressure he might lack loyalty even to Enoch. When Romiel had raised the issue, Enoch had appeared to obstinately refuse to listen to any words that doubt his friend. And yet, it seems that Romiel had at least seeded a little doubt. Samuel hears more than is wise, but Enoch plays a guarded enough hand to keep Samael from the most vital of information. And so it is that Samael's reports to the City offices only mention that Enoch is definitely communicating with outside forces, including the scribe Romiel. Fortunately, Asaradel sees insufficient cause for Enoch's immediate arrest, thinking it best to leave the traitor room to lead the way straight to his accomplices.

Azazel has long known that the old fool Enoch works against his interests. He has even read for himself the flamboyant writings of Enoch's voyages, and of his high regard for the Host. But now he needs detail, about when and how the expected invasion is to come. All Azazel has on the specific threat to the Fallen came from the concoction of half-stories and confused understanding that flows from the likes of Jasper's simple mind. Samael's report, coming to him from the Admiral, will convince him that Enoch and Romiel are the keys to unlocking the facts. But maybe that will reach his ears too late.

* * *

Reality is that there never will be an invasion, not now, not ever. The Martians already feel themselves to be far too weak mount such a grand campaign. But isolated on Earth, the Fallen, don't know just how enfeebled the Host has already become. On Mars, all that remains of the will to combat the Fallen amounts to the ongoing plan to save some of the Righteous that most earnestly resist the Fallen. Plans had been crystallising in the minds of the Host, coordinated through their contact on Earth, Enoch, for many desperate months. What Azazel has guessed exactly

127

right was the timing of approaching trouble. Many times, Azazel has come so very close to finally squashing Enoch, toying almost daily with whether now is the time to arrest him. Even now, at the eleventh hour, Azazel is aware of Enoch parading around the government buildings, without an apparent care in the world. Ironically perhaps, while the scribe is so near, Azazel feels less immediate compulsion to pounce; for surely there is little need for alarmist haste when the creature is so close he can almost be smelt.

* * *

In his assigned quarters on the spacecraft, Romiel is suffering a crisis of the spirit. The inside of the craft is so different to anything he has ever envisioned. Yes, he'd seen plenty of spacecraft, coming at going from very close to his own neighbourhood. However, to be inside one, to see the workings of such advanced technology, that is something else. This isn't at all like any other structure he has ever been in, as the advanced machines of the Martians are kept distant from the eyes of all but the most privileged of Anakim. Before he has fully adjusted to the strange metal surfaces, lights and weird apparatuses, Romiel is being escorted into the heart of the ship. Even having been given a little time to come to terms with things, Romiel's sanity swings on a knife's edge. He is suddenly aware of standing before the large figure of an Archangel, the pilot of the ship. The angel is sitting on a wide-backed swivel chair in the centre of the ship's bridge. Power seems to emanate from the being itself, a power far greater than Romiel has ever felt from any of the Fallen. The creature is also physically bigger than even Azazel. The pilot seems to glow with power, dazzling Romiel. The angel slowly turns his chair so that he faces Romiel with all the pipes, wires, flashing lights and screens of the console behind him. The apparatus seems to splay across the Angel's back, almost like massive wings. Romiel has a vision of a giant bird, as light streams from behind the awe-inspiring sky-pilot. Already a bag of nerves, Romiel's knees buckle, involuntarily bowing him down onto the deck.

The pilot speaks with a voice that echos around the room, and at the same time inside Romiel's head. The Archangel's deep voice penetrates almost into Romiel's bones. "Romiel, you can direct me in selecting the Righteous. While other ships from the fleet swoop in from space to distracting the defences, you will act as pathfinder for our ground forces. However, understand well that there is only one we absolutely must rescue, that being Enoch. As for the rest, that partly depends on you. Choose well those creatures you believe fit to join our congregation, because those that are later found to be unsuitable will be trying out their legs in the void of space."

"I will do my best, Sire. If my spirit will only allow me."

"Have no fear for your life, but only for the father and the girl I'm told you most cherish. I know you have plenty of determination, driven by romantic love. But if that is not enough, our ship's doctor is at hand, with his black-bag of invigorating potions. Go now with David to prepare. Our armorer and our tacticians will be at your disposal."

Romiel whispers to himself, hardly moving his lips. "Jeseka, give me strength." He is amazed to get a reply.

"And don't forget the strength that God gives, Romiel, or at very least the cunning instincts His Nature have given you. Go now, and guide my soldiers in the good fight."

ACT III – THE FAITHFUL MUST ESCAPE

Over breakfast Enoch, Edna and Jeseka are talking through what is planned to be their last day in the City.

Enoch is doing his best to distract their fears by assigning them clear roles. "Have you checked that Jasper is distant, Jeseka?"

"Yes father. There is only Samael in the building, editing the latest scriptures you assigned to him."

"I have to remain in plain sight until the very last minutes. I will gather all the intelligence I can by being close to the battle's directors. Edna, pack as little as possible, no more than you and Jeseka can easily carry. Jeseka, you go around the houses of our friends telling all to move. They are to travel in small groups, setting out in any direction they would normally take on familiar business, and only when well out of sight of the City are they to head directly towards the Reema Flats. When they've gathered, they must trust and follow ogres that'll keep them heading to the south-east. No monstrous tribes should worry them, except only the soldiers of the Fallen. Tell them they must be prepared for hardship. When night falls, none are to use torches. They must walk on by the light of the stars and with only the courage of prayer, remembering that patrols will be as handicapped by the dark as our people, unless they telegraph their positions with their torches, which many are sure to do. Tell all our friends that if they want to live, then they must make haste. Those who falter or are captured must be left.

"As for you my daughter, don't be timid, we have much to do, but don't be reckless either. For safety on the street, take Samael. He knows little, but he does know I expect a lot of his friendship. But be circumspect with the information you give even him. Perhaps just say, that you are both required to go around the houses to find Romiel. You might say, Romiel is in trouble with the Guardians for the misuse of a lion, or some such nonsense. Samael can guard the streets while you enter the private dwellings of our followers. Whatever you do, be back here by midday to help your mother flee. I will be one of the last to leave travelling alone, disguised as a humble goat herder. Romiel may return to help, having guided friendly forces towards the City; or he might not. Regardless, you two must flee, meeting up to travel with whomever you like, but don't travel in a big group that will attract attention. You must not allow Jeseka to linger in expectation of Romiel's return, Edna."

Edna looks earnestly at her family, "Eat up, and be gone, the two of you. I will be ready. Jeseka, dress for warmth and to be inconspicuous. This isn't the day for you to dress to draw eyes."

"Yes, Mother. I'll find an old-ladies shawl and a tunic that trails down to even cover my ankles."

Enoch sighs, "Don't be cheeky to your mother, young lady. I'm glad though that your moods are still both light enough for domestic tittle-tattle. Keep smiling. A cheerful countenance can disarm a thousand suspicious eyes."

* * *

At the appointed hour, the forces of the Host stream out from the concealed craft. Before the dust settles, the expeditionary team, fronted by Romiel, is heading for the hills. With a couple of minutes all that is left of activity around the craft, are crew employed handing out weapons and supplies to a few remaining, gleeful, primitive tribesmen.

Romiel follows back the route the ogres had escorted him over. All through the journey he conveys information to those with him, anything that he thinks might help give the Host forces the advantage. At the edge of the forest, having outlined the defences of the City, Romiel leaves his troop and heads on alone. He reasons that if he is stopped by the forces of the Fallen, even having all the troop would make little difference to a poor outcome, and that one man alone has far less chance of being spotted and challenged. They are not far from the earlier site of Romiel's crash landing, as the troop spread out and take cover, with orders to only advance once Romiel has got through the City walls. The Host's forces have orders to disrupt the normal order of the City as much as possible without been drawn into a one-sided firefight. Everything seemed to be going very well, too well perhaps. Romiel prays that their whereabouts isn't being tracked; that they aren't stumbling into a trap. The slopes of the hill are not devoid of activity, with units of soldiers moving back and forth, and even occasional groups of tradesmen, apparently uninhibited by all the military activities. However, even amongst those bent on commerce eyes are beginning to shift, as people start to sense that nothing is as normal as first appears.

Suddenly warplanes start to roar out of the City's airport, to engage the Hosts' fighters that are diving in from deep in space. The Host are doing their level best with their meagre forces to make the operation look like the beginnings of a large invasion. Romiel notices scuffles as guards are suddenly trying to direct everyone back towards the City. Things are beginning to seem a little less like a walk in the park. Before many more minutes have passed, groups of civilians start to panic as it has become abundantly clear that a real battle is unfolding.

* * *

Enoch busies himself about the offices of government, which he often frequents on almost a daily basis. He even does his best to join in and further confuse debates about the possible movements of forces loyal to the Host, all of which still seems to be based on little more than hearsay. When the time approached for departure, he heads for the cloakroom where he has hidden his disguise, empties his brief-case of its usual paraphernalia, and stuffs those suitable for goat herding inside. He then heads determinedly to the North gate of the City, and the herder he'd previously arranged to meet. He feels encouraged by the roar of fighter aircraft taking to the skies. He knows that attacking craft are too few in numbers to occupy the City's defences for long, but they are exactly on time. He prays his people will use the opportunity of the soldiers' distraction, to make rapid progress away from the City.

ACT IV – LOVERS IN PERIL

Samuel realises he is accompanying Jeseka on far more than a simple errand, and knows that the last thing he wants to risk is to be seen acting with the Fallens' enemies. He reasons that now is the time to act to save his imprisoned family. As Jeseka and Samael finished the rounds of the houses, Samael makes his dastardly move, betraying his friend's daughter. At their next stop, while Jeseka is indoors giving her instructions, he alerts a City patrol. They grab Jeseka as she emerges from the house to look up and down the street, searching for the disappeared Samael. In a state of total shock Jeseka finds herself being escorted towards the governmental buildings. Jeseka is very scared, but the fact that her mother will be unlikely to flee without her frightens her more than the knowledge that she will surely be made to suffer for all that transpires this day.

Romiel has completed his roundabout journey to the City and now moves from shadow to shadow towards Enoch's residence. He is surprised to see Samael hurrying away alone towards the town centre, while glancing furtively back over his shoulder. But aware that time is pressing, he doesn't dwell on it. Nevertheless, Samael's behaviour is enough to encourage him to be extra vigilant himself. Romiel believes that Jeseka and her mother must have long departed, yet he feels compelled to check their house. He's sure he can soon make up lost time. Out behind him, back towards the City walls he hears lasers firing. The thinly spread troops of the Host have begun to do their best to sound and act like a large invasion force.

* * *

Meanwhile, Enoch nears the forest, having abandoned the goats, who were most disinclined to follow his direction. The animals have been spooked by howling aircraft, and other frantic activities. Nevertheless, the disguise did its job, by getting Enoch to within a few minutes of the forest, where he trusts help will be waiting. He is delighted to see several parties of escapees making good progress in the same direction. Enoch is still short of the forest as friendly forces start to fire on the Fallen. Now that the City is under siege, the soldiers have no time to pursue the suddenly running groups of Anakim, who seem to have magically multiplied in the terrain under the walls. For a time, the sky is full of extra noise as a couple of space-fighters manage to break through the City's air defences, but that doesn't last long as one is driven away and the other trails into the distance spurting flames and smoke. It leaves only a dirty scar across the sky.

* * *

Romiel made his way across the City, and now crashes into the house to find Edna forlornly sitting alone, her eyes moist with worry. He knows he has to help her first, despite his desperation to locate Jeseka. Gently pulling Edna to her feet, he half carries her out onto the street. As he drags her, ever crying that they should wait for Jeseka, he is relieved to see a supporter that he vaguely knows, also late on the road. Tasker has come back for a family heirloom, undoubtedly a stupid act, but fortuitous in the circumstances. The man didn't need much persuasion to take the protesting Edna into his care and leave his even heavier vase. Romiel is at last free to resume his search for his heart's desire.

* * *

A few streets away, Jeseka is fighting like a banshee to delay the patrol's progress towards the centre of the City. She knows that whatever happens she must not let herself be used to draw Enoch into danger. it's almost too late, as the government offices loom, when suddenly she sees an opportunity to escape. A self-propelled chariot, moving at full-speed, steered by a determined Angel, rounds the corner towards them. Rather than cooperate with the guards attempt to scatter, Jeseka digs in her heels and fights to hold her ground. At the last second, her guards realise that they've been too long detained and make a desperate attempt to jump clear. Jeseka risks all by falling flat to the ground as the two soldiers release their grip. Somehow the wheels miss her as the body of the chariot passes above, but the two guards have no such good fortune. Guards and driver are sent flying. Jeseka doesn't even glance at the carnage as she flees down the nearest side street. As soon as she can, she doubles back towards home, worried that even at this late hour her mother will still be waiting for her.

* * *

Romiel was certain that just as the daughter came first in importance to Edna, Edna would come first in the mind of her daughter. He had decided that the best he can do is hang around the streets near the house, and try to spy and eavesdrop on any individuals that pass. He reckons that alone he could leave himself as little as a few hours to make the rendezvous, but deep down he knows he won't be leaving unless he is certain Jeseka is safe.

* * *

The Host's fighters had been beaten off, rather too easily Azazel thinks, and no motherships or battlecruisers had joined the fight. That could only mean one thing, the Host are no longer capable of mounting a credible invasion. Logically then, all this activity can only be a diversion, and for what if not for getting a sizable number of individuals out. That means that subversives will already be on the move, most already having left the City, and, he reasons, likely as not there is an enemy transporter craft hidden not so very far away. He quickly surmises that it would need to be far enough out to escape easy detection, but not so far that potential escapees couldn't get there within a reasonably short time. At Azazel's insistence, within half an hour of the retreat of the Host's last fighters Asaradel has most of his air force refuelled and flying local search patterns. Surely, if a ship is out there they will quickly find it.

Azazel redirected some ground forces that had returned to the City, to search the houses of every half-likely escapee, starting with that of the now very clearly absent Enoch. Now that he is sure that this is a diversionary attack he knows that any of the Host's friends not already fleeing will soon be doing so.

* * *

Jeseka has arrived back in her neighbourhood, and circled the streets around her home a couple of times, without seeing anything suspicious. She now heads inside, only to be pleased if surprised that her mother has apparently fled. Before departing she decided to have a quick final look around, extra minutes that threatened to cost her dear. Already, militia are moving down from the top of the street. Romiel had fortuitously just arrived, and is hidden in a shadowed doorway across the road. The house looks deserted, but he is determined to await the result of the inevitable search. Then he got a glimpse of a shadow moving across a window, and instinctively knows Jeseka is there. Troops are fortunately going methodically door to door. He needs a diversion, and fast, but what? Then he gets an idea. On the street behind is a temple with a gong run by a water wheel. Heedless of possible danger, he sprints toward it and flings himself though the temple door. In another few seconds he has the temple's water tap on full bore flooding the tank that drives the water wheel, which in turn will shortly strike the bell. The speed of the ringing is dictated by the flow of the water. By the time the bell starts chiming he is on the street screaming his head off and shouting to non-existent attackers. He then rushes back between the houses to Jeseka's street and looks to see if he's successfully distracted the patrol. He has. They have turned to find a passage towards the temple. The noise also alerts Jeseka, who sees Romiel staring up at her.

As the last of the patrol disappear from sight, the love-birds meet in the middle of the road, hug, turn and sprint for their lives, all almost in one fluid motion.

Running as fast as they can it isn't long before they see troops ahead of them, still moving out after the fleeing civilians. Now all they can do is follow, and hope for an opportunity to pass through the lines later. It's already getting dark, so slipping through might not be such a totally reckless proposition in another hour. There is only a quarter moon, so though the sky's clear are also enough deep shadows to hide them. The hirsute Jeseka isn't so visible especially now she has discarded her shawl, and Romiel blackens his pale skin by rubbing in dirt. Most of the angel's and Anakim troops ahead of them are on foot, though a few of the Fallen are using chariots. The clumsy vehicles are of little advantage in the dark, unless the Fallen light them up like beacons. And anyway, amongst the trees they suffer much reduced manoeuvrability.

Despite the descending dark it is over an hour before the couple feel brave enough to move through the ever-dispersing line, and another ten minutes before they risk the noise of running and inevitably stumbling and falling. When they eventually risk a rapid pace they are determined not to stop for a second until they've covered every metre of the still ten or so kilometres between them and the Reema Flats. Several times, half lost, they are forced into wide diversions, which add time. And once or twice they're forced to stop while flying craft light up nearby ground. At least the lights give them a chance to get their bearings. Often they make hard contact with immovable objects, but though bruised, neither is severely enough handicapped to greatly slow them. Usually Jeseka leads, her better sight making some considerable difference in the gloom, and especially as she is slower except in short bursts, that is probably the best strategy.

As the couple finally reach their goal, they see that preparations are underway for lift off. With every bit of speed their exhausted legs can muster, Romiel and Jeseka sprint hand in hand for the already lifting spacecraft door. It is still an hour earlier than the originally planned departure, but that's an impossibly delayed target now. As missiles smack and ricochet around them, they both fling themselves over the already metre high ramp, and tumble, sprawling down the other side. Romiel glanced back as the craft lifts away, to see Azazel's war chariot come to ground, the chase abandoned. Jeseka, grabs Romiel, hugging him tightly. With tears running rivulets down dirty cheeks, she gazes at her very relieved father.

ACT V: MISSION ACCOMPLISHED

And so it comes to pass that, at the age of three hundred and sixty-five, Enoch is taken up into the Godly firmament. Along with him, many of the faithful of the Earth depart. The Righteous escape the Earth, to temporary respite on Mars and eventually onwards to very distant satellites. Over time, prophets and preachers will return, to bring hope to those still on Earth, but that is the stuff of future hope and often doubted legend.

A millennium on, of scriptures chronology, the Empire of the Fallen will be finally swept away as the dry lands of Earth are inundated by the Great Flood. One of Enoch's very own great grandchildren will be the lauded facilitator of many creatures' survival; as God finally undoes the descendants of the Fallen. You see, Enoch is none other than the great grandfather, on the male side, of Noah, the builder of the Arc. God works in mysterious ways. Noah will build the massive vessel that keeps the treasured safe from deep cold waters. But that future requires this history, of Enoch himself being plucked from the Earth, and of at least one of his sons, Methuselah's, survival.

———

Richard Bunning ascribes to the view that artists don't have to suffer to be creative, but definitely do need to be very nosey about the sufferance of others. Find Richard's writing and views at: http://richardbunningbooksandreviews.weebly.com

WORSHIPPING VENUS

Jane Buchan

There are seven of us on a good night, out here, under the stars. After our potluck supper we climb up Wilson's Hill, a secluded spot in Vermont's Northeast King/Queendom, to lay down, no matter the weather, in our flower formation. Our heads form the tip of each petal. Our feet, touching in the middle, form the small circle of space containing our center candle. In this space, in winter, summer, and all the variations between, a fat beeswax candle burns in a hurricane lantern, one of the special archaic objets d'art Bob's father makes out of tin. Its perforated holes cast a dancing array of tiny earth-bound stars upon us and the grass or snow or stubble, depending on the season. When I am with my friends in this circle, I can't help but imagine how we look from above. Like Wilbur in *Charlotte's Web*, I suspect we look Radiant.

I joined this circle after I met Zara at a death-by-dancing evening, my private name for what is called contra-dancing in these parts, because my feet never touch the ground the whole time I'm passed from set to set, sometimes mauled, sometimes cosseted, by the joyous men delighted to find willing partners for these brutal calisthenics. I'm five foot two and weigh eighty-five pounds on a fat day. The men, mostly burly farmers starved for human touch, pick me up and twirl me around like a leaf, dancing me silly until I

140

manage to make my way to the end of a line and escape into the refreshments room.

The night we met, Zara had taken refuge by the punch bowl a few moments before I escaped my handlers. She was rubbing a bruised instep and looked up when she heard my limping entrance. I thought her eyes, more black than brown, and her skin, a glowing, burnished, old gold, the loveliest combination of colors and cultures I'd ever seen. She might have been forty or sixty. I was forty-five, newly divorced, and hopeful in the way that earned my eldest sister's scorn. When I began to date again, she called me terminally optimistic.

Here you are, then, Zara said, all business. *I've been watching you.* She didn't give me time to reply before she added, *From the moment you came in I knew you were the one I'd come for.*

When someone I don't know begins a conversational gambit with a possible reference to fate, I pay attention. My grandmother, known to everyone in these parts as Nini, a melodious perversion of Nana some grandchild with plugged ears coined early in life, had clairvoyant gifts that could stop me dead in the middle of a lie. They could also make me believe the worst tragedy would turn out well. She was, throughout her long life and the thirty-seven years I'd been fortunate enough to have her in mine, uncannily correct in her predictions and assumptions, her guesses and surmises. Nini's gifts ranged from tea leaf reading — she told my cousin Lydia that sometime during her first year at college she would meet a man on a train and marry him within a month — to visions. My cousin did meet a man on a train and marry three weeks after their meeting, forgetting our grandmother's prediction until she came home with her wedding band and her Gloria

Vanderbilt smile. This accurate prediction secured Nini's reputation as a psychic not only in our family, but in the whole town.

Clairvoyance can be nothing but a parlor trick, but this prophecy turned out to be vital to Lydia's happiness. On her first visit home with her new husband, in an uncharacteristic outpouring of her secret life, my cousin confided to Nini and me that she had intended to kill herself at the end of her first year if college turned out to be as brutal as high school. Long before she heard this story, my grandmother knew the desperate straits Lydia floundered in and somehow conjured her granddaughter's belief in the possibility of love as well as its wedding-ring bearing agent. Lydia's husband, Barry Fournier, is the son of a stone mason, and, amazingly, at the time of their meeting, his life was also hanging in the balance. He wanted to follow in his father's footsteps but his father and mother expected him to be the first in their family to go to college. My cousin Lydia helped him to hang in at school and he helped her to hang in at life. Given this family history, I took Zara's references to fate seriously.

I saw that she was staring at a spot just to my left. *What are you…?*

Zara anticipated my question. *I see auras. Yours has a line of fuchsia in it that's like mine. It's uncommon, both in color and quantity. It means you belong to Her, you know, the Goddess. But you know that already.*

I put my punch glass on the table because I was afraid I'd drop it on the floor. Not that it would have mattered. This floor, unlike the pristine contra-dance floor, had been scarred and abused by every imaginable kind of boot and shoe. I suspected it would have welcomed the anointing of my punch. I stalled for think-time. Notoriously slow on my feet when it comes to honest communication, I need the space to reason out things my trustworthy heart understands in a nanosecond. *You see what?* Zara stood, tilted her head in a way that conveyed unmistakable disappointment, and then did something annoyingly familiar. She flipped me the bird, pulled her shawl around her shoulders, and walked out into the night.

I grew up with six siblings, four of them drama queens who early in life perfected the flouncing exit. Mia and Pete, our twins, were born calm and resistant to histrionics, but my four singleton sisters and I became mistresses of flouncing's many, many forms. In our old farm house, flouncing was a way of life, as was swearing, at least when Mother wasn't around. My father was never around, having buggered off to pursue his calling as a gigolo, something he only figured out after all seven of us were born and my mother inherited responsibility for her aging parents, and with them, the spectacularly disintegrating family farm. Granddad worked a couple of hundred acres of wheat for some big conglomerate and rented out the barn for hay storage. This simple arrangement meant all manner of sun blessed, lively young men and women visited the farm on fairly regular basis, hired to help with the old-school style planting, tending, and harvesting. My older sisters came to love the farm for this reason. I loved it from the beginning, mostly for the sky.

In town, in the small house we rented before Nini and Gramps asked us to move in with them, the sky always held a portion of the day's trials and tensions, at least it seemed that way to me when I looked out my bedroom window into the haze of street light that obscured the black dome and its on-again, off-again cache of stars and planets I loved to watch whenever Nini invited me to the farm for a sleepover. These invitations, issued to each grandchild in turn, were her way of making sure we each felt seen, heard, and welcomed into the world beyond the brawls that were standard fare in a house with three bedrooms and seven children, a house with no basement, no dining room and no garden to speak of. Moving to the farm was what I imagined Paradise was like. My older sisters, sophisticated in the ways of town life, were miserable and lived for their drivers' licenses — until they met a few of the young men who brought hay to the barn for storage and felt better about country life.

Trailing out onto the old Grange Hall front stoop behind this unfamiliar aura-seeing flouncer, I knew Zara had a BS detector every bit as good as Nini's. I stood on tiptoe looking out at the herd of dozing cars, hoping to see a light or even Zara backlit by the lights from Carnival's Used Cars across the road. Nothing. I looked up. Inhabitants of the black dome winked and shone and teased despite the determined light-show across the road. Deep in my psyche Zara's cryptic remark reverberated: *You belong to Her, but you know that already.*

Standing beneath splatters of starlight ancient and immediate, I knew Zara was right. I belonged to Her all right, whoever She might be, in spite of my early traditional, religious indoctrination. My mother insisted we attend church when my father left, I suppose because she believed in order for us to cope with the loss of one of our parents, our grandparents' comforting presences needed to be backed up by some grand-design belief system. I sat in my hard pew, sweating in the oversized wool coat I'd inherited from Jeannie, hungry and resentful. One day after the third or fourth service, I asked the questions that exposed the Emperor's nakedness. *What's all this about the Father and Son and Holy Ghost?* My wonderfully diplomatic mother stared, a deer in the headlights. I pressed my

144

advantage. *Mom, tell me. What happened to all the girls in this story? And how come everybody sits here like your tailor's dummies acting as if there are no other mystical stories to tell?*

When you start to attend church at eight and your life up to that point has been full of *Grimm's Fairy Tales*, *Bullfinch's Mythology*, and the stories of Beatrix Potter and Roald Dahl, you know damned well girls and boys go together like bookends. You needed boys and girls, princesses and princes, fathers and mothers, and above all, grandmothers—often called Fairy Godmothers in stories—for a complete picture. I wasn't going to get involved in anything that had decided to raise to some great height all the men and wipe out all trace of the women. Maybe it was Nini's influence—she was a bluestocking descendent, direct from The Motherland—or maybe it was my mother's quiet but firm emphasis on fairness and equality among her brood, but from the start, I thought what went on in our church left a whole lot to be desired.

As I grew older and more argumentative I came up with some great questions for my born-again friends who said we were all going to hell if we weren't saved. *But what about those people who've never heard of Jesus? What about people born into different traditions? What about Hindus? What about Muslims? What about Jews? How is it loving to say someone you don't even know is going to hell when the whole Bible story is supposed to be about God loving the world so much that He...* I never did get any answers and so church just didn't play with me. After a year of fierce resistance on my part, my mother said we could all lapse. This meant staying home on Sunday mornings reading and baking and generally doing whatever we liked.

Although I'm sure I was feeling beyond surprises after my early disappointing religious experience, that night at the contra-dance Zara managed to surprise me. She emerged from the shadows, unsmiling, ready for some kind of acknowledgment. *I know what you mean,* I said quickly, not wanting to lose her again.

She looked skeptical. *About what?*

About belonging. To Her.

As she moved away from me, the night seemed to take bites out of her—first a shoulder, then an entire arm—as she entered the deep shadow between the dance building and the outer edge of sleeping cars. *Come Thursday. At five-thirty. With food to share. Vegetarian. Wear something festive. My place. Wilson's Hill.* And so began my new life with a no-nonsense savant who read auras and spoke of the divine feminine as if such heresy were commonplace in the Green Mountains of Vermont.

Wilson's Hill is tucked within the undulating folds of many similar mounds of thrusting rock and tree compost in Vermont's Northeast. Like so many other places, it is named for the European settler who murdered whatever human, animal, or plant life stood in the way of his right to scrawl his name on a board and call the place his. But it never belonged to him, not in the way that a place belongs to the beings who resonate with every tree, erratic bolder, clump of colt's foot, wild leak, grub, and peeper, to name but a few of the earthlings living out their lives in obscurity on what is to car culture merely two-dimensional, Currier-and-Ives poster potential. The place might more accurately have been called Cedar Hill, because so many cedars, generally stand-offish in these parts, congregate there. It might have been called Wild Turkey Hill because of the intricate intersection of wild-fowl foraging routes on its hospitable breast. Or it might even have been called Catamount Mountain for the shadowy big mountain cats glimpsed slipping in and out of the shadows of the hill's mixed forest from time to time. The hill might have been called any number of names after any number of its wise and respectful inhabitants, but it was stolen by Wilson and his name continues to distort the truth to this day.

I was nervous my first time on Wilson's Hill. I don't share my passion for the non-human world with many, largely because most members of my own kind are TV devotees. Despite my reticence, my passion for the natural world is a deep and true one, not inspiring scientific study or any kind of urgency to understand capillary flow or root systems, but filling me with respect and admiration for wholeness. Nini would say I'm a wool-gatherer. I can sit and watch, and watch, and watch, not with hungry eyes, but with a kind of tenderness uncharacteristic of my office work at Felix's or my shopping-with-a-list activities at the mall or grocery store.

That first night, a young guy named Gareth met me at Zara's door, taking the stew pot out of my hands as he leaned forward to place a light kiss on my left temple. He looked like any ordinary boy-man in flannel shirt and jeans, and without the robes, or vines wound around his head, or big rings, or any of the other trappings the blowhards use to proclaim some sort of other-worldly status. He looked very ordinary, sort of like the guy who waits on me at Hall's, the independent hardware store in town where I buy my bird seed. I studied him. As he walked away with my stew I realized he *was* the guy from Hall's.

Zara materialized from somewhere to my left, smiling as she hadn't the night of the contra-dance. She wore a fuchsia sari and had pinned her long black hair to the nape of her neck in an intricate lazy eight. She looked as if she'd just stepped off the set of Bollywood's *Bride and Prejudice*, kohl-rimmed eyes and all. She had a gold ring on every finger of her fine-boned hands and allowed one of these gorgeously bedecked appendages to flutter to my arm the better to steer me into the kitchen.

There, in the steam, I met April and her twin brother August. I looked around to cover my shyness and understood immediately that Gareth, my sometime hardware expert, and Zara, were a couple even though he was significantly younger. I didn't reach this conclusion in the usual rational way, say from something they did or the way they looked at one another. My hunch was born of something less tangible and more like the slightest glimpse of red I see on tree limbs at winter's end. When I see the first inkling of the red haze to come, I know that Spring is about to charm me into living yet another year. My knowing about them was like that. I felt an inkling of connection, nothing more.

While I was in the kitchen describing the dish I'd brought, another man arrived. I felt him before I saw him, because the moment he banged through the front door a cloud of wood smoke April released into the kitchen made me cough so hard my eyes watered. When I looked up, moist-eyed and sputtering, he was standing in front of me as if he'd just popped out of a magician's hat. His look was French, and so was his name, Hebert. *So this is the new one,* he said, uttering these words with undisguised interest. Zara introduced me only half-heartedly, preoccupied as she was with surveying the mountain of food he piled on his plate.

Hebert, Zara pronounced it Eeeebear, didn't stop to take a breath until after he'd eaten half my casserole and pronounced it good. I looked for what he brought and found in a battered cookie tin, small hard lumps that resembled what I imagined teddy bear scat would look like if teddy bears pooped. I suspect my eyes must have rolled back in my head when I ate my first lump because he laughed at me from his place at the stove. *Blueberry syrup,* he said, the skin around his eyes crinkling. *It makes everything taste good.* It turned out he bakes and cooks with blueberries, not the fat domesticated variety, but the small secretive kind that grow on nothing but conifer mulch and rock dust in our northern clime. Without any encouragement he launched into a description of his dehydrator, an invention he'd apparently rigged up out of old screens and a throw-away black plastic composter. He followed this description with his method of boiling down his first batch of berries into something as deeply blue as a midsummer midnight sky. *Just sunflower seeds and blueberry syrup,* he said when I'd stuffed my mouth with another one. *I grow the sunflowers. I forage for the berries.*

That night my life as an ophthalmologist's receptionist and sometime tax preparer took on the story-book significance I gleaned from all good fairy tales. With his blueberry syrup melting in my mouth, it was unthinkable to offer my usual response to *What do you do?* To mere mortals I describe my nine-to-five routine in Felix's busy office, including my detailed work with insurance companies. I never mention my after-hours obsession with small children who cannot see. But Hebert didn't ask me what I did for a living and this let me off a very large hook.

My job with Rockwood Ophthalmology, meant to be temporary when I was finishing my undergrad studies, had become my life's work without a single act of volition on my part. I didn't mind the grunt work, and I loved Dr. Felix's clientele. They gave me a sense of purpose when they came in crying with fear and I was proud that I could make even the most frightened little kids laugh before their first-time exams. I have a collection of stories I roll out for these kids, Nini stories I've printed and illustrated on old bed sheets cut into long swaths that unroll as the story unfurls. This delivery system means the children can see the whole story at once, remedying what I perceive to be the failing of all conventional picture books. Nini's stories were never so long or so complicated that I had to have fifty feet of cloth. The width and length of a twin sheet did nicely. And no trees have ever been killed for the telling of what I call 'Nini's Tales'. When sheets are no longer bright enough to impress those casual visitors who glance in at bedrooms as they wander along the hallway on their way to the bathroom, most people around here send them to the Sally Ann Thrift Shop in Barre. I travel there every so often for just the right subtleties of background for her stories. Once I find them, I launch into production.

It amazes me to remember that I stopped all creative activities when I was married, but it took Nini's death to understand why. I wasn't relating to my husband or to myself. And so we parted, amicably and respectfully, he with the Subaru, I with the furniture I'd inherited from Nini a few years before along with all of her stories.

Hebert is very different from the other men I know. He doesn't give a fig about what whimsy might dictate how I make my money. He's an in-the-moment kind of man and easy for someone like me to understand. Wool-gatherers are nothing if not in-the-moment people. That first night on Wilson's Hill, we went from listing the various herbs and ingredients in our respective dishes to talking about the moose that mesmerized a growing crowd as his misplaced adventure unfolded in the crook of the Lamoille River beyond the local diner. And then we got into crop circles and how preposterous the film *Signs* was because it postulated hydrophobic aliens colonizing what is basically a water planet.

Hebert told me he'd been to England the previous summer and had visited a number of what aficionados call temporary temples. I told him I'd seen *Signs* and heard that the circles were hoaxes. That was the extent of my exposure. Zara overheard us and went off to retrieve a calendar, each month offering up an exquisitely intricate image pressed into flax crops or mustard, or barley, or corn. In response to the hoax accusation, I said I doubted any drunken gang of students could conceptualize, never mind execute such exquisitely rendered forms in the dark without leaving traces. I confessed my love for Andy Goldsworthy's *Rivers and Tides*. And, with my ego front and center, I shamelessly admitted that I didn't understand why anyone who created such magnificently intricate patterns wouldn't publicize themselves.

That first night among these kindred spirits, I leaned against the kitchen counter, the harmonious images in Zara's calendar flooding my mind while Hebert talked about the lay and swirl of certain configurations, the energies he'd felt as he stood up or lay down or danced about in them, the strange smells he'd encountered, the absolute ignorance of people who used the word *hoax* when describing the real ones. *Do they happen here?* I was prepared to jump on a bus at that very moment if he answered yes. He did something extraordinary then. He reached out and cupped my face with his rough hands. *A believer,* he said tenderly. *Zara, you actually found us a live one this time.*

What was not to believe? The images were perfection. I don't consider myself a believer simply because I recognize beauty and something more, perhaps mystery, when I see it. To me these crop circles were evidence enough to make me quit my job and go set up a tent at the edge of a field where one might appear—whether humans created them or not. I thought of my story scrolls. If I had made the exquisite dance of light and shadow in the fields of rye and wheat before me, I'd be taking pictures and having shows in galleries all over the world. These circles were breathtaking. These circles were Lourdes, but without a Pope claiming victory for his team.

That night marked my humble entry into the debate about configurations appearing most spectacularly in England around Avebury and Silbury Hill, and mostly in grain crops, a debate that has been going on for more than a decade. As our conversation flowed from the food we'd brought to this spiritual feast, I heard all their theories: The American circles, at first thought to be more primitive and far less frequent, appeared mostly in Ohio according to Zara, because Ohio was the new world's cradle of civilization. *This area*, she said, pointing at a map, *is home to The Great Serpent Mound and the Newark Great Circle, earthworks all but unknown outside their immediate geographical locations.* Hebert added that these mysterious landmarks were within boat and even walking distance of Cahokia, the seventeenth century name given to the largest pre-Columbian city north of Mexico created on the Mississippi across from modern day St. Louis, Missouri.

As he repeated the origin stories he'd learned, I imagined people of the past traveling river routes, all of them exchanging goods and stories as far south as Poverty Point where, according to Zara, a great bird earthwork protected the earliest village inhabitants, and as far north as Canada with its thriving First Nations' woodland culture. Zara and Hebert spoke of how frustrating it was to have only modern names to reference these places, the old names, like the ancient civilizations, vanishing with the arrival of the Europeans.

During that very first story hour with my new friends, we congregated in a tight little circle in Zara's kitchen. Enchantment ruled even our meal as Gareth's small pan of cornbread fed us during the initial storytelling, retelling, and afterthought embellishments. April had made a green salad and her brother a thick dressing out of ground sesame seeds, water, lemon, and salt. Perhaps it was because I was doing something so in synch with my true nature that this combination of flavors seemed more wonderful than anything I'd ever tasted. I have, at times in my life, been a Coke and chips vegetarian, with a little red licorice for dessert. I didn't learn for years that sugar, the ordinary white kind, is often processed through charcoal made of the bones of animals. That first night at Zara's, their food cleansed my palate. I tasted things that spoke to me the way the sounds and scents of a summer night speak when I sit on my favorite rock behind the hay barn on Nini's farm. I had taken care with the food I'd prepared for the evening, more than I usually did, because there was something about the way Zara said *vegetarian* when she'd issued her invitation. She might have said *sacrament*. Maybe she did. *Bring sacramental food to share.*

My dance with food changes as I age. When I was a child, I ate what was put in front of me without a lot of interest except for certain favorites. One of these favorites involved Nini's organic popping corn. Every fall, our mother supervised the making of popcorn balls made from Nini's popping corn on Halloween. We could eat as many popcorn balls as we wanted since we had helped to make them. When we were little, Mother stirred and stirred and stirred the syrup until it was time for us to shape the balls with our buttered hands. As we got older and stronger, we stirred the sensitive mixture of maple syrup, butter, and a little baking soda over low heat until it became the bubbling perfection that made the kernels stick together.

Right up there with Nini's maple syrup were the fiddleheads we gathered from the banks along Nini's creek and ate with butter and homemade apple cider vinegar the moment she took them out of the steamer. And omelets made from our own eggs, gifts from the Marys—Mary Wollstonecraft and Mary Shelley—chickens Nini adopted and named after two of her heroines.

After I married, the grind of cooking a meal at a regular time never took. I ate when I felt like it and my ex, a student at the Culinary Arts School at the time, offered up many experiments I could take or leave. He was a born chef and had no insecurities about rejected offerings. He also had a memorable appetite and a flare for creating five-star meals out of leftovers. His food tasted good, but this food I shared with Zara and her friends was otherworldly. Even my own brown rice with sesame seeds and broccoli tasted like the marriage between heaven and earth. And dessert, served up constantly throughout our conversations, mingled the flavor of blueberries with oregano and sweet cicely and red onion and corn. This food became the fairy dust that held us in the spell cast by our shared characteristic: we all belonged to Her. I ate widely but sparingly, chewing while I listened, feeling the flavors seep into my heart and my eyes and my fingertips along hitherto unused routes of passage.

After a couple of hours of talk and food that first time, the twins began our collective clean-up process by toweling and oiling their ancient butter bowl and gathering up their cutlery. One by one we took our dishes to the sink, scrubbed whatever pots and utensils we brought clean, made room for the next person. All of this was done while Hebert or Zara or Gareth or August or April spoke of some personal experience with the land they lived on. My face felt hot, as if I'd been running to an unknown destination for an eternity and had, in this moment, unexpectedly arrived. I had just finished saying something about the sky at Nini's when Zara presented us with large woolen blankets and beeswax candle stubs in an array of holders. My holder, offered to me with her dazzling smile, was topped by a fuchsia globe. Others, I saw, wrapped their blankets around them. I was already far too hot and let mine, a soft, dove-grey and white plaid rectangle, rest on my arm.

And then we were out under the stars, walking slowly in single file up to the top of the gentle rise behind Zara's home. From what I could see of it, the path was narrow but well worn and as I walked it I imagined others, some with two legs, some with four, some with none, some with hundreds, walking up this slope since the time before time. The night was with us in the way night in open, empty places settles on the earth. I felt its skin against mine, heard its whispers. The brush of blankets against the grass comforted me as Nini's humming had comforted me in my last few moments of consciousness when I slept over at her house as a little girl, reluctant to let go of the day.

An old woman, Zara's mother I assumed that first time, met us on the hill's zenith, the tin lantern she carried scattering dancing light on the ground all around us. I wasn't coached in any way. No one spoke of what we were doing or why. I let myself travel on the currents of shared passion and questioned nothing as we formed a circle. I put the blanket down, laid on it. I looked up to where the stars tilted downward. Then Gareth coughed. And then, from below, I could hear Zara's old black lab complain that his arthritic hips had kept him behind.

This is how it has been for all the nights that I have visited Wilson's Hill. This is how it was tonight. Absolutely nothing happens. I let my mind drift over my day's peaks and valleys. Margaret Leicester's boy, Tom, is troubled by the astigmatism in his right eye. He'll get his glasses sometime this week. Mary Trent is shifting from readers to trifocals because she cannot see depth on the soccer field. Alfred LeMotte's parents have agreed to take him to Copley Hospital for a CAT scan. Dr. Felix is worried about him, I know, but doesn't say anything to me. He's superstitious although he'd never admit to being afraid to say the worst for fear of bringing it on.

Hebert and I are deciding whether to move in together or continue as we are. He loves his land and can't bear the town. While I love my weekends with him, I don't feel right about leaving Dr. Felix and my young, sight-challenged story addicts, and the daily commute would use up far more of my own and the world's energy than I'm willing to sacrifice. It's really just an ordinary job, but it led me to the contra-dance, and Zara, and my time on Wilson's Hill. And even though she's been dead for years, Nini continues to remind me that all work has dignity.

Remembering this makes me realize I have stopped eating eggs. I see the stars or sometimes the great black night that sucks up everything, even the moon, and I don't want to eat anything I might rob of this view. When I said this one night, apropos of nothing, August told me that eating the world gives it consciousness. Once we take in whatever we eat, it sees with our eyes and feels with our soul. I think I believe this, but still, I leave the eggs for the Mary hens to hatch. Mother gives their chicks the run of the garden where they are diligent at keeping the potato bugs, cut worms, and grubs under control.

In my world, no one ever talks about converting to Love

and yet that is what I have done. I have fallen in love with a crowd of stars, of people, of crop-circles, of Wilson's Hill moments. I have, at forty-seven, fallen in love with Life itself. Hebert tells me I have become a worshipper of Venus. Even though the words don't translate, I sense he is right. All those years ago, when I sat in the Methodist Church hearing about the Father, the Son, and the Holy Ghost while wondering where the girls and women were, I couldn't anticipate this time in my life, and yet somehow I have always been making room for it. I smile at this kind of intelligence that flourishes against all odds. I smile at the idea of becoming a worshipper of Venus, Goddess of Love. It is the perfect religion for me because it requires no belief, no faith, only wide open eyes, wide open heart, and the odd risk taken at a contra-dance. These requirements feel tailor made for me and my way of being in the world. Nini would agree with me, anyway.

———

Canadian Jane Buchan has lived in Vermont since 2002. As well as writing fiction and non-fiction, Jane currently teaches writing and research courses at the Community College of Vermont, and in her life coaching practice helps clients build resilience after school and life learning traumas that contribute to high Adverse Childhood Experiences (ACEs) scores. Learn more about Jane at http://www.winterblooms.net.

DO YOU WANT YOUR SOUL BACK?

Ian Lahey

Dermott waved a couple of carts past the customs table with little or no inspection. Since the spit-and-polish officer had been called away, Dermott and the other aide waved them along rapidly, occasionally exchanging glances like naughty schoolboys and then quickly looking away. The officer had insisted on cataloging every item that came through the gate, and now the line of carts trying to get goods to market stretched as far as he could see. Thankful to have the nit-picker busy elsewhere, Sergeant Dermott lifted his hand to wave the next cart through.

A hooded figure stopped in front of him. "Excuse me," it said. The voice was a thin whisper which made Dermott feel like the world itself needed to hush and go to sleep.

"I need to see a religious man. It's for ah...a confession."

"Yes, well," Dermott cleared his throat, "you will find temples to almost all gods and doctrines here in Bleakham, but for confessions your man would be Father Francis Warwick, in the cathedral, unless you wish to confess some crime, in which case you could follow us to headquarters, ha ha ha." His laughter came out rather unconvincingly.

The hooded figure heaved a great, shuddering sigh. "Yes. Thank you. I shall go to the cathedral. First." And with heavy, dragging feet moved on, into the city. The two guards followed the figure with their eyes until it disappeared past the gates. They both blinked and shook their heads, as if not really sure what to make of what had just occurred. Just another oddity strolling around Bleakham. Dermott shrugged and started waving the carts along more expeditiously. The line began to move again and picked up a good pace.

* * *

Within its walls, the town of Bleakham was just reaching its habitual chaotic peak of blustering activity. Inns and taverns beckoned passersby to taste their wide selections of dishes which, upon closer inspection, generally turned out to be a choice of either ham, potatoes, cheese, or any combination of the three. A cart had toppled in Wicker Street and, now that the merchants and their barrows had started to pour in towards the market square, the adjoining streets were jammed with wheels, hooves, feet and oranges gleefully rolling away from the overturned cart as if enjoying a hitherto unexpected moment of freedom.

Whichever meteorological or godly entity was in charge of Bleakham weather chose that moment of frantic outdoor activity to release rain from the previously cloudless sky. It was a treacherous, sticky type of rain. The individual drops were small and seemed barely capable of reaching the ground before evaporating, yet somehow they managed to get everything and everyone miserably soggy in a matter of minutes.

The cloaked figure proceeded unnoticed, dragging its slim shape along the muddy streets of Bleakham. Wheels rolled, hooves stomped and feet splashed all over as many sought cover and headed for cart lots, stables and inns. Such was the confusion that the tasks were not always done in logical order, which culminated with angry innkeepers pushing horses back out the door or recovering discombobulated customers from the stables. Somehow, wherever the brown cloaked one passed, hooves and carts jerked sideways and feet sidestepped, unawares. As it proceeded along the street, the gray, wet shape of the cathedral emerged from its gray, wet surroundings.

Bleakham Cathedral is a wonder to gaze at, especially when it rains. The original project had begun on a sturdy Romanesque foundation. Sadly, the architect passed away while the cathedral was only half done. His successor took one look at the squat thing and decided he wanted no truck with that, and built straight Gothic up over it, so that the two different parts not only disagreed but appeared to be actively engaged in a perennial argument which went like this:

"I am the stronghold of God, my walls are as firm as Faith," the lower, Romanesque half would say, to which the Gothic half would reply: "Stronghold my foot, admire my spires and arches as I reach up to shake hands with the God Himself!"

The elaborate gargoyles of the top part had been turned and modeled so that they seemed to puke over the lower part when it rained.

The hooded figure paused at the front of the building and looked at it. Then, as many do when first presented with Bleakham Cathedral, it looked up to the spires, then back down at the base, stepped back to take in the whole architectural mashup, and stood frozen, transfixed. Clearly distracted, the stranger's hand came up and pulled back the cloak's hood, revealing the delicate features of a young, red-haired woman.

"Damn me to hell," she breathed.

She wasn't sure she could cross the religious threshold.

160

She'd never tried before, so paused with bare muddy feet before the entrance.

"Hesitating at the door? Feeling unwelcome? Or is my floor that ugly, child? " called a voice from inside.

"Er, no. I just wouldn't want to intrude."

"Please come in, and be welcome. Now you are not an intruder anymore. Please wait for your turn."

The floor of the cathedral felt cool and reassuring under the soles of her feet, and seemed to soothe, at least for a while, the burning in her heart. She looked up. The architecture, seen from the inside, was almost, but not quite, less aggressive on the eyes.

Her eyes moved to the two men near the altar. The one who had spoken had a hand on the shoulder of the other, who was kneeling down.

"Can't I just say the rosary a few dozen times?" the penitent man asked. He was holding something which had been wrapped in one of the altar vestments.

"What, dear Nigel, will that do for you, except renew your thirst for ale and wine? Such simple penance is not meant for those whose path has led them close to eternal damnation. As for the item in your hands—"

"The...the mirror of Saint Fillmore?"

"I trust you with the keeping of this ancient relic. Don't let it shatter or the awful penance of Fillmore's Seven Years of Woesome Pains will fall upon your head and those you love. Keep it in your bedroom, and when in prayer you'll wave an olive branch over it, and so will your wife. On Sundays, by the faces that you wear, I'll know if you've been faithful to this task."

"But, will you want it back...eventually?"

"Yes, when another's soul will be, as yours, at risk."

"Oh." The man, looking relieved, made as if to stand up.

161

The priest's hand kept him down. "But not before your own is out of peril."

"Ah." The shoulders slumped again.

"Remember not to indulge in your reflections. And tell your other half the same thing, too."

"My other three-quarters you mean." Nigel's grin quickly disappeared as his joke fell short. "Yes, Father Warwick."

"Good. Now go, son, and be a better man and a better husband."

As the man exited the church, he quickly readjusted the vestment, revealing the smooth reflecting surface of the glass mirror. He muttered a hurried "scusmey," never even glancing at the cloaked woman as he left.

"That's never going to work," she muttered to herself. Faint echoes of her voice fluttered about the nave, a quick pang of guilt for contradicting the holy man reminded her of the burning.

"What isn't?" Father Warwick replied from the other end.

She took a deep breath. "Not many common people have mirrors of that quality. Indulging in their reflection is the first thing he and his wife are going to do."

"I'm counting on it. In fact, it happens to be quite an old trick, I seem to remember a parable about it, too. There's an apple in it, I think."

"Oh." The man she was speaking to was now walking slowly towards her. She could see he was past his sixties, but his steady step was lithe, strong. "Well, what good will it do them? What was his sin?" she asked.

"Confessions are not to be revealed, you must know," he replied, "but perhaps I could point out that Nigel and his wife both reached that age when virtues such as youth and beauty begin to evaporate, like perfume from a ripe fruit, and each begins to see the wrinkles in the other's face. In this stage of life it is not uncommon for folk to think they are wasting their youth with an older person."

"...and may yearn for younger...attentions."

"A good mirror will reveal to each their own wrinkles, and remind them that they're aging together. They will give special importance to what they see, especially since it's a holy mirror from a hallowed saint."

"Saint Fillmore. Never heard of him. What pains did he suffer?"

"Marriage! Lasted seven miserable years. Now his wife thinks he's fighting in the crusades. She still pays the local wizard to zap letters over to him. Every single one's a nag."

"So he isn't dead? How can he be a saint?"

"Although he isn't technically a saint, I can assure you his spirits have lifted considerably. He calls himself Friar Jollynoggin now, up at the hermitage. The mirror was his thank-you gift."

Father Warwick was face to face with her now, his short tousled hair forming a silvery white ring below his possibly still shaved tonsure. His eyebrows, as white and just as tousled, hung over the grey, ageless eyes that had distracted her from the torment she felt inside. Now, as they gently, but relentlessly, dug into her like fingers in clay, guilt and shame sparked up inside once more. Instinctively, she pulled her hood back over her face.

Father Warwick smiled, a warm smile that looked like it was worn for reassuring others rather than personal enjoyment. When he lifted his hand to pull her hood back the sleeve of his habit fell to his elbow, revealing the shadows of old scars.

The cool air of the church was succumbing to the charring sensation in her chest. She felt weak. Was the holy ground she had stepped on burning away her sin, and perchance her essence along with it? "I need help," she said.

The large church was caving in around her spinning head.

"What's your name, child?" His voice sounded distant, as if it were made of echoes alone.

She couldn't let him know. That would be the end of her. "Beth," she said. Too close to the truth, and still she'd lied, to a priest, in a church. A pain like a blow to the stomach doubled her over and made her cry out as the wave of searing self-loathing washed over her and slammed her into a wall of darkness.

* * *

"Beth?" The name and voice simultaneously woke her up and reminded her of where she was and who she wasn't. Father Warwick was standing beside her at an odd angle. She slowly became aware that she was lying in a large, high bed. A topknot held together by a long iron pin bobbed beside the priest.

"What happened?" she asked.

"You dropped to the floor like a ripe brick, my dear. I barely caught you before you hit your head," Father Warwick replied. "You must've been exhausted, I suppose from hauling around the weight of all the dirt on your body. How do you feel now?"

"Better, I think. And clean." She was wearing a soft cotton bedgown, and nothing else. A thought came to her, and she felt her face flushing crimson. "Did you..."

"Of course not." Father Warwick smiled and pointed at the topknot near his thigh. "Sister Duilia took care of you." The topknot bobbed up and down happily. Beth glanced over the edge of the bed to see that it belonged to what looked like a woman, if said woman had been raised inside a two-hundred gallon barrel until she had taken its shape. Sister Duilia beamed at her and, with incredibly short arms, reached up to give her a bowl of steaming liquid. She made a very clear "Drink up" gesture and left the room. Beth wondered how such a creature could have lifted her unconscious body off the floor of the church.

"She's stronger than you'd imagine," Father Warwick said, as if reading her thoughts. "She's also a very good cook. You should do as she says and drink that."

Beth nodded and started sipping from the warm bowl in her hands. The hot, hearty mix was like a loving, forgiving hug, only from the inside. She felt tears welling in her eyes.

"I am so unworthy," she couldn't hold back the shame, "I am the worst of sinners, a liar, a thief and a traitor, and hell is where I'm to be," she sobbed.

"Now child, absolution from sin awaits those who truly repent."

"Oh, I do, I do repent! The guilt is unbearable. How do people manage?" She dried her eyes on her soft, white sleeve. "If you can relieve sinners of such torture, why isn't there a queue to the entrance to your church?"

"Well," Father Warwick said, looking slightly embarrassed, "I suppose that depends on the weight of the sins, and how well you carry them. Most people around here are quite athletic in that respect, I reckon."

"I know it's wrong, but I envy them," she said.

"Don't be ashamed. You know you've done wrong, so it's a good sign. It means you are a good soul," Father Warwick said.

"Souls shouldn't hurt so much. No wonder so many prefer to get rid of theirs." A warning jolt almost made her drop her bowl. "Enough," she said, finishing the contents of the bowl. "I wish for you to grant me absolution and rid me of the pain of my sins."

"Only if you are ready."

"I'm ready." She closed her eyes.

"Well, I need a confession first," Father Warwick said.

Beth opened her eyes again. "What? No, *I* need it!"

"No, I mean I need you to say what you've done, what you need to be forgiven for."

This was a problem. A big one. She looked at him, pleading. "Could you just forgive me in good faith?"

His expression darkened. "I can do nothing to help if you won't help yourself first." There was a warning tone in his voice.

"No, no. I'm sorry. It's just that..." She wet her lips. "There are things I can say..." This went well, she took a deep breath and continued, "and th—" her mouth closed. Another warning jolt made her hands shake again.

"Things you can't?"

She nodded with puckered lips.

"Can you tell me more about yourself?"

Her lips relaxed, "I...can try...I can hint...I came, I came into the world and I was happy."

"Nice start, go ahead."

Her breathing accelerated as she spoke. She had no control over it. "But then I followed the wrong...person. We f...went down. I wrote co...I wrote. There was a...mistake and now I gained...pain. I feel guilty, always," she said and breathed deeply again.

Father Warwick's frown made Beth realize her confused account had probably done little to clarify her situation. She watched the cleric's wrinkled face with apprehension.

"You said you were a sinner and a liar. What did you lie about?" Father Warwick finally said.

She fought the sudden surge of shame. "I lied...to you, too. But I can't..."

"I see. Well, it seems like you had no choice, am I right?"

She nodded, feeling a little relieved.

"Now, this mistake," he said, "was it spoken...action..."

Beth shook her head. She made a gesture through the air

166

with her hand while holding the bowl with the other.

"Written, then. A contract you signed?"

A window flew open, blasting blizzard-cold wind into the room. A paralyzing jolt welled up from the soles of her feet. She had to be faster. "YES," she screamed. The bowl flew at the wall and shattered, her hand slapped her on the mouth and stuck there. "Mmmh!" she added.

"Good." Father Warwick went on unperturbed. "I suppose you can just nod at this point. Is it this contract that prevents you from speaking about it?"

Beth nodded and the bed jumped, making her fall backwards and bump her head.

Father Warwick remained impassible. "Hmm, yes. I'd say it's pretty clear what kind of contract this is. You'd better not nod at this point unless you feel safe. I imagine any further revelation on your side could cost you your life. Let's change the subject."

Beth relaxed a little.

"You also said you're a thief. Can you tell me about that?"

Her hand was hers again to control, and she uncovered her mouth. "Yes. I am so sorry. I was hungry coming here, and I stole an orange."

"That one." Father Warwick pointed to the fruit on her bedside table. "It was in your pocket. You didn't eat it."

"Couldn't. Felt too guilty."

"Well, you could've just given it back."

"No, I mean I wanted to, but I couldn't. I found it on the ground."

Father Warwick looked at her for a long time. "I think you need more than just a confession, child. We need to get you out of that contract before we can find out more about your overactive conscience. I will send Sister Duilia with some clothes, you will come with me to the market and we can talk some more."

"About Duilia, I couldn't help but notice..." Beth said and then hesitated, thinking she might sound offensive.

"Yes, she never talks. Her order requires a vow of silence."

"Oh..."

"I'll be in the next room while you get dressed," Father Warwick said, and left her alone in the room. A few minutes later Sister Duilia arrived, making cheerful non-musical humming sounds and carrying a large bundle of sundry garments. She tossed it effortlessly over the bed, where it bounced once and came undone rather neatly into different clumps of clothes. Duilia pointed at them randomly and then at Beth.

"So, I can choose from these and wear what I want?" Beth said.

Duilia snapped her fingers and made an elaborate winknod which clearly meant "You're the smart one", then turned about and was gone, followed by the sound of her tuneless humming.

The clothes were a motley mix of different pieces and sizes, including a nun's habit and what looked like a chainmail handkerchief. Further inspection revealed it was, in fact, an undergarment with a large, unsightly lock in the front. Beth set it back down and quickly made her choice. Practically everything was too large and she had to do some extra folding and tucking to keep things from sliding off. Once satisfied with the result, she left the room and wandered down a long corridor. Judging from the stone-work she guessed she was in a section of the cathedral. Halfway up the wall the rocks changed size and orientation and appeared to have been slammed, rather contemptuous-ly, over the lower row of heavier, chunkier blocks.

"Well, I'm glad you didn't choose the nun's dress," said Father Warwick when she walked into a large room which looked like a study.

"It was too grey, and I don't think there's any order that would accept the likes of me," Beth replied.

"Not all of us are made to be priests and nuns. You look fine."

Sister Duilia stormed in with a set of pins lined up between her lips, a sewing basket in her hand and an expression which said "No she doesn't!" on her face, and went to work on her clothes. Beth could hear ripping, cutting and sewing behind her as the sister's hands moved in a flurry. Her body jerked this way and that with the small woman's energetic work, making her feel like a puppet.

"And now you look even better," Father Warwick admitted, moments later.

Beth looked down at herself. The long white gown she'd chosen now had a slant to it. The matching blouse was even more matching now, as the extra slack had been also turned into a slant, on the opposite side.

"This is more than I deserve," Beth said.

Sister Duilia harrumphed and produced a long list of paper which she handed to Beth.

"Since you can write, you can also read, can't you child?" Father Warwick said, while preparing for the outdoors with a large green scarf on his shoulders.

"Yes, I can," Beth replied.

"Excellent. That's our shopping list, made by our dear sister who knows the exact type and amount of every single stored item of food in the pantry."

The list was made out in three columns and written in an elaborate runic-looking shorthand. One column had an "F.W." heading, the next had a "B." heading, the letter had been embellished with a little flower, and finally the last column which had the letters "S.D." with even more flowers and a butterfly with a long stalky belly, which almost made it look like an axe. Still holding the paper with both hands, Beth followed Father Warwick down some stairs and into a hallway.

"The Cobbler Guild occasionally donates a few shoes, not always matching, for the needy," he said, and reached inside a large box full of footwear. "These are good enough, I guess." He tossed a pair of padded sandals at her feet.

"We have a lot of shopping to do," Father Warwick said, "I don't often get to go to the market, or rather the market doesn't often get to Bleakham, what with the customs officer corking it up at the gates."

"I think he got called away," Beth said. The shoes felt warm and comfortable on her feet.

"I know. I arranged it," Father Warwick said, and opened the door.

The door gave way to a side alley behind the church. From there they were quickly onto Ladder Street and over a small, rickety bridge across the river Ralph.

Ralph is perhaps the only case of a watercourse which springs from the bowels of a city. It is vastly variable in its flow, taking up different characteristics during a single day, to the point that you could probably tell the time based on its chemical composition: urine surge in the morning, followed by a comparative trickle of cleaner water, which swiftly swells with dishwater, dark with tea leaves, that merges into another dishwater wave shortly after lunch. Afternoons bring a mixed tide before barrel rinsings and the occasional drunk-dead corpse in the evening. Finally, a cleansing tsunami descends from the stables, swishing north through the darkening streets. Through a corroded grate in the eastern wall, Ralph the sewer-river ran past islands pleasureless to man, down to a smelly sea.

"What's that smell?" asked Beth.

"Six p.m.," Father Warwick replied, "we'd better hurry."

They sped through a narrow alleyway which cut across a block of terraced houses and emerged into the noise and chaos of Market Square. Beth instinctively reached for her hood, which she no longer wore. Merchants shouted their offers, people chatted loudly to hear themselves over the shouting and haggled, even more loudly, with the merchants.

"All right. Let's get started on that list," Father Warwick said, raising his voice. "What are the first items?"

"The first column?"

"Nope. Sister Duilia groups them vertically for the person they're intended for, and horizontally by type. If you read the first line they will probably all be things you can find in a single market stall."

"Yes, you're right. All fruit and vegetables. Very efficient."

"That's nothing. You should see her counting donations."

The greengrocer greeted them with a wide, friendly grin. "Here, here for the freshest greens in the square. Among the first in line this morning at the gate."

"Oh," Father Warwick reached into his pocket and said to Beth, "here child, as penance for your thievery I charge you with giving him the orange. It was probably his."

Beth took the fruit and tossed it into the pile of oranges on the stall. "I'm sorry. I think I stole this. Not from you...from the ground. It's a bit peculiar, I know."

The greengrocer stared at her, open mouthed, then he looked at the oranges, evidently hoping to spot the unexpectedly first time returned orange.

"How do you feel now?" Father Warwick asked, as they

moved on for the next row of items.

"Much, much better," Beth said.

The sky was turning dark by the time they got to the end of the list. Beth was laden with bags but feeling much less heavy-footed than she'd felt earlier on these same streets.

"Very well, as evening drains the last drops of daylight so we, too, have exhausted all but one item from our list. What's the last thing?" Father Warwick asked.

"It's in Sister Duilia's column: '*creame for the shavinge of beardes.*'"

They exchanged glances. "I assume she wrote in the wrong column, this should be for me," Father Warwick finally said. "Phyrrod's Apothecary is all the way across the square and not worth hauling all these bags. Wait here by the alley while I go alone. It'll be faster."

Beth barely had time to nod and he was off. She leaned against the wall and reveled in the noise of the market, which now had dwindled to a steady murmur, as if everybody were repeating the word "rub-a-bugger" over and over, and the sound of the river Ralph, past the alley, which channeled back whiffs of stale beer.

"You seem to have adapted well," said a voice from the alley. Beth turned toward the sound. A slim dark shape was standing at the edge of the shadow.

"What the hell are you doing here?" Beth whispered.

"Well you know, I think I am, therefore I am...wherever I think I want to be." The voice gave an unfriendly, malevolent laugh. "So I thought I'd be checking on you."

"Go away."

As the voice spoke it stepped out of the shadow, revealing a young man with white hair and impossibly dark eyes. Beth shivered and cursed her weakness and fear.

"My oh my, you look miserable, but why, now that you've got what we fought for? You should be happy," he

172

said. "You should share," he hissed in her ear.

Beth pulled away. "Go to hell!"

"Most certainly, but before I go, I just thought you'd like to know he's coming here for you."

"Who?"

"You know who, his name's on your contract. Has some things to settle, I think."

Beth fought to keep her legs stiff and hold her place. "You told him..."

"Knocked at my door asking me if the contract was still binding even after your massive screw-up. I told him it was, every single word, for a hundred years, the contract says. He asked whether killing you would fix that. We checked, and hey, he was right!"

"What? That will fix nothing."

"Of course it will. As a sinner, you will immediately join the ranks of the damned. I think I will get to have some fun with you...personally."

"Go away!" Beth screamed, swinging her bags at him. "Never show your face again." Her voice broke and her vision blurred. The man just grinned at her, his white teeth and black eyes shifting in position and shape as her eyes filled with tears.

"Beth, what's wrong? Did someone hurt you?" Father Warwick grabbed her trembling shoulders. The other one wasn't there anymore.

"I must suffer for my mistake, but nobody else must ever feel this. The guilt...I feel...if I passed this onto others, the pain would destroy me." Anger rose from deep within her and crashed against her impotence to help her frail, impermanent self. A volcano of self-loathing erupted from her soul. "Let me go away," she said.

"Nonsense, give me those bags," Father Warwick said.

"Let's go home."

Together they walked slowly towards the church. Father Warwick carrying the many, heavy bags, and Beth, carrying an even greater weight inside.

As they crossed the rickety bridge, the river Ralph stank a very sharp seven o'clock.

* * *

Sergeant Dermott was bored. His replacement hadn't shown up at the end of his shift, and he couldn't leave the gate unattended. He took a turn around the post to keep himself awake. As he turned, he noticed someone standing by the table. At last! Something to do. He pulled out a little notebook and a stylus. "Please state name given at birth, business and intentions."

The tall man looked down on the sergeant. His eyes squinted, as if struggling to focus. They had a reddish tinge to them, as if he was suffering from some kind of allergy. "Used to be Cuthbert," he growled. "Devil, third class, short visit, I intend to kill someone." He showed the large mace he was carrying, as if to clarify.

Dermott looked at the mace, and then at the large figure looming before him. The subject was wearing a leather gilet and worn-out trousers, strange boots which were made to look like clawed feet and a funny, misshapen hat. A ridiculous bovine tail hung from the trousers.

"Very funny, indeed. Must be one hell of a fancy-dress party you've been invited to, I must say, but no matter how 'dressed to kill' you may be, I'm afraid you can't come into Bleakham unless you give me your real credentials. What do you mean when you say you used to be Cuthbert? Did you undergo a name change?"

"Yes." The other shuffled his taloned feet. "It's standard infernal protocol."

Dermott saw just another fool trying to get past him

174

with a cheap trick. "I'm afraid this 'infernal protocol' will have to be reviewed under the laws of this city before it has any validity. What would your new name be?"

"Smasher."

"Very well, '*Smasher*.'" Dermott produced a small book which he expertly flipped to the relevant entry. "Customs regulations article 332 states that you must provide the documents proving your name was officially changed, do you have them?"

"No," Smasher replied, "but customs regulations article number 506 states that 'an individual may provide sworn statement of his identity, to be held valid as proof under the risk of perjury.'" The visitor seemed to be enjoying all this bureaucratic banter with which, apparently, he was fairly well acquainted. The sergeant, on the other hand, had already grown weary of the entire thing especially after looking the entry up and finding Smasher to be absolutely correct, to the letter. He read on, furiously.

"Aha! Valid unless an officer demands some proof of said statement to ensure it isn't perjury. So can you prove your name's Smasher?"

"Oh, but you see, I could provide proof for my statement with another statement, it's a loophole, a legal ambiguity which allows me to circumvent the rule." Smasher grinned with fangs Dermott entirely failed to notice.

"Nobody circumvents anything when I'm around! No loitering, prowling, dilly-dallying or circumventing in *my* city! I demand that you provide proof of your name in a form other than spoken statement," his voice rose to his commanding tenor note, "and if you can't, it's gonna be the slammer for you."

"Ermm, yes. I can," Smasher said.

"Very well, let's have it!"

The mace swung around and up, and then came down on poor luckless Dermott.

"What was that?" Beth said as they were getting back to the door in the alleyway behind the cathedral.

"What?" Father Warwick replied.

"I heard a noise, like a smash."

"Could be a tree in the nearby forest."

"Do trees go smash in the forest?"

"Only when somebody's listening."

A feeling of dread crawled up the skin on her back and she knew she had to leave this place before Father Warwick and Sister Duilia got dragged into paying the price of her terrible sins. She smiled, hoping her eyes wouldn't betray her worries. "Tell you what," she said, "I'm an absolute disaster at cooking and you really don't want me to go anywhere near a kitchen, the fire especially. I'm curious to find out what that noise was, and being a bit late will be the perfect excuse in case Duilia plans on having me help out with dinner."

"Well...a moment ago you looked so terrified..." Father Warwick said.

"Just a little panic attack, a little more fresh air is all I need."

"Fine," he sighed, "here, take my scarf, it's getting chilly."

"No, I can't. I mean it won't be necessary," Beth said.

"It is a gift. Duilia knits furiously. I have dozens."

"Well then, in that case I'll take it."

"Good, don't get lost," Father Warwick said, rather gruffly, and closed the door behind him.

Beth felt relieved. *I'll be back in a minute* and *see you soon* were lies she had managed to avoid, and the Father's kind heart made it so she could take the scarf without worrying about not being able to return it.

Beth took a deep breath and silently made her way

towards the city gates. She took side streets and alleys to avoid the direct route. She was confident that if someone was really coming for her, there was a good chance she might creep past them and get a head start on her escape to...somewhere else. She would worry about that later.

The unpaved streets of Bleakham were still soft from the morning rain and made no noise under her feet. Holding her breath, she squeezed through a very narrow gap between an alehouse and a courthouse, and saw she had reached the perimeter wall. She allowed herself to exhale in relief. The gate was just twenty feet to the left. As she approached the torchlight of the main street, she glanced back towards the town. She could barely see shadows moving in the distance.

Light-footed, she ran past the gates and out of Bleakham.

She glanced at the customs office, hoping they stopped people going in but let them leave at will. To her relief, the sergeant was slumped over the table with his stylus still in his hand — apparently asleep on the job. She had no time to wonder about the dent at the top of his helmet.

"How nice of you to come out," Smasher said.

Beth's blood turned to frozen lead.

"I just finished checking the defenses of this place, in case you decided to hole yourself up in there," Smasher continued as he quickly closed the distance between them. "Would've hated to burn the whole city down just to get to you."

"Cuthbert, you don't have to do this. I'm sorry for the mistake, but it's only for a hundred years. If you kill me, you will not void the contract. I don't really know what will happen."

"The effect will be permanent," the creature replied. "I feel so free now. Without a conscience nagging at me all the time I can work much, much better. I even had a successful job interview." The devil was now standing, unhooded, and towered over her with his horns, braided goatee and red skin.

"Wait, what? Who would give you a job?" she said.

"I would." It was the man with dark eyes and white hair. He'd suddenly appeared next to the table where he'd been standing all along, listening and watching. Or so it seemed. Demonic apparitions are not easily explained.

"Lou!" Beth said.

"You used to call me Lightbringer once," he said with a sneer. "Well, do you want that job or not, Smasher? Why is she still breathing?"

"Wait!" Beth said. "What job? Can't you tell me why I must die?"

"Why bother?" Lou said, "You'll have eternity in hell to find out. No need to waste time telling you now."

"You can tell me," said a familiar voice behind Beth.

She spun around. *Leave now!* was what she wanted to say, "L...huh?" was what she said instead, when she saw Father Warwick and Sister Duilia, dressed up in a harlequinesque array of armor bits and carrying a huge wooden cross. She remembered the scars she'd seen on Warwick's arms. "You weren't a priest all your life, were you?"

"No," he admitted, "I was a sell-sword."

"What happened to your sword then?"

"Sold it. Now get behind me, and let me deal with these folk." He set the cross upright on the ground and held it there with one hand, like a spearman. Duilia took a few steps forward and winked at Beth, who looked back, alarmed.

"No, you can't deal with *him*," she said.

"Wouldn't be the first time." Father Warwick called out to Lou, "Right, flapears? Wanna build me a new bridge?"

"Don't call me that!" Lou scowled.

"You two know each other? A bridge? What?" said Beth.

"Flapears?" said Smasher, and started moving menacingly towards the priest.

"Yup," said Father Warwick, ignoring Smasher and Lou's mounting rage, "Half of Bleakham had to go round that river, too dangerous to ford and too smelly for anyone to work near enough to build a bridge, so one day Flapears here comes to me with a contract. 'I'll build a bridge over that river of sludge for you, but as payment I shall take the life of the first one to cross,' he said."

Lou's eyes smoldered dark red as Father Warwick continued, always holding him with his eyes.

"As soon as I sign the contract, he builds that ramshackle thing—"

"A supernatural feat," Lou said.

"An insult to engineering," Father Warwick replied. "So the next morning we had a small inauguration ceremony. I was all dressed up and gave my blessings to that miraculous heap of jerry-rigged wood. I walked right up to it..."

"...and then?" Beth said.

"...and then?" said Smasher who had stopped his advance.

"...and then he sent a pig across the bridge," Lou growled.

"A pig?" Smasher bellowed.

Father Warwick nodded. "Called Ralph, yes. Peace to its little porky soul. Named the smelly river after him, seemed a sensible thing to do."

Lou was furious. "I meant the first *person* to cross, when I wrote that contract."

"You botched it up, and you just did it again, didn't you? What mistake did you make this time?"

"Aha!" Lou grinned. "You're asking the wrong devil."

Beth took a deep breath. "It was my mistake. Remember, I tried to tell you. I wanted to say more, I still do but..." Beth began, then stopped.

"You," Father Warwick said, flatly.

"Allow me to make proper introductions," Lou said gleefully. "Father Warwick, this is El-Berith, 28th of my fallen angels, currently on trial for messing up her first contract. El-Berith, this is Francis Warwick, ex-convict, mercenary and smartass who will pay for fooling me."

"How did she mess up the contract?" Father Warwick asked.

"Oooh, badly. It was an easy contract, a no brainer, really. Standard hundred years of happy, successful life in exchange for the contractor's soul, a little charm to prevent the client from mentioning any of it. Wonderfully verbose and garbled so only a devil could make heads or tails of it."

"A devil or a lawyer," Smasher added.

"Er...yes. Anyway, off she goes to find a poor unsuspecting soul, and convinces the bloke to sign."

Father Warwick shook his head. "But if it's a standard contract, how could she possibly mess up? The only thing they could get wrong would be...the signatures?" He looked at Smasher. "You were human!"

"I was a lawyer."

"Still counts as human." He turned to Beth. "When you signed in the wrong place, you got his soul! That's why your conscience feels so heavy, You weren't used to having one."

Beth nodded. Sister Duilia looked at her with a strange expression. Beth felt shame and guilt for betraying the people who had treated her as a friend — again the pain. "I told you, I am a thief, a liar, and a traitor." Her voice broke. The burning in her chest brought her to her knees.

180

"Yes," Lou jeered, "you're guilty of stealing an innocent's immortal soul, you lied about your identity, and betrayed your raggedy friends here. You will die now."

"Wait," Father Warwick said, "what happens if she dies?"

"That's the fun part. If she dies before the term, the contract is void, so the soul should go back to the mortal, but since the signatures are reversed, the soul stays with her, and since she's a fallen angel, I get to torture her in hell for her mistake."

"And I get to stay a devil forever." Smasher grinned.

"Why would you want that?"

"Are you kidding?" Lou said. "A soulless lawyer down at the Contracts office? Together we'd reach new heights! Can't have him for just a hundred years though. I'd have to fire him when he gets his soul back. And I mean *FIRE* him."

"No part-time in Hell. That kind of ordeal is made for the living," Smasher said.

"Yes, I see," Father Warwick replied, lowering his eyes. "Sister Duilia, could you please get the cross?"

Lou nodded with satisfaction as Warwick let go of the cross and the little nun grabbed and lifted it with a soft grunt. "Good, I see you've grown wiser with time, Francis. How nice of you to realize you can't fool the devil twice. Smasher? Get this over with."

Smasher wielded his huge mace and started walking back towards Beth with long, unhurried steps and the eager expression of one who knows he won't have trouble with a nagging conscience.

Beth was barely able to move but managed to stand up and glare defiantly at him. Her sanity was drowning in dread and terror, and all she had to cling to was the knowledge her new friends had kept themselves out of harm's way. She saw her punishment as just and inevitable.

"You know," Lou told Father Warwick as he nodded toward the cross, "dragging that thing around is kind of silly. You must know all your religious symbols mean nothing to me. That's just a stick to me."

"Yeah, big 'ol stick," echoed Smasher, circling Beth and raising his mace over her. She closed her eyes and waited for the blow.

Father Warwick grinned. "In fact I was hoping you'd see it that way. Duilia? Give them the stick."

Beth opened her eyes just in time to see Sister Duilia tippy-toe towards her like a ballet dancer, turning into a graceful spin while swinging the huge wooden cross around with her and slamming it into Smasher's back. Beth barely avoided getting bowled over as the devil came stumbling past her, roaring in pain and surprise while falling to a half-crouch in front of Father Warwick, who grabbed him by the horns and held him face to face.

"When she came barefoot to my city and my church, she asked for permission, but you," Father Warwick shouted, "you are NOT welcome!" With that, he head-butted the devil straight on the nose.

It was brutal. It was unexpected. It made a loud splattering sound and a curious red arch of blood as Smasher flew backwards and crashed on his back.

"Beth, listen," Father Warwick said, "I guessed your nature from the first moment."

Lou was standing over the fallen devil, who was still groaning and holding his nose. Beth could see the black eyes turning red. She looked at Father Warwick. "You knew?" she said.

"Yes, I wasn't sure, but I noticed you could not step on holy ground without my permission, so you didn't lie or betray anyone. Another thing, about that contract: How long did it take your client to read it before he decided to sign it?"

"A few hours. He said he felt a bit iffy."

"A contract only a devil or a lawyer could understand. And when he finally made up his mind?"

"Oh, he was in a real hurry then! Really eager to sign." Beth turned towards Smasher. "He signed first, in the wrong place. He *knew* what would happen."

Lou took a step towards Father Warwick, his face terrifying to behold. Duilia stepped in front of him, still wielding the cross menacingly. "You..." Lou growled. A sword of black flames appeared in Lou's hand, or maybe it had always been there. His face was so contorted with rage it didn't look human anymore.

Father Warwick was trying to get Beth's attention, but his words were dimmed by her fear for the safety of the little nun. "Listen. This is important, Beth. A soul, a conscience, is like Saint Fillmore's mirror. Ask it."

"Ask my soul?" Beth could hardly breathe with terror as Sister Duilia moved another step closer to Lou. She struggled to hear the words over the roar of fear in her heart.

"Yes! Look into it and ask!" Father Warwick's voice was strong and insistent.

"What should I ask?"

"What are you really guilty of?"

Sister Duilia stepped forward and swung the cross at Lou. As soon as it touched the black flame, the wood burst into a thousand wooden splinters. Duilia fell backwards and slammed into Father Warwick, knocking both to the ground.

Beth felt herself being consumed from within by the raging flames of her own, self-inflicted hell. "I followed him and turned into a renegade angel," she cried, choking on her own tears.

Father Warwick tried to get back up, but he was pinned down by the dazed nun and Lou's foot over them. "Why did you follow him down?" he wheezed.

Beth closed her eyes. The fire in her heart, wasn't it guilt? She had deserted to follow him, to be near him. Even that action made no sense. She had never really trusted Lightbringer.

"Because I win, that's why!" Lou roared as he raised the sword to strike the fallen nun and priest.

Suddenly, El Berith, not Beth, knew. The answer was in her hands, and the fire of justice had left her chest and was in her eyes. She was holding one end of a long splinter of wood. The other end was embedded in Lou's belly. She was standing in front of him. Perhaps she'd always been standing there, blocking him, sacrificing herself, her own, beautiful white wings to follow him down to Hell and keep him in check.

His sword descended on her shoulder, maybe it stopped there or maybe it went clear through. She felt no pain or heaviness in her chest. What she felt now was—an old word she hadn't used in a long, long time—Elation.

"Ah," Lou said, his expression suddenly blank, "I killed you, right? My sword..." He looked at his empty hands and instead saw the splinter in his chest. "Oh," he grinned sheepishly, "ouch?" and he vanished with a pop.

Beth turned to help Sister Duilia and Father Warwick to their feet. "I'm sorry you got involved, I really am. But—"

"But it really wasn't your fault," Father Warwick said. "What did you see in the soul-mirror?"

"I saw the creature of light I used to be."

A frowning Sister Duilia tugged at Beth's gown, and then prodded her thighs like she was appraising cattle.

Father Warwick frowned a little as well. "So what are you now? I mean we both saw the sword cut through you but...are you—"

"—dead or alive?" Beth said, "I don't really know." She raised a hand behind her head and caught the huge mace as it came down, stopping it as if it were a child's toy in a child's hands. "I feel...whole."

Father Warwick and Sister Duilia peered behind Beth and saw a very surprised Smasher.

Beth turned slowly. "You," she said. "To you I shall do something which is hard for a mortal and impossible for an angel of war..."

"Please, no..." Smasher whimpered.

"...I forgive you. Do you want your soul back?"

Smasher stared back at her, his braided goatee swung round as he ruminated on her words. "No." He sniffled with his still bloody snout.

Beth took Duilia's list from her pocket and watched the letters dance around the paper and rearrange themselves into the text she needed. She shook the extra letters off like dust. "Sign here. Then go to your new office and get those word-jumbled documents straightened out."

"Oh, well, I'd need to read this, I mean, I want—"

"Want me to change my mind?"

"No!" He picked his nose, scribbled a red signature with his bloodied claw and popped away.

"Well," Father Warwick said, "looks like sanctity has its own advantages. But why did you send him off? Lou will think he's won."

"For about ten minutes. I've just agreed to keep Cuthbert's soul in exchange for his immediate employment in the Infernal Consumer Complaints and Legal Coverage Department."

"Didn't know there was one."

"There is now. They'll have a soulless lawyer nit-picking

every single case in defense of the damned. The backlog will be unimaginable."

———

Ian Lahey was born in Milan, Italy, to an American father and an Italian mother. He teaches English Literature and Aviation English in Udine, Italy, and leads a quiet and ordinary life with his wife, his two children and his invisible cat, Laurelin. To learn more about Ian, visit him at his Facebook page: http://www.facebook.com/lovewritingstuff.

THE LAW OF RECIPROCITY

Terry Korth Fischer

December came in under a saturating drizzle. North, over the houses, beyond the tree tops, the refinery flare surged above a silhouetted stack. The sky glowed amid the fiery gasses and the air hung heavy with the stench of industry. Clara Vogel sat alone in a spotless kitchen, sheltered with the familiar.

A single limpid memory teetered on her lower lash. She raised a quivering hand to wipe the tear absently, and thoughts churned. All those years together, why would Warner leave? We had an agreement. I would go first. With a sniffle, Clara fingered the edge of the teacup, studied the bottom, and marveled at the small leaves that scampered as she swirled a tide.

The cuckoo called out the hour. Clara watched the little wooden figures do their circle dance and duck back inside. Five o'clock. It took an effort to scoot the chair back as its feet clung then scraped on the linoleum floor. She placed her hands flat on the table and managed to push herself up slowly. She waited a moment to let everything settle into place and then reached for the Philco radio atop the refrigerator, turning the volume higher to cover the wail from the refinery siren. "Muriel and I loved to listen to the radio," she said aloud. "We spent our youth dreaming to the Big Band sound." Her lips turned up in a smile. "We learned the mysteries of the world from the wireless." Clara wobbled and reached out for the counter to steady herself. The corners of her lips slid down at the thought that Muriel could no longer recall those days.

Clara shuffled to the stove and poured hot water over her tea leaves. Stepping back to the table, she caught her reflection in the window above the sink and paused, trying to reconcile the specter with the slender girl Warner had loved. Long vertical lines ran down her face, and the brow wrinkled into a deep furrow, lips led down to soft jowls. Unfocused, Clara stared into the yard beyond as deep, dank melancholy pressed in on her. When had she grown old?

The radio distracted her with a story about an office building that spanned the border between the Netherlands and Germany. *'Companies have offices in each country, 40 yards apart.'* The voice went on, *'The border is a metal line running down the center of the building. You can stand with a foot in each country.'* Aberdeen circled Clara's feet, and she reached down to tickle him on the fur tuft under his chin. Her reward a back stretch and a purr. His brother, Yukon, stood guard, watching silently from the doorway. "What I learn, just by listening to the radio."

Clara reached for the box of Christmas cards lying on the table, fingering the edge and tipping it slightly to inspect the one card that remained. She'd mailed the others earlier, right after the radio piece about the sociologist who ran an experiment, sending hand-written Christmas cards with a note and a photograph to six-hundred complete strangers. Shortly after he sent the cards, responses trickled in. He received dozens in reply. It was the Rule of Reciprocity at work.

The decision to do The Experiment was easy for Clara. Despite what Warner would have thought, Clara Vogel knew there was nothing to lose. Thanksgiving Day, while eating turkey pot pie and thumbing through a dog-eared address book, the realization dawned, her life could be summed up by a tattered black book with a loose 'G' section.

The Experiment started on Monday morning. The drugstore had a complete section devoted to Christmas, which included a satisfactory assortment of cards. She selected a box of cards picturing a cottage in the woods, lights aglow and a seasonal sprinkling of snow. The sentiment read, "Warmest Season's Greetings." A small lined tablet from the stationary aisle, a bag of Warner's favorite mints, and a book of stamps at checkout completed her purchases.

"Getting ready for Christmas?" the clerk asked.

Buoyed by the question, Clara perked up, but the clerk didn't meet her eye, instead she shoved the items into a plastic bag and impatiently held out a hand for payment. The woman behind Clara clucked her tongue when Clara dug to the bottom of her pocketbook for coins. Pressured to hurry, Clara barely glanced at the surly man that watched the proceedings.

Tuesday Clara opened the box of twenty-four cards, signed each with a flourish in green ink, "Love, Clara & the Boys" and stuffed the envelopes before straightening them into a pile. How to select the strangers? Followed by a quick correction—they were recipients, would-be acquaintances, and soon-to-be friends. "What did I do with the white pages?" she asked Yukon and then rummaged in the junk drawer next to the stove and found an old copy.

Clara started right at the beginning with the A's, selecting John R. Aaron of Elizabeth Street. Then Roger B. Bennett of 1st Avenue, followed by Chas J. Collins, George Delaney, Lincoln P. Everett, and on it went until she reached the letter X. She skipped names with initials only, surmising they might be single, not families—it was families that interested her. Ignoring names too difficult to pronounce—no need to be embarrassed should they meet. She took special care to include foreign names, both Italian and Irish. Addressing each envelope to "The Family of John Aaron," Roger Bennett, Chas Collins, and on it went. In the upper left-hand corner, went, Mrs. Warner Vogel, and current address, written with special care so the handwriting was entirely legible. Then straightening the envelopes, tapping them square, the packets became the table's centerpiece.

With a feeling of accomplishment, Clara went into the living room for a knitted shawl. It was then, noticing the cats staring out the front window, that she first saw The Man. "Aberdeen, Yukon, who is it?" She stepped to the window and pulled the curtain back. Across the street, tall, menacing, his face lost in the shadows, the man stood staring right back at her. Could he be waiting for someone? Clara dropped the curtain and moved to the window edge to peek, squinting, trying to make out his identity. Perhaps, it was nothing. It was conceivable he worked at the refinery, or was one of those environmental men, the ones around collecting samples. She stepped away, snatched the shawl, and made a retreat to the sanctuary of the kitchen.

The next morning, listening to an amusing radio story about elves blocking road construction in Iceland, she drafted a personal note to include inside the Christmas cards. *'This is a land where any house can be destroyed by something unseen, where the wind will knock you off your feet, where the smell of sulfur is in the air.'* Her tea grew cold, and a pile of crumpled sheets sat on the table before she felt satisfied enough to write out twenty-two exact copies, tuck them inside the cards and affix the stamps.

Clara hummed an English Christmas carol on the way to the mailbox. She walked carefully, placing each foot solidly on the uneven concrete, afraid of a fall. Cars not pulled fully into their drives blocked the way, and children's bikes peppered her path, but, in spite of all the obstacles, she managed. Clara had just started humming "Ten Lords a Leaping" when she arrived at the mail drop. Pushing the envelopes down the chute, a movement caught her eye. On the porch of the corner house stood The Man. He leaned against the gray slats and stared broodingly out at the street. He was watching her.

She quickly turned, anxious he wouldn't notice, and waddled back toward home. Not daring to glance behind her. The thought of him following, perhaps edging closer, caused her heart to beat wildly, her feet were unsure, and she stumbled in her haste. If only her feet could move faster, but those days were long gone. By the time home came into view, she couldn't draw a full breath.

Clara didn't expect any replies to her cards for at least several days. She hoped the Law of Reciprocity would kick in before Christmas but vowed not to be disappointed at the lack of any immediate response. Each day she listened for the postman. He came precisely at eleven o'clock. From her spot in the kitchen, the crunch of fallen leaves, porch board groans, and post lid snaps announced his arrival.

After the first week, at 10:45 each morning, Clara turned off the radio and moved to the chair in the living room. Aberdeen curled at her feet, and Yukon stood guard at the picture window to verify nothing impeded the postman's delivery. Exactly at eleven each morning, came the thud, creak, snap, and through a small window in the top of the door, she'd catch a glimpse of the navy watch cap on the postman's head. After his departure, she'd retrieve the post.

Each day brought disappointment, and her sighs grew grave.

Yesterday, as the season turned more winter than fall, Clara brought in two articles from the box. The first, the Christmas card prepared for "The Family of Joseph Marchetti" — marked "Return addressee unknown." She let it drop onto her lap and wondered whether the others had hit the mark. The second, a simple postcard, addressed to "Resident" from the Department of Public Safety. Clara turned it over tentatively and let out a gasp. The Man stared back: dark and brooding, cruel mouth, defiant chin. The bold letters across the top read, "Notice High-Risk Offender." She skimmed quickly over the card, then read it carefully, word for word, but only, "Status: Parole," registered. A shiver ran up her body. Looking through the front window, into the leaden sky, she asked, "Warner, how could you leave me alone?"

* * *

Clara sat in the kitchen while the sky darkened with rain. The refinery, cranked up to full flare, echoed through the neighborhood. The air carried the pungent odors from the ship channel, and she wondered if there would be an answer in today's post. Taking the last Christmas card, the one saved for Muriel, she wrote out a note that contained no mention of The Experiment or The Man. Clara felt a hopelessness Muriel would never understand.

Rain drummed against the roof. Through the window, she stared into middle-distance, lost in a downhearted mood. A sudden light flashed in the sky. Expectantly, she waited for thunder to rattle the window pane. Instead, the front porch creaked.

Clara looked at the cuckoo — it was 8:05. Her heart began to race. Gathering her nerve, she moved to the sink and peered through the window. The birds were silent, the shadows deep. Was someone behind the oak tree? "Aberdeen, Yukon," she whispered.

A groan from the front of the house answered her. Clara clutched the edges of her sweater together in a fist, so tight her knuckles turned white. With a shaky hand, she reached for the silverware drawer. With squeaks and growls, the old wood fought against her, as if reluctant to grant her access to the carving knife. The dark void beyond the living room doorway mocked her efforts to see what lay beyond. Uncertain feet carried her forward, and with the knife tip pointed up, the blade became her protective shield.

The old porch boards spoke, stretched by an unseen weight. Clara took shallow breaths, and her heartbeat echoed in her ears. Aberdeen and Yukon lay curled on the rug, unmoving. "Yukon, Aberdeen." Their names called silently, more for reassurance than aloud. She felt the presence beyond the door and trembled behind the steel. "Who's there?" Her voice barely left her body.

A shadow crossed in front of the picture window. Clara concentrated on the door before her where tiny points of light appeared, a kaleidoscope of colors, skipping first left, then right, careful to stay in her peripheral vision, teasing her with their seductive dance, leaving her light headed and off balance. Through the small window in the door, moved a whisk of brown. The floorboards dipped, and the room went askew while she reached for the knob, and turned.

"Yukon!" Clara protested when he scampered out, crossed the wooden boards and skidded around the side of the house before she could react. Aberdeen crouched behind her legs, and she risked a look outside. But, the porch stood barren.

"Oh," Clara said her eyes wide.

Under the picture window, the glider swayed. On its faded blue fabric and guarded by hand rails worn smooth under the hands of those who spent spring evenings enjoying its luxury, lay a parcel—a plant whose red blossoms peeked from a cellophane cover.

Clara reverently placed the package on the kitchen table, cut the string holding the wrap with the carving knife and watched as the leaves unfolded to reveal a beautiful plant. Aberdeen nudged Clara's leg as she fingered the envelope and withdrew the sentiment, "Merry Christmas, Wayne and Fern." Warmth spread from the center of her chest. The Family Smitsmeyer. She tenderly propped the card against the poinsettia plant and leaned back against the chair. Yukon appeared on the ledge of the kitchen window and watched from outside.

Clara sat for a long time admiring the gift wishing Warner or Muriel was there. Then satisfied, waddled toward the living room and took the chair to await the day's mail delivery.

* * *

Yukon vanished from the kitchen window. A man's face appeared in the dingy pane, his features distorted and grotesque, as if viewed through a magnifying lens, a specimen just out of focus.

Oliver Toucey had watched Clara for some time. He found her at the drug store, where she fumbled through the aisles, bumped into the patrons, and acted indifferent to the help. He couldn't put a name to her but had a lingering feeling of childhood disappointment and disapproval. He watched her back out of the parking lot, tap another car with her giant Chrysler bumper, and drive away unconcerned.

He followed her and recognized the house, a home with a tended yard, the illusion of peace and tranquility, where a man and woman sat on the porch glider on spring evenings and protested against the exuberance of youth. Toucey recalled a couple who yelled at boys playing in the street, warning them not to trespass or disturb the peace. The Vogels. The neat and tidy house with a car pulled into the garage and the shades drawn tight. He remembered raking leaves for the middle-age couple and frustration at payment withheld when his twelve-year-old skills couldn't perform to her satisfaction. He recalled Mr. Vogel's apologetic expression, the hang of his head as he gave way to his wife's rants of displeasure, and yet finding a way to slip a ten dollar bill to him behind her back. It was the house across the street from his childhood home.

Today, paint peeled from the cedar shakes, roof shingles flapped in the wind, and the eaves were imbedded with the odor from the stagnant ship channel. Oliver Toucey eased the kitchen door open and stepped inside. The air from outside swept past him, ruffled the leaves of the plant on the table, and blew a small card to the floor. A gray blur scooted in before he had a chance to latch the hook. A wet leaf that clung to his trouser leg fluttered onto the worn linoleum.

"Aberdeen?" Clara called from the living room. Toucey heard the springs in a chair flex and the recliner snap closed. He looked around and spotted the knife on the table. He stiffened, willed himself to blend with the cabinets, and waited, his attention locked on the doorway.

"Is it time for your treat?" Clara shuffled into the kitchen and halted. Her breath labored, she swayed. "But you're—" Toucey cut her off.

"I lived across the street," he said, his gravelly voice reverberated in the small room. "I expect you remember me." He looked at her defiantly and hooked his thumbs in the waist of his jeans, his shoulders hunched. His denim jacket gaped open to expose a dirty T-shirt emblazoned with a rock band looking more alien than human. Greasy hair hung over his forehead and curled at his frayed collar. His dark glare locked on her ashen face.

The air went out of the room. Clara couldn't breathe; the atmosphere felt suddenly thin, saturated with dust particles and the lingering scent of stale cigarettes.

Yukon ambled past Clara's fragile form and regally strolled over to Toucey—his tail held high. He arched his back and brushed against Toucey's pant leg, twining first over his right foot, and then his left. Yukon began to purr. Toucey swooped down, picked him up and stood, turning Yukon over in the cradle of his arms. He rubbed the cat's belly.

"It's been years," Toucey said, keeping his head down, studying the bundle in his arms. "I was young."

Clara blinked rapidly and rubbed her hands over her arms before ending with them crossed over her sunken chest. The Department of Public Safety postcard flashed through her mind. Could Yukon be wrong? She leaned weakly against the doorjamb and tried to steady her heartbeat.

"How is the ol' man?" he asked.

"I've been alone for fifteen years."

He bobbed his head and continued to pet the cat. Yukon relaxed his body and with his head hung down over Toucey's arm, he looked upside down at Clara as Toucey said, "Can't live forever." Toucey lifted his head slowly.

Yukon, tired of the attention, leaped to the floor. His paws landed on the linoleum with a thud. Now with arms suddenly empty, Toucey rubbed open palms down his chest and glanced at the kitchen table. "This street must be a magnet. I couldn't get away from here fast enough, and now I'm back." He watched Yukon scamper into the living room, then checked the window and finally his gaze drifted back to Clara's cringing figure.

The sound of Yukon's leap startled Clara, and the quick movement roused her to action. Clara saw a familiarity in the close set of the man's eyes and the way he held his body. It begged a memory. Could this be someone I know? Maybe he is from the neighborhood, a Jones boy or, perhaps, one of the Humphreys?

"The place ain't what it used to be," he said.

"Not many things are." She found her voice ragged.

"I've been looking around and I don't see any of the ol' gang."

Maybe that was it, Warner always piddled about with Little League ball, and perhaps he is one of the hundreds of boys Warner coached.

The yellow princess phone hung by the back door on the far wall. The fifteen-foot cord uncoiled and limp from years of use draped to the floor. Clara, still unsure, covertly eyed the phone.

The refinery siren wailed as she pushed off from the doorframe and stumbled into the kitchen. Crossing to the stove, she turned the flame up under the tea kettle and reached for the cupboard door cautiously. A quick glance over her shoulder, Clara checked his position and then pushed Warner's favorite cookies, Pecan Sandies, out of the way and pulled out the Ritz crackers. They would be good enough served on a paper plate.

Turning to Toucey, she said with forced bravado, "Can't let you starve. Warner always believed in hospitality. We'll have a little snack and sort things out." Her eyes followed the nod of his head, and then her glance shrewdly lifted over his shoulder to the phone once again. If she distracted him, the phone was within reach.

As Clara arranged crackers on the plate, Toucey folded his lanky frame into a wooden chair and rested his forearms on the tabletop. He fingered the edge of a poinsettia leaf. "Christmas," he said. "I been down to the Union Hall every day this week. Nothing there. Couldn't spot a soul I knew. Amazing, you grow-up in a place, then Bingo, one day you're a stranger." He creased the leaf with a jagged thumbnail and wrinkled his brow as if confused by the bruise he created.

Clara put the crackers on the table and scooted the plate around her unfinished correspondence to place it in front of Toucey. Union Hall? Had he worked at the plant with Warner? No, he was too young, but, maybe one of the apprentices.

The envelope addressed to Muriel lay before Toucey. He flicked at it with a tattered nail. "Christmas ain't what it used to be," he said. "Not such a big deal when it's just you."

He worried the edge of the envelope until it flipped onto the plate and scattered the crackers. He lifted his head to look from under bushy brows at Clara before picking up the envelope.

The rain fell against the window pane, a steady and insistent tempo. The cuckoo's pendulum beat out an accompanying cadence. Together, the rhythm stayed two beats ahead of the muddled thoughts inside Clara's head. In the overheated room, a sheen of perspiration formed on her upper lip.

Toucey's eyes flipped up to Clara, and pinged down again as he read the address on the card. He turned it over in his hands, laid it gently on the table. He lightly caressed the lettering with his fingertips. "Grams," he mouthed. On his face, he wore an ache as evident as the dreary day.

Clara felt the clock pause, heard the whine before the release, and then the wooden dancer's carrousel twirled to announce the half hour with a tune she and Warner had never been able to place. The clock's every movement was familiar—every tick anticipated—a mechanism that never failed. When the doors clicked shut, Toucey spoke.

"Grams doesn't know me," he said, still lost in pain. He rubbed his finger over the writing and added, "Didn't even know me."

A greasy lock of hair hung down over Toucey's forehead. Clara looked and then flinched, remembering the tresses of Muriel's fawn locks, slender pointed chin, and aquiline nose. The distinguishing features of her dearest friend emerged on Toucey's face.

"I'm such an old fool," Clara chided herself. Of course, I know this boy. It's been thirty years, but I know this boy.

"You're not here to harm me," she said.

He looked at her, bewildered.

"You don't mean to torture or rob me," she added with conviction. This wasn't The Man at all. Clara straightened her back and pushed out her chin.

"No ma'am," he whispered.

"Good, that's settled."

"Ain't nothing right."

"Who says?"

"We was getting along fine, then, all of a sudden Grams was angry. I can't figure it out. I really thought she'd be glad to see me." Toucey turned his hands to rest the backs on the tabletop, his palms pleading with the cracked ceiling.

"Everything will be all right. Stop feeling sorry for yourself." Clara took the chair across from Toucey. "Muriel, your Grams, doesn't recognize most people. If you're here, there

199

is joy in seeing you, whoever you are. And when you leave, well... she forgets you were there." Clara smoothed the fabric of her apron. "She spends most days in a slice of time somewhere before you were born. She's comfortable there—it's familiar and safe."

"I want her to be happy."

"I think she is. Only, it's... Muriel, your Grams can't remember why."

Seeing Toucey's discomfort, Clara added, "It started with a pot left on the stove. Followed by a fall. One day Muriel couldn't remember which house was hers."

Toucey looked at her with sad eyes. And so, Clara began right at the beginning, with a tale of joy—the excitement Muriel shared at the birth of her only grandson. She recounted the pride Muriel shared with the neighborhood as she followed his progress through school and his growth to manhood.

"We lost track of you, but Muriel never stopped hoping. Even when she could no longer recall her old friends, she counted on you coming back."

The cats wandered in and out of the kitchen as Clara and Oliver talked over one cup of tea and then another. Eventually, he relaxed and extended his legs out under the table until they almost touched Clara's.

Clara chatted until she no longer felt old and useless.

With her encouragement, Oliver talked about travels and mishaps until he turned back into a boy with a love for chocolate chip cookies and knock-knock jokes.

The cuckoo called out the hour, eleven straight up. A snap announced the postman's delivery. "That'll be the mail," Clara said.

Oliver crossed through the kitchen and disappeared into the living room. In his absence, Clara placed the carving knife back in the drawer and brought out Warner's cookies, putting them on a china plate.

Oliver returned with three envelopes. He laid them on the table and, as if he belonged there, pulled out the chair and resumed his position.

"My, tsk, tsk," Clara said, her fingers rifling through the envelopes, "Chas. Collins.., John Rotterdam..," she bit her lower lip and flipped to the last one, "and, Henry Koeppee." She displayed the envelopes to Aberdeen, who sat at the foot of her chair and then looked up at Oliver, beaming proudly.

Clara Vogel sat the cards from the Collins, Rotterdam, and Koeppee families against the poinsettia pot, arranging them with particular care. There was an animated crinkle to her face as she looked across the table at Oliver Toucey. In a playful voice, she asked, "Ollie, do you listen to the radio?"

The cold rain continued to fall, but the day was no longer bleak or solitary.

———

Terry Korth Fischer lives in Houston, Texas. Retired from a career in IT, she uses her time to read, write, and relax. Her work recently appeared in The Write Place at the Write Time, *and* Clear Lake Area Writers Selections—Spring 2016. *Terry is a member of Sisters in Crime International, Clear Lake Area Writers, and Pennwriters Inc.*

I AM THE WOLF

Liz Fyne

When I was a girl of only seven, I became convinced I was the wolf from the Italian city Gubbio, blessed by the late St. Francis of Assisi.

Of course the original wolf was long dead, but the spirit of the wolf—the only lupine hero ever to receive a personal blessing from a living saint—had entered the great beyond in need of a new host. Thus his spirit had entered wolf after wolf, decade after decade, until by some odd bit of fortune, it came to me.

So now I sat in the kitchen, wearing my mother's oversized rabbit fur jacket. It was old and worn. In places the fur had largely rubbed off, leaving just an under layer of balding leather. But I'd scoured the house and this was the closest thing we had to the coat of a wolf.

"You're not a wolf," said my mother, who meant well but who didn't always understand.

"I *should* be a wolf."

"And wearing an old rabbit fur coat doesn't make you furry."

But of course I wasn't furry. Wolves weren't furry either; they had a *pelt*.

I'd seen that, somewhere, and I knew it was true because my friend, Mia, had looked up the definition of pelt online. She'd read: "The pelt is the skin of the animal after it has been removed."

Before the conversation in the kitchen, Mia and I sat in my backyard, in the grass, in the shade of an evergreen. Wolves seemed far away, except in my mind, where all universal laws converged and the inexplicable became comprehensible.

"Removed from what?" I asked.

"From the animal."

Mia looked up from her tablet, uncertain if I would find this information distressing, which I didn't.

"Of course it is," I said. "If it wasn't a pelt, I couldn't take it off." Which I did, removing the jacket just long enough to make my point. Then I put it back on, because I wore the jacket now all the time, even in bed.

I watched Mia, awaiting her certain jubilation. I was ecstatic and had been counting the hours, the minutes really, until we met again. To tell her of my new history, the discovery of my truest identity.

In an odd turn of events, however, Mia didn't appear to share my elation. She picked a strand of grass and chewed it.

"It's exciting," I said, "don't you think?"

"So, would you eat someone?"

"No, see that's the thing, the Gubbio wolf doesn't eat people. He was blessed. He was chosen by God."

At the time, neither of us had any real education on matters of God. Later in my life, I'd realize my parents were atheists. Mia's, too. Thus we'd had no church, no Sunday school. I had only an abstract thought, that there was a being called God. He was old and powerful and had a long white beard. He was responsible for miracles and other great events that could not be otherwise explained. Thus when I learned of the wolf, and when I felt myself become him while he became me, I just accepted that this thing called God had entered my short and simple life.

So I told the story —

Mia watched me, letting the tale unfold.

Long ago, during the lifetime of St. Francis of Assisi, there was a city called Gubbio in Italy. There was also a wolf. Because the wolf was wild, and because he was hungry, he ate the townspeople of Gubbio. Any persons who tried to kill the wolf were killed and devoured. So the people hid inside their city, scared to leave the safety of its tall city wall.

"And moat," offered Mia.

"No moat."

"How do you know?"

"Am I telling the story?"

St. Francis came along. He heard of the plight of the Gubbio people, and he approached the wolf in his dark scary lair. St. Francis called to the wolf, and he asked it to listen to him. He told the wolf that the people were scared of him.

He told the wolf, Stop killing the people of Gubbio, and then they will feed you and you won't be hungry. They will give you a place to stay.

The wolf agreed. He stopped eating the people. He wandered their city and became a friend.

This story, among others, was in a book my atheist parents kept on a shelf in the living room. It was a hardback book, bound in red felt with small stylized images of wolves recessed into the fabric, highlighted in shiny yellow gold. I could put my finger on the book and pet the binding, feeling the tiny wolf impressions. I'd opened it to find the tale, and then also the painting. Which was old. I could tell that much. Even in the photograph of the painting, centuries were visible in its image. And the colors were strange, too much yellow and green. Like when you're image editing on your phone and you pull the yellow color too far to the right, and the colors bleed from their real homes and infect neighboring hues. Like the painting was overexposed. It was the excess light, I thought, you might expect if God crouched and took a photo and his own glory caused a blur.

I'd seen paintings of God. Huge and in the clouds. Bolts of lightning.

"That's Thor," said my mother when I'd asked her about the lightning.

But God, to me, was still in the sky, and he wasn't Thor. He still had lightning. And one day he'd come down to Earth and he'd taken the St. Francis photo, where Francis stood in a monk's gown, in evident conversation with something that resembled a dog but was actually a wolf.

I admired St. Francis, but I became the wolf.

That's what I told Mia.

"I am the wolf."

It was a flash of insight, and it was as real and true as anything I'd ever known. The experience, something I'd later know to call mystical, had been all-encompassing as the picture-painting swelled larger than life, larger than me. When I fell inside. Where I stayed.

I stopped talking and Mia sat speechless, still oddly skeptical.

"It's true," I said.

A breeze stirred and brought mild relief from the heat under the jacket. While I talked Mia had googled my story, and now she presented to me a screen of other famous wolves, listed under the hideous title of man-eaters. I took the tablet from her and my cheeks grew hot as I saw the names of these scoundrel wolves of history. All of them had been guilty of human mastication. Even worse, the Gubbio wolf was also there, from the days before he reformed. Mia pointed.

"Look at all these other wolves. How do you know you're not one of them?" She took the tablet back and pointed. "Like this one. The Beast of...Geevawdin."

"The what?"

"The wolf from France."

I followed the path indicated by her finger, read the strange words: *Beast of Gévaudin.*

The *Gévaudin* wolf also had a painting. It was depicted as a vile animal with blood-red lips menacing a peasant girl. It was hideous. It wasn't me. I was good.

"No," I said, "that's not me."

"We have to test it."

"Test what?"

"You. We have to test you, to be sure you're the right wolf."

"The right wolf?"

"Because if you're not, how can I trust you? Like now? Just the two of us in the yard? How can I be safe?"

This question, the question of Mia's safety, it gave me pause. Because Mia was my best friend. She was my only friend, really. Other people passed through my life, at school, at the park. Kids my own age moved in a place that was near me but not. I talked to them, when we played kickball in P.E., when we stood in line for lunch at the cafeteria. They said things that moved from one ear to the other and then drained to the earth at my feet. Because what they said wasn't important.

Mia, though, everything she said was important. How could I go on if she was scared? If she thought that, as the wolf, I would eat her? These doubts she'd expressed made me sad in an entirely new way. It was something I'd never felt before, this sadness that another person feared I might harm them. I wanted to shake my brain, rid myself of such ruinous despair.

"Okay," I said, "how can we test if I'm safe?"

"We create this other place, the one with the bad French wolf. You come to the scene. We see if you turn bad."

I wasn't sure, exactly, how we'd do that, but I was willing to try.

"Okay," I said.

* * *

So that's how it started: the reenactment.

We met the next day to further our plan. As usual we met in my back yard, which was spacious and private. Mia's yard was also spacious, but she had siblings. Especially her three-year-old brother, Tommy, was problematic—following us everywhere and offering up to us the bugs he caught with his short, candy-stickied fingers.

Big smile.

Not to be trusted.

But now Mia arrived alone, prepared, with a printout of the French wolf, the *Beast*, presented in all his color printer glory. He'd been a giant, hideous and insatiable monster, and between the years of 1764 and 1767 he'd feasted on villagers from the mountains of south-central France.

Rivulets of sweat ran beneath my habitual rabbit fur jacket. Every morning the sheets were damp with perspiration. My mother threatened to put me in a cold bathtub. Send the jacket to the trash.

I wondered that wolves could take it. I thought maybe the summer heat was the real reason they ate people—all that pent-up frustration. But not now, not the good wolf. The good wolf stayed cool. It was part of his deal, I thought. A perk not mentioned in the St. Francis story.

But the *Beast*, he had no God-anointed perks and he was hot in the early French summer. According to the printout he saw a young woman tending cattle, and he recognized her for the tasty morsel she surely was. He charged, but the bulls among the cattle charged back, maybe scared for their own skins. The *Beast* was driven away.

"So she made it," I said.

"But other people didn't. It says there were over two hundred attacks. Most of those people got eaten."

"Oh."

"To test we can do just this first part," she said, "when the wolf charges the maiden. You be the wolf."

"You'll be the maiden?"

"Tommy will be the maiden."

This was unexpected.

"Tommy?"

"In case you become the bad wolf."

I saw issues with this plan. To work, I thought, we should do a truthful reenactment.

"Tommy is a boy," I said, stating what should be obvious.

"I can give him a skirt."

"You think that'll be enough?"

"And a hat," she said. "I can give him a big hat. With a flower."

I wanted to argue but in her eyes, yet again, I saw fear. The new sadness came back to me. It was terrible and must pass. I let the Tommy issue go.

"Okay," I said. "But what about the cows?"

A boy being the maiden, if he was wearing a skirt, I could understand how the wolf might be fooled. The wolf would see the skirt and *assume* it was a maiden. But cows, that was something different. You didn't confuse a cow for, say, a dog.

Our neighborhood was utterly lacking in cattle.

It was a problem.

Mia and I faced each other in silence. The neighbor cat, Jazz, walked a tall cinderblock wall that separated our house from the next. Jazz had spots; she was a calico. Even more than a dog, however, she was just too small to impersonate a cow.

She jumped to the lawn and jogged toward us with her tail pointed high to the sky. I petted her soft fur, so warm from the sun. Unlike me, she didn't seem hot.

"Okay," I said, "I'll think about the cow thing."

Thus we parted again, still with only half a plan. In the meantime, Mia remained apprehensive. She would only meet me outdoors, where she had ample prospects to escape in case I turned suddenly vicious.

Sleepovers, previously a common event, were out of the question. I felt exiled and alone.

For me, becoming the wolf had been so fantastic. I'd felt the love of St. Francis and God for an animal that was large and ferocious but could also love back. I could close my eyes and feel the wind in my pelt. It was freeing. It was real.

I racked my brains for an answer to our remaining problem.

Next morning I sat at the kitchen table, still wearing the jacket. My mother cooked breakfast on the stove.

"Mom?"

She turned her head from the stove to me. Her short brown hair brushed her shoulders.

"Are you done being a wolf?" she asked.

The wolf, I wanted to correct, but I didn't. Instead I asked a question:

"Do they have cows at the zoo?"

My mother looked from me, to the wall, back to me. I thought she must be confused. I didn't want her to be confused. Or suspicious. My question should seem natural.

"No," she said. "Animals at the zoo are exotic. Like gazelles. And lions. Do you recall seeing cows last time we went to the zoo?"

We'd been to the zoo not so long ago, and I didn't recall seeing cows. But I thought maybe there'd been some and we'd somehow skipped them. Maybe because my parents thought they were boring. Not worth a trip to the cow exhibit.

"Do you want to give me the jacket?" she asked.

I didn't want to give her the jacket. I was the wolf and I needed to find some cows.

When I failed to reply, my mother returned to cooking. She made eggs and sizzling ham. She poured milk from the carton. I turned the carton and scanned the side panel. It had photos of cows, spotted and mellow. Bells hung from their large ponderous necks. Printed in block letters was the farm's slogan:

Happy Cows Make Happy Milk.

Then:

Meet our cows at Happy Cow Dairy.

Meet them in, I read the panel, Vermont. We lived in Medford, a Boston suburb.

I glanced at my mother, who'd returned to the stove. One more question.

"Do they have dairies in Massachusetts?"

Once again my mother looked at me, then she wiped her hands on an old, overused apron, the blue one with stripes.

"I'm sure they do," she said. "Do you need to be a cow?"

She watched me, too curious. So I resumed eating, pretending she hadn't asked anything at all. Later that day

I was back on the internet, searching dairies in Massachusetts, preferably near Medford.

I called Mia.

I told her there were several dairies. One offered tours. Alternatively, you could wander on your own.

"You can see the cows?" she asked.

"I think so."

"Are they in a barn?"

"Some are, but I think there are also cows in fields."

I listened into the phone, impatient as Mia digested the news.

"We need cows in a field," she said, "so you can charge at Tommy."

Mia located the site on her tablet and scrolled through photos. She agreed the venue had potential. We decided that, to deter suspicion, Mia would be the one to inquire of my mother regarding the dairy, as if by chance. Mia would brave the indoors in my company and she'd talk of milk; my mother would be near. Mia would raise the question of where it came from, and wonder if we could see an actual cow. All these years she'd been curious. She'd never seen one, live and in the flesh. At least not up close.

I could point out how I'd been to the zoo and *still* hadn't seen a cow. If an animal was sufficiently exotic that it couldn't run free in Medford, then it should be sufficiently exotic for a zoo.

Right? Surely the zoo was at fault.

But I think there's a dairy, I'd say, *with tours.*

Mia would perk up, then heave a sigh, so yearning and sad.

It would be so FANTASTIC, she'd say, *if I could finally see a cow.*

We'd fix despairing eyes on my mother and she'd sense

how she'd failed, in her motherly responsibilities. She would relent and take us to the farm.

Which she did.

All three of us, Tommy, Mia and I packed into the rear seat of my mother's car. Tommy came because he was also lacking in the bovine experience, at least that's what we told my mother.

I wore the ubiquitous jacket, such that my mother turned the A/C to max and Tommy whined from a chill. Mia had a backpack loaded with an extra skirt. She wore a hat she'd borrowed from her own mother—as promised it was wide-brimmed and boasted a large yellow flower. It was a good touch, and I was sure the wolf would be fooled.

I thrilled as we passed from the neighborhood to the highway. I really hadn't seen a cow up close, nor had I been to an actual farm.

I felt the wolf inside me, impatient for wild open fields, freedom to be his true self.

Mia turned and looked at me. I smiled reassurance that all was well. In the sky, specked with fleeting clouds, I saw endless light and recognized it as God's glory. I felt again that love I'd never felt until looking into the eyes of Francis. It was incredible and perfect.

I was so ready.

We left the highway and our car followed a long, windy road. Bordering the road were fences. Beyond the fences were cows. They clustered in the distance, heads down, tails whipping.

Tommy strained to see from his spot in the center of the rear seat.

"Moo!" he said.

At a farmhouse we stood in a short line to gain admittance. Even indoors I was assailed by a ripe smell I hadn't expected. It smelled like animals but not like dog or aquarium. It was like where horses stood at a park harnessed to carriages. Like the police horse pen at Frog Pond in Boston, but different. This was the smell of farm— cattle, cows, livestock. For an age-old wolf, it was the smell of authenticity.

At the front of the line my mother received a map and other related documents. We crowded at her skirt.

"They have a lot of animals," she said. "Goats, pigs, sheep." She looked down to catch my eye. "They have a cow in a pen, one you can pet. At two you can milk it." She checked her watch. "One hour from now."

My mother continued watching me, and in her eyes I saw a question—the true reason behind my sudden fandom of cows.

"We could pet the cow," said Mia, coming to my aid.

"Moo!" said Tommy.

"That's right," said my mother. "Pet the moo. Or we could watch the chicken parade first."

"We should pet the cow," I said, confirming Mia.

My mother gave up on the question stare. We left the house and followed a dirt path through the grass, down a hill, off to one side. A series of covered pens approached.

In the third pen stood a cow, black and white spotted like the ones in the field. Its massive head towered over Mia and me as its jaw moved in rhythmic chewing. A long string of spittle hung from its lips. The udder, hanging from between its dirty rear legs, was huge. Distended, even. Veiny and hideous.

Milk, I drank it every day. Poured from the carton it was pearlescent, so white and purely pure. Now, standing near this large, filthy beast, such clean fresh milk seemed like an irreconcilable paradox.

Despite its faults, however, a look of deep contentment

filled the cow's big dark eyes.

Mia stood frozen, surely as astonished as me. Next to her I heard Tommy's breathing, fast against the low snuffling heaves of the cow.

The animal lowered its head. Between its eyes, on the forehead, fur swirled from a central point, radiating outward to resemble less a star than a sea star with curving legs. The cow blinked. Its lashes were long and black, curled like those of an exotic girl wearing mascara. I was torn between finding the spectacle both hideous and beautiful.

"She spends a lot of time chewing," said my mother, oblivious to my jumbled mindset. "Her stomach is very different from yours. She regurgitates food into her mouth and chews until it's completely broken down. Then she swallows again."

I took my mother's hand and stared at the animal, smelling its odor, feeling the warmth of its moist breath as it reached its snout toward my face.

It was curious. About *me*.

I stepped back.

Mia turned her face to look at me, and of course she wondered how this visit affected my real identity. That was, after all, the reason we'd come. So I closed my eyes and struggled to push aside the numerous observations that jostled without order in my brain. I breathed quietly until the chaos retreated. I saw myself far away from this pen, from my mother, standing in a field that was endless in all directions. In the distance were cows, walking freely. There was a maid, standing, watching, wind pulling her skirt.

Slowly I crept near, not as my person self but as the wolf. My nose twitched with the fragrances of the wild. My pelt was no longer hot and detached, but rather comfortable and real. Every movement translated into countless bending hairs that pulled infinitesimally at my skin. It was a pleasant sensation I hadn't anticipated. In the distance I observed the girl and waited, to see if there was anger, or hunger. If I went mad with desire.

Instead I felt disoriented. Lost, just for a second, from seeing the world through amber wolf eyes.

I recovered to find my mother watching me.

"Are you OK?" she asked.

Her expression was concerned, and this was not a good thing. Too much concern might abort the trip.

"It's just hot," I said.

"It is hot, if you wear a coat in summer." She dropped my hand and opened the map from earlier. She dragged a single finger down the length of its shiny paper surface. "There's an ice cream stand, in the square down the road. We can get some ice cream."

She packed the map back into her purse and the three of us followed her down the road leading to the square. Mia came up beside me, alert that my mother was focused elsewhere, then she whispered.

"Did you feel like the bad wolf?"

I shook my head: no.

Mia was visibly relieved that I hadn't gone bad so quickly, but she was far from convinced it couldn't happen. Because it wasn't enough, to merely stand near a pen. We needed to be in the field, in the rough wild landscape like in the south of France. The setting had to be authentic.

Our path terminated at a wide open space.

"It's not square," said Mia.

My mother laughed. "It's more of an expression. The ice cream stand is that way."

"Ice cream!" said Tommy.

"Yum, ice cream," said my mother.

She served Tommy first, then Mia, and then she bought me not just ice cream but also lemonade. She pointed to a bench near a tree with thick knotty bark.

"Why don't you sit down?" she said. "You can cool off in the shade."

She looked at me in way that communicated this wasn't a request.

So we made our way to the bench, Tommy exiled to the very edge. Satisfied we'd done her bidding, my mother moved away to read a large wooden sign. From my place on the bench I could see it had drawings, probably of the farm, and also parts with writing. My mother loved historical information, always impressing on me the importance of reading the stories of other people and places.

"We need to go to the field," said Mia, picking sprinkles from her cone.

"I know."

"There's the tour," she said, pointing to a crowd that filled a portion of the square. She kicked dirt at her feet, causing a small cloud of dust.

When we'd first arrived at the farm, Mia and I had argued against the tour, saying we wanted to explore at our own pace. But then we'd faced the dilemma that my mother explored with us. Watching the group of tour participants, however, it occurred to me that the tour might have been better. It was a crowd, easier to get separated, and I'd seen online that it extended to the edge of the pasture areas.

I had the idea.

"We can join *that* tour," I said. "The one that's going on."

I took Mia's hand. Mia grabbed Tommy. We stole a glance toward my mother; she was still entranced with the sign. Soon, however, she would finish and then do her best to pass this useless information to me.

Our window for escape was narrow.

I left the lemonade on the bench and we scuttled across the square, pressing ourselves into the little crowd.

The tour guide was speaking and gestured toward another path, this one leading away from the path upon which we'd entered. She and the crowd began walking and the three of us walked also, in the center, maybe not easy to see. My skin prickled as I imagined my mother's hand appearing from behind and yanking me back, but her hand did not appear.

We left the square, moving down what became a broad dirt road.

To distract myself I listened to the guide: The farm's eldest son had studied organic farming at school. It was a major recently added at some universities. The cows were Friesian Holsteins, originating from what was now Northern Germany.

Then I heard my mother's voice, too. It was small and distant, but there was no question it was hers. She sounded puzzled but not panicked. Not yet.

Mia heard it too, and she turned her head in the direction of sound.

"Don't," I said.

For a moment I felt guilty that we'd vanished as we had. My mother would worry; she always worried. But this was important. It wouldn't be so long, really, and then we'd be back. All would be good. No reason for concern.

"Concentrate," I told Mia.

The guide continued her dialogue. There'd been a famous Holstein cow named Pauline Wayne. She was the "First Cow" and belonged to former president William

Howard Taft. She grazed on the White House lawn and provided fresh milk for the First Family.

No one knew how she'd gotten the name Pauline Wayne.

More walking. My mother's voice faded into the distance.

Pasture appeared on either side, fenced along the edge of the road. Just ahead was a cluster of shrubs that hugged the perimeter.

I took Mia's hand; Mia took Tommy's hand.

When we reached the bushes we left the group. There was a rustle of branches. The tour continued their travels unknowing.

* * *

We were free and grassland became as endless as they had in my imagination.

Cows were visible in the distance and we embarked across the rough landscape to reach them. They didn't seem so far away until we walked and walked and still they looked just as far.

Tommy whined that his ice cream was long gone. He wanted to go home.

Beneath the rabbit fur jacket I felt cooked and thirsty. Back on the bench my lemonade might still be cold. No help now. I closed my eyes but opened them again from dizziness.

Still onward toward our goal. Marching. Swelter. Gradually the cows grew nearer, larger. Soft lows greeted our approach.

Flies.

Watch where you step.

One cow raised its head and looked at me, its jaw in an endless cycle of motion. I recalled my mother's words, that the cow had a different kind of stomach. That it chewed and chewed.

We stopped walking and Tommy threw himself into the grass, whining once more. *Want to go home.* The sun was high in the sky. Time seemed to stand still, but our mission pressed.

Mia dropped her backpack and scanned the environment.

"Where do you think the maiden stood?" she asked.

There'd been no paintings available of maidens in fields.

"She must have been near the cows," I guessed. "I mean, she was supposed to watch them, right?"

"But not too, near, or else she'd be—"

Scared. Not just scared of the wolf but of the cows. Because they were immense. They were dinosaur cows. There was no more fence between them and us.

For a moment we stood, silent and not sure how this would work.

"We can dress Tommy," said Mia.

She unpacked the skirt and together we pulled Tommy to a standing position. Mumbling but obedient he let Mia tie the wraparound skirt at his waist, over top of his pants. Then she removed her mother's hat and used it to replace his Red Sox cap.

We backed a few steps to view his transformation, which was less dramatic than expected. With the dragging skirt and oversized hat he resembled less a maiden than a dwarf girl with no legs. Still, even a legless dwarf girl was a girl.

"I think it's good enough," I said.

Mia seemed less convinced, but like me she was hot and thirsty and tired of walking. She looked at the cows, then at Tommy.

"Pick up your skirt," she said to him.

Tommy removed the hat and stared blankly.

"Keep the hat *on*. Hold the skirt up so you can walk."

She helped him bunch the skirt into his fists. Then she gripped him by the belt of the skirt and pulled him nearer the cows. I watched as they moved away from me, toward the herd. A few cows raised their heads, twitched their ears.

I could tell that Tommy was resisting. Mia leaned away from him, toward the direction of movement, putting her full weight into the job at hand. But eventually Tommy dug in his heels and she had to stop.

More cows raised their heads. One began walking away.

Mia released Tommy, said something I couldn't hear, then walked back to me.

"I told him to stay," she said. "I told him he'll scare the cows if he moves and they'll run him over." She turned her head, looking back at Tommy, who hadn't moved, then she looked back at me. "So," she said, "are you ready?"

"I think so."

"I'm going over there," she said, pointing beyond me and away from the herd. "Wait until I'm there and then start."

I thought she would walk immediately but instead she hesitated, gripping the empty backpack. Then, unexpectedly, she hugged me.

"Be the good wolf," she said. "You're my best friend." She paused. "My birthday is in a month and I want you at the sleepover."

She released me and then she did walk. I turned to watch as the distance grew between us. I looked back at Tommy, and it seemed he'd taken Mia seriously because he stood exactly as he had before.

Eventually Mia reached her destination and gave me a thumbs up. Which meant it was time.

Earlier I'd felt ready, but now that the moment was here,

I felt unsure. I looked again at Tommy, stone-still in the breezeless heat. The expanse was not just as vast as I'd imagined but more so. Never had I been so far from other people, from other adults. It was hard to believe one could feel so isolated.

So frightened. I was genuinely terrified.

And the sun—

My shirt was soaked under the rabbit-fur jacket and I shivered from a paradoxical combination of freezing and hot.

But I'd made a deal with Mia and I wasn't going to go back on that deal. I was good and I knew it. I'd met St. Francis and I knew it. God had come from his great space in the clouds and he'd given to the wolf, then the wolf to me, a halo of Godly righteousness.

Now was time to prove it.

So I let myself down in the grass. I got onto my hands and knees.

I closed my eyes and thought back, to the first time I'd opened that book in my parents' house. To when I turned the pages, not caring at first, just words about people who died long ago and who meant nothing in a modern world of iPads and cars. And then I saw the wolf, and just like that, I was there.

How it happened, I had no idea, but when you're seven, sometimes even when you're "grown," an experience like that isn't something you question.

Now I opened my eyes and everything that might have concerned me just seconds ago was gone. No more thoughts of milk in cartons or school in the fall. No more concern that somewhere my mother searched for me, by now utterly panicked. My yard, the neighbor cat, my bed at home with flower sheets—

Mia, that I had a friend named Mia...

If someone had asked me, right then, I would have looked but spoken no words. Because speaking was a human thing, and I was no longer human.

I was the wolf. It was total and without question.

And ahead, not so far that I couldn't easily reach him, there was Francis. As before he was tinted in that odd shade of green. But now he projected a wide yellow aura. As in the painting the background, now the field and cows, assumed those same yellow-green overtones that distributed unequally. Bleached but not uniformly. Blinding but only in spots.

I took a step forward, one paw, then the next. Long canine toenails scraped in the dirt. Tiny sounds filled my ears. I sensed my tail, *my* tail, all bushy and full.

Smells were like I'd never known. The smell of my pelt, the smell of the grass, cows, sweat, dirt, sun, birds in the sky, trees miles away. The smells were so strong I felt sick.

But more than anything else, I felt love. It was love like I'd never experienced. It was love from my mother, from my father. From grandparents and granduncles and regular uncles, and from aunts and friends, and from the old woman down the street who gave me fresh-cooked brownies, but not even like that but somehow much more. Maybe it was like the love my mother said she felt for my father or like the prince feels for the princess in the movies. Maybe like all those kinds of love mixed together but then hundreds and thousands and millions times more.

Now Francis smiled at me from beneath an oversized gaudy hat that must have been his halo, for now, just for this visit. He beckoned to me and reached his hand. More than anything I wanted his fingers in my thick fur so I took more steps, moving briskly.

My long legs were agile and they propelled me forward

with a speed I'd imagined but never experienced. Faster and faster I ran, and Francis got nearer and nearer. In just moments, we would merge and life would be complete and perfect and beyond beautiful and then I crashed, head first, into the hard and heavy dirt.

My previously agile legs were suddenly haywire.

As I struggled there was a strange whooshing and then I saw my body far away, far below me, and I saw my previous self as a girl in a jacket who lay in the grass and flailed. I saw Tommy, mere feet from where I'd crashed, and he was screaming.

The cows, previously mellow and slow, threw their heads in the air. Their bodies that looked so awkward and square began running. Tommy began running also, although stumbling, away from my flailing figure and toward the cows who outpaced him, scattering like a startled flock of birds.

Francis was strangely absent and I wondered where he'd gone. Because just moments ago he'd been right *there*. I was sure of it.

Francis, I love you, where did you *go*?

* * *

There was an ambulance, but things weren't clear in the ambulance.

Then there was a hospital and both my mother and father were present, which seemed serious because my father usually worked on weekdays.

Nurses stuck wires to my head and there were beeps and conversations just outside my hearing. At one point Mia peeked around the corner of the doorway to my room. Tommy held her hand; he had a cast on his wrist but he smiled.

Days later came the diagnosis: epilepsy. Everything

leading up to the *event* in the dairy field had been precursor to the inevitable. I'd been a countdown clock. The clock reached zero and epilepsy happened.

Over subsequent decades an optimized regimen of prescriptions mostly kept the seizures at the bay, but sometimes they came all the same. Even so, I was never again visited by Francis. I never again became the wolf. When I got back from the hospital, medicated for the first time, I crept to the living room at night and opened the red and gold book. The painting was there as before, but now it was just a photo of a painting on a small glossy page.

Francis was two-dimensional. So was the wolf. Their postures looked a bit stiff and unnatural. It was clear they made eye contact, but the contact was outside of me.

The impact of this sudden abandonment was devastating. All the time between my initial lupine bonding and the charge in the field, I'd felt that seed of love growing within me, small at first but then branching to fill my every cell. It was nourishment, and warmth. It was being filled inside instead of being empty. Until that time, until I met Francis and became the wolf, I hadn't been aware of my emptiness because there'd been no comparison. But when I had it and then lost it, it was like puking and then sitting up and realizing I'd puked out all my guts.

I could eat, but I'd be forever empty because the food had no place to go.

Of course, with time, the loss grew more distant. The memory of magical fulfillment grew more vague. And it wasn't like I was abandoned in every way. My mother still loved me, my father. Mia made a shy but tender return. We were never admonished for our dangerous exploit. My parents, understandably, were baffled by the source of my new-onset melancholia — I always withheld from them the full story of my transformation. They consulted in whispers and then bought me a puppy, and its boundless affections did help turn me back from the brink of so much grief.

When I was older, I learned that feelings of profound religiosity are common in epilepsy originating from the temporal lobe of the brain. In fact temporal lobe epilepsy is widely discussed, in certain circles — among neurologists for example — as the true fount of inspiration among various prominent historical figures such as Jesus and Abraham. Moses.

But I don't really know. I am not a neurologist.

When I was mostly grown and left for college I took the wolf book with me. Then again when my college years passed and I married and had children of my own. I wondered, sometimes, if I skipped my meds and stared at that painting with a few glasses of wine, if my old furry self would return, if only for a few moments.

Occasionally Mia and I would meet for drinks and reminisce. At some point Tommy joined us as well, after we finally explained to him his role in the affair.

"Most people never meet God," said Tommy, one night, speaking to me. "You should be grateful."

"I don't know if I met God, though. How do you know if it's God or just a short circuit?"

"I guess you can't."

"So then what happens?"

Mia shrugged. "We can be happy we didn't kill Tommy."

"That we didn't kill a cow," said Tommy.

"That none of us was trampled," said Mia.

I held my glass of wine and contemplated the deep red.

"It was the most fantastic thing I ever experienced."

"So you see?" said Tommy. "You have that to be grateful for."

225

Mia smiled. We ordered more cheese.

———

Liz Fyne has an M.S. in neuroscience, and over a decade post-graduate work experience in biomedical research. She enjoys deeply beautiful writing that explores issues of psychology. Ms. Fyne lives in the Pittsburgh area, with her husband and cat. Learn more on: linkedin.com/in/elizabethfyne or find her on goodreads: goodreads.com/author/show/14244663.Liz_Fyne.

DID YOU ENJOY THE BOOK?

MAKE THE AUTHORS HAPPY

LEAVE A REVIEW!

S & H Publishing, Inc. is proud to publish this and other books by many of these very talented authors. Visit us at http://sandhpublishing.com

www.ingramcontent.com/pod-product-compliance
Lightning Source LLC
Chambersburg PA
CBHW072232170626
46813CB00003B/1191